"CORD THE HUNT

The pirates had him ___ ___ ___ ___
him, one at his back with weapon drawn, and
one somewhere off to the side. Still, the odds
were the best he was going to get.

Cord's tail tip curled around the pommel of
the knife hidden in his boot. He was raising
his arms, pretending to surrender, when he
suddenly twisted around. The tail-held knife
slashed up against the pirate captain's groin,
while Cord's right elbow smashed into the gun-
wielder's throat. The blow to the neck sent his
opponent reeling back, but the man still gripped
his dart gun—and if Cord couldn't change that
fact quickly, he'd find himself one very dead
dartboard. . . .

THE ALIEN TRACE #2
TIME TWISTER

TIME TWISTER

The Alien Trace #2

H. M. Major

A SIGNET BOOK

NEW AMERICAN LIBRARY

PUBLISHED BY
THE NEW AMERICAN LIBRARY
OF CANADA LIMITED

NAL BOOKS ARE AVAILABLE AT QUANTITY DISCOUNTS
WHEN USED TO PROMOTE PRODUCTS OR SERVICES.
FOR INFORMATION PLEASE WRITE TO PREMIUM MARKETING DIVISION,
NEW AMERICAN LIBRARY, 1633 BROADWAY,
NEW YORK, NEW YORK 10019.

First Printing, December, 1984

2 3 4 5 6 7 8 9

SIGNET TRADEMARK REG. U.S. PAT. OFF. AND FOREIGN COUNTRIES
REGISTERED TRADEMARK — MARCA REGISTRADA
HECHO EN WINNIPEG, CANADA

SIGNET, SIGNET CLASSIC, MENTOR, PLUME, MERIDIAN
and NAL BOOKS are published in Canada by The New American
Library of Canada, Limited, Scarborough, Ontario.

PRINTED IN CANADA
COVER PRINTED IN U.S.A.

For John and Sue T.,
who lent research materials,

and particularly for Bubbles Broxon,
who suffers cruelly from cats.

And also for Robert,
who had faith, sort of. . . .

PROLOGUE

The space yacht, its sides blazoned with the blue-and-silver badge of the dukes of Komonor, drifted in tandem with a larger but less aristocratic vessel. The connecting personnel tube between the two ships suggested a mating of great sleek beasts. It was more of a rape.

The pirates had searched every compartment and taken everything of value: the works of art, the begemmed wine cups, the jewelry in the ducal stateroom. Now the crew and passengers were lined up before the pirate captain, an amazonian woman with curly, grizzled hair.

"A fine lot you are," she said disgustedly. Most of the yacht's crew were neatly uniformed—or had been, when the renegade spacer overtook them—though one slender young man wore a crumpled, grimy steward's uniform. "I was sure I was going to bag the duke himself," she continued, "or at least one of his sons. The ransom would've set me up for life. I don't suppose as how his high-and-mightiness will pay all that much for a concubine," the captain concluded, turning balefully to her one nonuniformed captive.

The girl scowled and bit her lip, glancing toward the blue-skinned Komonori crew. They stood straight and expressionless, except for the disheveled steward, who met her glance nervously.

"Don't frown like that," the pirate captain admonished. "You'll give yourself wrinkles and bring down your price. These spur-of-the-moment captures never work out right. Yance," she called, "how's the transfer coming?"

"We've got it all aboard."

"And the radio and subspace drive?"

"Smashed." Yance grinned.

"Good man. We'll be going, then."

"What about them?" The second-in-command jerked a thumb at the crew.

"We've got about as many prisoners as we can take. There's no market for ships' crews anyway—too many on the block lately. We'll take her along, though. Pretty girls always sell."

For a moment, the captain thought the girl would speak. But though her lips quirked a little, she said nothing; not a usual reaction for someone captured by pirates.

The windowless room adjoining the duke's study was ice-green, like the inside of a glacier, small, plain, and furnished sparsely. Ashek used it for interviews of the most private sort. In the heir's experience, to be summoned to that room meant nothing good was to come. He covertly studied his father, the duke, since the latter's attention was not on him. Ashek's blue skin was so suffused with blood that it was almost slate-colored. His thin, harsh features were set in rage. Kenek, the heir, was devoutly thankful he had never incurred his father's wrath to such a degree. He stole a glance at the others present: his youngest brother, M'Sen, and Yevren, the half-Komonori police commander. Yevren was impassive, but M'Sen was nervous and looked unkempt. His ceremonial braid was not even decently smooth.

"So," Duke Ashek said, voice as cold and sibilant as wind blowing across an iceberg, "I hope you have had a pleasant excursion, M'Sen? I confess I was . . . startled to be informed by three separate sources that my youngest son, my concubine, and my yacht had all vanished."

"Father . . ." the slender young man began.

"Be silent. Since you were the culprit, it was naturally less of a surprise to learn that the yacht and my son had reappeared, *sans* woman and furnishings. My only lingering curiosity is to know why the raiders did not take you. Not knowing you, they might well have had some notion that I would pay to get you back. You may speak."

It was not a happy family gathering. Kenek watched his brother's growing discomfort with apprehension. M'Sen was on the verge of tears, a state to which Ashek had reduced him on several occasions in his younger years. But, never, Kenek reflected, for such good cause. Their father might have been less stern with M'Sen if the boy had resembled him more closely. Kenek thanked the gods that he himself favored the duke, being tall and lean, with sharply molded features. M'Sen's comparative lack of height and his soft, boyish face were legacies of his mother's family, and a source of provocation to the duke. The lad didn't look like a leader of men, and Kenek doubted Ashek would ever succeed in badgering him into being one.

With a convulsive swallow, M'Sen managed to stammer, "Father . . . sir, I disguised myself as a crew member. I . . . I didn't think you'd want me to be abducted by those people." His voice died at the look on the duke's face.

Kenek interjected hurriedly, "Sir, is there really any need for Yevren to be present?"

The half-Komonori waited deferentially by the door, giving no indication that he had heard his name spoken. Kenek knew he would respond only to a direct question or command, and perhaps not then, if it did not come from Ashek. Those who did not know Yevren often overlooked him: he was not a commanding figure even in his blue-and-black uniform. He was as tall as Kenek, very nearly as tall as the duke, and more strongly built, but the stillness of his whole bearing and his lack of expression made him a cypher.

"The theft of ducal property may be considered to fall under his jurisdiction," Ashek replied. "He will remain until I decide whether to turn you over to him or to punish you myself."

M'Sen almost moaned.

"So you posed as one of my servants," Ashek continued. "How brave, how noble of you! Of course, the crew would never betray one of our house, but I wonder that Edwina did not give you away."

M'Sen began a stuttering explanation, which was cut off by his father. Kenek was increasingly uncomfortable: it took no genius to guess that the concubine had probably felt sorry for the young fool. Or, perhaps, had fallen in love with him, or thought she had. . . . In any case, it presented no very good picture of the Komonori Empire's second most powerful family. Yevren, on the other hand, gave no sign that he had drawn any conclusions whatsoever. He was here, he must be paying attention—but he would not embarrass his employer by showing surprise or interest. With a skill born of long practice, Kenek suppressed a shiver.

"What I wish to know is, why did you do it?"

The words hung in the air like icicles. The wrong answer might bring an avalanche down on M'Sen. Kenek wondered whether he would still have three brothers in a few minutes, or whether the total would be reduced to two. It was of no real importance to him, as he was the heir anyway.

"It was . . . I didn't . . ."

"Yevren, give me your weapon," Ashek said, and

extended a hand without looking at the policeman. Without a word, Yevren slapped his disruptor smartly into the duke's palm.

"Now," Ashek said, "unless you tell me why you committed the colossal impudence of taking my yacht and my woman, I shall assume your intent was treason. You have until the count of three. One."

"Sir," M'Sen said shakily. "You've always said I didn't show as much initiative as Kenek, Senek, and even Annen . . ."

"Two."

"I wanted to show you I was like them—like you. Bold. Daring. It wasn't as if you cared about Edwina. You don't—didn't—send for her for days at a time. She's not even special in bed. . . ." M'Sen seemed to feel he had gone too far, but the duke had asked for an explanation. At least Ashek had lowered the disruptor and stopped counting.

"So it was all for the sake of a prank?"

M'Sen nodded miserably. His father was not going to be amused, Kenek observed with a mixture of satisfaction and pity. Though why M'Sen had ever imagined stealing the girl and the yacht would be a good idea baffled him. M'Sen would have done better to have stayed with the pirates. At least they would have kept him alive. . . .

"A prank," Ashek repeated. He was not given to repetition. His thin nostrils dilated, his mouth a hard line, he said, "Get out of my sight, you fool. Let me not see you again until I send for you, and remember this: if you occupied even one place higher in the succession than you do, I would kill you. Get out!"

Even Kenek winced at the duke's tone—though not visibly enough to attract his attention. He understood the source of the duke's anger well enough, but still was dismayed by it. Duke Ashek was not a warm-hearted man, but neither was he in the habit of flying into rages. Kenek could not recall any previous occasion when his father had raised his voice. Still, given the circumstances . . .

"I must get her back," the duke said in almost his usual tone when M'Sen was gone. "And Senek and Annen are to learn nothing more about the matter than that the yacht has been raided while M'Sen and one of my women were aboard."

I'm sure he was aboard her, all right, Kenek thought irreverently. It was not a witticism he would have cared to utter. Not in front of his father. Instead he asked (since being heir to the duchy gave him some privileges), "How are you going to find her, sir?"

"I think," the duke replied, "that that is a job which calls for a specialist."

Chapter 1

Bounty hunters seldom rate much respect, even from those who require their services. This was a fact of which Cord had long been aware. Bounty hunting was just about on a par with Catching, back home on Mehira. Except that it paid better. Much, much better. And it was possible to conceal his profession when not actively engaged in it.

Unfortunately, he was very much at work right now, sitting in a grand but chilly hall, waiting for his soon-to-be employer. Cord was clad in wide trousers, his tail accommodated in one leg, a long fur-lined coat over his broad shoulders, and yet he was still cold. Komonor was farther from its sun than his homeworld. It was the last planet he would have visited if there had been any choice. There wasn't. He needed money; the Komonori Duke Ashek needed a hunter. Ashek was willing to pay a great deal for Cord's skills, which was, after all, the bottom line.

If he had not needed the money, Cord mused, he would have walked out of this white, inhospitable room. The tracery moldings around the high ceilings reminded him of frost, as no doubt was intended. The only color was pale blue: it tinted the floor and some of the upholstery and did nothing to lend the room warmth.

So he waited, having made himself as comfortable as possible in a chair. It was hard and straight-backed, but, as he noticed, the great chair on its dais was of similar pattern and no softer. He passed the time by polishing his sidearm.

He had not reached the height of his profession by being unobservant. He had already guessed that the carved screen to the right of the dais was a door. His pointed ears swiveled at the whisper of the door's movement, and before it was fully open, he had returned gun to holster and buffer to pocket. He rose to meet his prospective employer.

The duke was a surprise. He was unaccompanied, and he moved with feral grace. Cord had expected someone . . . softer. If not degenerate, at least dissipated.

Ashek seated himself in the chair on the dais—almost a throne, really.

"Sit," he said. "Do you always come armed to interviews, hunter?"

"No," Cord replied. "Only when the interviewer comes of a culture which values a show of strength. What I have learned of you, my lord duke, suggested that you would not be offended by the sight of a weapon. Indeed, that you would think little of me if I arrived unarmed."

"True—and perceptive. My informants advised me that you were successful and scrupulous in fulfilling your contracts. They overlooked your intelligence and your polish."

Cord bowed slightly, acknowledging the compliment. Now he forgot the low temperature and his boredom. His interest was roused.

Ashek was tall and thin rather than muscular, but without any suggestion of frailty. Age was difficult to guess in different species; if he had been Terran or Mehiran, Cord would have estimated his age at between thirty-five and forty standard years. The Komonori duke's skin was dusky blue—almost the shade of the tile floor. He wore darker blue and silver. His black hair was long and worn in a braid. His face was harsh, with a scar across one cheek.

Cord automatically opened his psychic shields to sense the duke's personality. Ashek's emanations were equally harsh and commanding. He would be a staunch ally or a relentless enemy. As he studied the duke, Ashek studied him in return, through narrowed eyes.

"I think you will prove adequate," Ashek observed.

"You haven't yet told me what the assignment is, my lord," Cord responded. "I may decide not to take it."

"You have a reputation for taking any case if there is profit in it." Ashek smiled thinly. "You will be well rewarded if you succeed."

"What is the nature of your problem, your grace?" A quick course in the etiquette of the peerage and another on Komonor itself had prepared Cord. One must not insult a potential employer by using the wrong form of address, after all.

"You ought to be aware that the Komonori Empire spans four solar systems, though many races have more and better ships than we."

Four systems conquered a thousand years ago by the then pre-star-travel Komonori, whose homeworld had been visted by a peaceful star-traveling race. The Komonori had commandeered that one starship and privateered their way into the galactic community. Surprisingly, they hadn't continued to push outward. Of course, even now, they were spread pretty thin in their four systems. The technology their subject races couldn't supply, the Komonori bought from other civilizations. They were able rulers but poor scholars and scientists.

"So I have heard," was all Cord replied. He doubted Ashek wished to be reminded that he came of pirate stock.

"We are much troubled by piracy," the duke continued, causing Cord to suppress a smile.

"Yes?"

"One of my ships was captured recently. Its subspace drive was destroyed, but its crew managed to make the nearest port at sublight speeds. The pirates took everything of value and also the one passenger."

"It's not uncommon," Cord agreed. On many worlds, including Komonor, slaveholding was legal.

"Naturally I cannot allow my property to be taken. However, your main mission is to bring back the ship's passenger."

"Who is this person, my lord duke?"

"A woman. Also my property."

Cord repressed an urge to sigh.

"I will need more information, my lord. If you'll tell me everything you know about the pirates and the woman, my chances of returning your—property—will increase."

Ashek's expression flickered, and Cord received flashes of irritation, desire, and fear. Reluctantly the duke went on to give Cord a lesson in history. Three groups of pirates preyed on Komonori shipping from time to time, Cord learned. It was necessary to extract it from Ashek bit by bit, not because he was unwilling to give the information, but because he could not understand its significance.

The Litheen raiders operated almost entirely in their own system, which was under Komonori rule. They were less pirates than a guerrilla force. With a handful of small ships they ambushed passing freighters. If the cargo was usable or salable, they took it. If not, they destroyed it. As a rule, they left the crew and passengers unharmed.

The Seti were better organized and operated in all four subject systems, and in others as well. They sold captured cargoes, and also the ships and passengers, through a large and secure base of operations. They had turned thievery into a thriving and profitable business.

The Ael fell between the Litheen and the Seti. They were clever. They chose their prey carefully, seldom getting a haul that was not easy to sell. They did not bother taking the ships, and they took the passengers only when they were sure to bring good prices in some slave market. On the other hand, they had been known to kill captured crews who might be able to identify them.

Ashek, having stopped speaking, was looking at Cord. Obviously he expected results.

"It would appear that we will be dealing with the Ael," Cord said. He was not going to explain the deduction. Anyone ought to be able to figure it out. Besides, why make it look too easy? "What would you like me to do about them once the woman is safe?"

Ashek regarded him thoughtfully.

"If Edwina is their prisoner, you may have to kill some to free her. If they have a fixed base—on a planet or planetoid—you need only report its location to me, and my forces will take care of it. If they operate entirely from their ships, then I would like you to bring back the leaders. Alive."

"I will do so if it is possible. You realize, your grace, that it might be difficult to do single-handedly. Particularly when your chief concern is the return of . . . Edwina, is it?"

"Yes. Yes, it might be. It is possible, too, that Edwina will resist being rescued."

"Oh?" A vista of potential problems rose before Cord.

Ashek flicked a button set in the arm of his chair. At once a servant entered, a very pretty girl with glossy dark hair that swung down over bare shoulders. She wore a tight bodice over full breasts and flaring pantaloons trimmed in fur. A scarf of the same fur was wound around her neck. The duke gave a command for refreshments; she bowed and left. Cord's eyes followed her ripe, round bottom as she went out.

When Ashek spoke again, it was on a new subject. "My family has served the emperor for more than nine hundred years; our duchy is seven hundred years old. I control more than three-quarters of this planet as the emperor's chief subject; I own the other quarter outright. For those reasons, it is not easy for me to appreciate any other viewpoint. Nor am I used to dealing with non-Komonori—or those who are not our vassals."

The servant returned and served first her master and then Cord with steaming mugs. They were works of art, he saw: fine, translucent ceramic painted with erotic scenes of great delicacy. One of the advantages of having wealth is being able to surround oneself with things of beauty. He resisted pinching one inviting buttock of the serving girl and sampled the beverage instead. It was hot, sweet, and mildly alcoholic.

"Other viewpoints, my lord?" Cord prompted.

"I was thinking of Edwina," Ashek said. "Granted, my experience of non-Komonori is limited, but Edwina is ... rather unusual. She actually told me that slavery was disgusting and immoral, and that she was not a slave because it was illegal."

"And what did you say?"

"I laughed—of course! If it had not been funny, I would have punished her, perhaps. But by then it was clear that she was ignorant, and so was not being intentionally insolent."

Rather unusual. The phrase made Cord's heart contract. He, too, had known a woman who might be described that way. But it would be too incredible a coincidence if the duke's woman turned out to be Julia McKay.

"How did you happen to acquire her?"

Ashek frowned. Cord could feel the duke unconsciously throw up a mental barrier. Then he said cautiously, "She was found wandering in a place she had no right to be. We were unable to determine how she had gotten there. I might have sentenced her to death for espionage or trespassing, if it had not taken so long to question her."

Cord was plainly puzzled.

"She spoke no known language, although she appears to be Terran. Finally she learned Komonori and Multi-Lang through quick-study tapes. Her presence seemed to be inadvertent rather than some plot, and she intrigued me, so I decided to keep her."

Cord found no difficulty in understanding that. Slavery was legal on this world. Anyone who was found trespassing on private property and could produce no identification or passport ran a risk of being claimed.

"She had no papers?"

Ashek was mildly surprised. "If she had, it would have been obvious what language she spoke. With hundreds of tongues spoken in the galaxy, for many of which we have no tapes, guessing was futile."

"Did she give no explanation?"

"No."

Cord decided Ashek was lying but decided not to press for complete data. Later he would learn more. Julia McKay's strange ability to be in places she should not be able to be nagged at him.

"Do you have a picture of Edwina?" Cord asked.

The duke pressed another button on the chair arm. A holopix image appeared between them, life-sized.

The woman was attractive but not beautiful. That was Cord's first reaction. She was no match for the girl who had served them. Odd. He would have expected Ashek to be content only with perfection. Still, the face had considerable appeal. And perhaps it did not convey the personality. Charm, wit, and warmth could add much to an unremarkable face.

He memorized the woman's features. Brown hair, wide-set gray-green eyes, snub nose, freckles, a square chin. She did not *appear* to be Julia McKay. But he would know for certain only when he felt her emotional aura. It was easy to alter appearance. On the planet Brunan, a tall person could be made short, skin color could be changed, metabolism speeded up or slowed. Julia had been on Brunan—who could tell what she might look like now?

"I will recognize her," Cord said firmly.

The projection disappeared.

"How much will you need for expenses?" Ashek asked.

Cord calculated quickly in his head, choosing an amount considered high but not exorbitant.

"The equivalent of fifteen thousand TerraBank credits. In assorted forms." To his surprise, the duke nodded. Sometimes the customer argued about expenses. Cord was prepared to explain the cost of chartering a ship and captain (as he expected to have to do) and of bribes. It was less humiliating not to be required to itemize.

"There is one more thing," Cord said. "Do you have anything of the woman's?"

"Her clothing. A few bits of jewelry. What do you need?"

"Something that is uniquely hers. What she was wearing when you found her—something of value to her."

"Her own clothing was ugly and unsuitable. It was destroyed. But there was a ring she had.... Come with me."

Cord followed the nobleman out through the concealed door and up a broad stair. It wound upward, to an atrium domed with glass. Looking up, he could see a few snowflakes drifting down.

Ashek opened a door and motioned Cord to enter.

The room was spacious, all white and pale green. The carpets which covered the tile were thick and soft, and many cushions were scattered around. A faint perfume was in the air. It took no great deductive ability to conclude that this was a woman's room. The duke went to a built-in dressing table and pulled open a drawer.

"She kept it here. Unless she took it with her. . . ." He brushed aside a pile of filmy material. "Ah." The duke held out a small object.

Cord took it, concentrating first on its appearance.

"I let her keep it, since it has no value—except aesthetically, perhaps. For some reason she treasured it."

It was a band of silvery metal with a strange lavender undertone. A line of—script?—ran around it, the snaky characters almost purple. It seemed too large for a woman's finger. Seeing it, Cord felt vaguely uneasy. He opened his shield fully to probe for emotional traces—and shut them down again quickly. It had a terrible alien feel to it that all but battered his senses.

Cautiously, Cord tried a second time, braced for the shock. The results were the same. Was it Julia's? His heart pounded. He thought so. Only once had he encountered an emanation so unlike any human's or humanoid's. And Ashek wanted her back? Cord almost laughed.

"Does it tell you anything?" the duke asked.

"Yes, a great deal. May I take it with me? It is helpful to have something of my quarry's for use in tracking."

Ashek found nothing strange in the request. Of

course, he himself admitted unfamiliarity with any ways other than those of Komonor, Cord reflected.

"Certainly. How will you begin?"

"In the spaceport bars," Cord replied, "where I can find out about the Ael—where they hide out, how to get in touch with them."

"It might be faster to have my police raid a few of the less reputable ones and question anyone they find."

"Faster, perhaps, but that method of questioning might alert the Ael. In this instance, your grace, covert action is called for, rather than a full-scale assault."

Ashek did not insist. "It is in your hands," he said, and summoned another servant to escort Cord to the door. He was toying with a crystal flask. Cord's last sight of the duke was of thin, sinewy blue hands tightening on the little bottle, breaking it in half.

The duke was still holding the fragments of crystal when Kenek and M'Sen burst in. M'Sen burst in, at least; Kenek, the most like Ashek in personality, followed with a brisk but dignified stride. Kenek would make an able ruler—someday. By the time he came to inherit his father's responsibilities and rights, the duke thought, he would be experienced enough to counter the emperor's machinations.

"He's gone," M'Sen commented unnecessarily. "Is he really the best of the ones you've hired, Father?" The boy looked as though he would have said more, although, indeed, he had already said too much.

"Cord the Hunter relies on intelligence rather than swagger," the duke replied. He feared M'Sen would never learn much discretion, but fortunately Kenek and two others stood between him and the succession. Perhaps he should not have forgiven M'Sen so easily. A few pains might have taught him some caution, some sense. This last escapade of his . . .

Kenek's measured voice cut off the duke's reflections.

"Yevren is here, Father."

Ashek brushed the remaining shards from his hands, letting them fall to the floor, before pacing to his office, with Kenek and M'Sen falling in behind him.

Entering the luxurious but functional room he used as office and library, Ashek nodded to Yevren, third in command of his police. Yevren bowed low, not presuming upon the fact of their blood relationship. His half brother, Ashek thought, was his most loyal servant. The old duke had been every bit as indiscreet as M'Sen—though Duke Sen had not been a fool. Still, his abduction of an offworld visitor had been reckless to the point of stupidity, and had needed to be hushed up. Money and influence alone were not adequate to gloss it over; after Yevren's birth, the woman was shipped offplanet to a sanitarium, so hopelessly addicted to an illegal drug that no one would have believed her story even if she had a chance to tell it. Yevren must resemble his mother: his skin was only tinged with blue and his eyes and hair were dark brown rather than black.

"Your grace commands?"

Ashek smiled. He felt a certain elder-brotherly affection for Yevren. After all, Yevren was no danger to him, unlike Kenek, who might eventually become impatient to succeed to the duchy. Ashek's bastard brother had nothing to gain from the present duke's death, and everything to lose. He owed all to Ashek: his position, his education, perhaps his life. A motherless half-breed, unacknowledged by his father, he had been the object of cruel and sometimes dangerous baiting until Ashek became duke and extended his protection over the half-grown boy. He had seen to it that Yevren was educated, even sent offworld for special courses of study, and had then installed him in the ducal police. On joining the police, Yevren had sworn fealty to him, but Ashek placed less faith in that than in Yevren's gratitude to him.

"Sit," the duke said. Yevren promptly did so, as the duke seated himself behind his great desk. M'Sen and Kenek stood to one side. "I have a mission I require you to perform," Ashek went on. "I am hiring ... certain mercenaries to locate my concubine. You are to follow them and to ensure that she arrives here safely. Is that clear?"

The pale, nondescript face remained a mask. "Entirely, your grace."

It was good to be able to trust the matter to someone who did not need to have its intricacies explained to him. Of course, Yevren had been present at Edwina's interrogation.

"Father," M'Sen's voice broke in, "why send Yevren, when he has duties here? I've already offered to go, since it was my fault the pirates got her. I didn't realize she was so important to you. . . ."

Kenek looked away from his younger brother in disgust; Yevren's expression did not change. He seemed not to have heard M'Sen's asinine suggestion—tactful, was Yevren. M'Sen had not been there when Edwina was first discovered, nor had he heard Edwina's story. Even if he had, Ashek doubted M'Sen could have been trusted to return the woman to him, if the fool could have found her in the first place. Ashek traced the long scar on his cheek with one finger. "Do you see this, M'Sen?"

"Yes, Father," he answered, sounding bewildered.

"When I was younger than you are now, I dared to question one of my father's orders—not rudely, mind you, and not before anyone else, but because I believed he was mistaken. He slapped me, and the ducal ring he wore laid my face open. It is clear that I have been too forbearing a parent: if you had been your grandfather's son, you would not have survived."

M'Sen flushed and bowed. Kenek looked angry, and even Yevren stirred. Ashek reflected that the words might well have touched a nerve there.

"Now—you are excused." Ashek did not speak again until both his sons were out of the room, the door closed behind them. "I need not tell you to be discreet. I am sure you will be. And your non-Komonori appearance will render you less noticeable."

"Shall I take action only if your mercenaries fail to keep their bargain, your grace?" Yevren asked.

"Yes." Ashek smiled and said, "One of them may yet return her to me without knowing the truth about her. Why should I—or you—interfere if one of them stupidly brings her back? You will do what you must do only to prevent her escape. But I do not want a scandal, Yevren. You know that laws are different on other worlds. Nor would I like to lose your assistance, which is valuable to me."

Spots of color appeared on Yevren's cheekbones, whether because of the implied praise or the suggestion that he might forget himself and do something to embarrass Ashek, the duke was not sure.

"My lord, since it pleased you to give me a commission in the police, there have been no . . . incidents."

"I am aware of that fact. However, as a member of the police, you have . . . outlets . . . which will not be readily available to you, off Komonor."

"Your grace," Yevren said earnestly, "the carrying out of your orders is always my first concern. Pleasure will not distract me from my duty. Twelve years ago, when I entered the police, I was still a boy. I am better disciplined now. And even before that, when you sent me away to school, I found ways to satisfy my needs without attracting attention or causing you shame."

"True. I know I can trust you in this, Yevren. The

only other detail you must bear in mind is that I have given Cord the ring."

The half-Komonori's eyebrows shot up: "Does Kenek know this?"

"No. The bounty hunter asked for something of Edwina's as an aid in tracking her. It seemed a good idea. And what harm? If she made no use of it here, it was because she could not. If she could have escaped, she would have—if only to avoid your 'tender ministrations.' "

When she was first discovered, wandering in the ducal residence, Ashek had wanted the woman unharmed; he would not permit Yevren to follow through with the threatened torture.

"Go, now. Provide yourself with anything you may need. My secretary has a letter of credit for you. And, Yevren?" the duke added, as his half-brother stood and made his bow, "do it quickly."

"Your grace, if it can be done, I will do it."

"Good. And perhaps when you return, and matters go as I expect, there will be a special reward for you. I understand our lord, the emperor, has several granddaughters. . . ."

"Yes, your grace. I thank your grace." The words were formally colorless but Ashek saw the flash of interest in Yevren's eyes.

Chapter 2

The duke seemed an undemanding client, Cord thought, walking through snow-glazed streets. He was willing to hire experts and let them do their work their own way. *But I don't think I'd care to fail him. Or to live under his rule.*

Komonor seemed a clean, orderly world, as much as Cord had seen of it, at least. He had visited many worse. The buildings were solid and practical, even the ducal residence, though it was luxurious enough inside. If you liked it chilly. This, Cord reflected, glancing up at the gray, matted sky, was springtime. A snowflake fell in his left eye.

There were many police constables. A single armed policeman was posted every few quadrants. As he approached the port, however, the constables traveled in pairs and brandished weapons. Passersby gave them a wider berth and sometimes an evil glance. The denizens of Port Row were enough to give any law enforcement officer bad dreams: poorly or flashily dressed, furtive or swaggering, secretive or boastful. The spacers' section is rough on any world, but Cord had noticed that the more oppressive the government, the less law-abiding Port Row.

Cord strolled past drug shops, sex emporiums which guaranteed to satisfy any craving, cheap eateries, pawnshops, and drinking establishments without end. A few were self-consciously quaint, cleaned up for the tourists. Most ranged from ordinary bars with ordinary vices to places that were no better than embassies of the underworld. Cord was looking for the latter. He would know the right one when he saw it—or when he felt it with his empathic sense.

The low, gray clouds were darkening with night when he spotted it in a narrow side street. It was old and not too prosperous. It lacked a holographic sign, making do with an old-fashioned flat projection showing a nude dancer surrounded by happy drinkers. Beneath, scarlet letters blazoned its name: the Joynt.

He walked in, giving the room a casual glance. It was not too large; probably there were private rooms in the rear. There were a few computer gaming tables, where the optimist could bet against a computer. Most were unoccupied. This was not an establishment for optimists. The other tables were three-quarters filled— with lone drinkers, with couples and parties. Many of them looked up when Cord entered. Some turned back to their drinking—or smoking, or sniffing—others continued to watch him covertly. He was aware of it, even without looking around. His mind was alert to the curiosity and hostility the bar's patrons radiated.

At the counter, he asked the attendant for ice wine. The barman, a sauroid, served him without a word. His forked tongue flickered out when he saw the Ismanian thirty-star note Cord offered in payment. His round black eyes sized Cord up; he gave back the correct amount of change.

"Anyt'ing elssse you want? Companion, maybe? It getsss cold here after sssundown."

"Later. Or maybe I'll run into a 'friend' who gives it away free."

"Heh-heh-heh," the sauroid croaked. "Never can tell. If not, asssk."

Cord took his drink to an empty table with only two chairs. It would be annoying if too many prospects joined him. It might make a good source of information dry up. He sat down, shifting his weight to avoid pressure on his tail.

The ice wine was good, much better than one would expect in such a place. Of course, it hadn't been cheap, either. At that, Cord was willing to bet the bar paid no duty tax on it.

He had not finished the ice wine in its tall, bell-shaped glass when the pilot approached him.

"You're no spacer," the man said.

"How can you tell?" Cord asked, knowing the answer and interested to discover whether the man would tell the truth or not.

"You don't dress like one. You don't even drink like one. There are dozens of signs—even the way you move."

Human stock, Cord appraised him. Middle height, slim, young but not innocent, semieducated way of talking. Maybe even well-educated, but with an overlay of roughness picked up in Port Row. The lines at the outer eye and mouth signaled a sense of humor. His coverall was well-worn but clean, with reinforcements sewn on at the knees and elbows, almost a standard uniform among spacers. The ship-and-orbit symbol on the breast pocket identified him as a pilot. No one could have mistaken him for anything else.

"You're right," Cord agreed. "I'm not. May I offer you a chair and a drink?"

"Thanks. My name's Connor Roi."

Cord gave his second-best name. His own was not famous, but modesty seemed safest.

When the waiter had brought their drinks, the pilot said, "If you weren't so obviously just visiting Port Row, I couldn't ask you, but since you are, what are you doing in a dive like this? There's no entertainment, the conversation's nonexistent, and you can afford better. So what's the attraction?"

"The excitement." Cord shrugged. "The hint of danger. The chance to rub shoulders with the real spacers and maybe even pirates."

"Pirates?" Connor echoed, his brows shooting toward the ceiling. "Now what would pirates be doing here?"

The question was meant to be rhetorical. Cord answered it anyway.

"Drinking. Screwing. Making contacts. Arranging to sell their latest haul."

Connor Roi laughed.

It was a pleasant laugh, with no harshness to it. The pilot was really amused, Cord noted, checking his psychic output.

"Why is that funny?" Cord inquired.

"Two reasons, my friend. First, if I were a pirate, I think I could find better places to do any of these things than the Joynt. Second, a pirate is the last person you—or anyone else of good character—should be looking for. Do you think a pirate would like being recognized as such by you? You'd leave your liver in the next alley."

"That could be a real problem. But I understood that on Port Row, it's never a real secret who's been out raiding. Everyone knows which pilots are tops, which ones are drugging up and aren't too reliable, who smuggles a little of this or that to pay his bills."

"Ah, those holodrama writers will say anything."

"But someone must know," Cord said. "After all, pirates live somewhere. Someone buys their . . . merchandise. Someone sells them what they need."

"Yes. The ones who need to know, do. The ones who don't are better off not knowing."

"This looked like a promising place," Cord observed, swallowing the last of his drink. He snapped his fingers to summon the waiter.

"Another bottle of the same," he ordered.

"Go easy on that stuff here," Roi told him. "It's not safe to be too ... relaxed around some of the folk hereabouts."

"I'll keep it in mind." Cord grinned. But when the bottle came, he filled both glasses. "You don't worry about yourself?"

"There is some honor among thieves. Everyone in Port Row—everyone who belongs here, anyway—knows Connor Roi. If I were dead drunk in the middle of the street, they'd move me out of the way of traffic, and I'd wake up with my pockets intact. You, my friend, would end up dead and robbed, because they don't know you."

"I will take care to avoid it," Cord assured him, letting his voice grow a little soft and slurred. He knew his tolerance well; even a bottle of ice wine, potent as it was, would not render him unable to defend himself. But he would seem to drink too much, and then see what happened.

Connor Roi was keeping up with him, and he showed no sign of intoxication at all.

The Joynt was filling up, the noise level increasing. Cord kept his psychic shields in place, screening out the mental "background noise." The brutishness of the customers' emotions was a dark ocean, lighted by an occasional flash of anger. The sauroid bartender's alien mental signal Cord read as predominantly sardonic amusement. A fist fight erupted in one corner. It was ended by a pair of bouncers who appeared from a door at the back. Cord, feigning alcohol-assisted abstraction, pumped Roi about his experiences and ship. To question a Port Row inhabitant about his doings or his past was suicidal rudeness, but the pilot bore it well. He even answered some of the queries, parrying others.

Cord played his role well. He was no more than

talkative and merry, full of questions, and even volunteered information about himself—false, of course.

The barman padded over to their table.

"You ssspend night upstairsss? Got lots of talented companionsss, any sssexsss you want. Not sssafe to go home ssso late."

"That's all right, Ektil," Connor said. "I'll make sure Rait gets back to his hotel."

Ektil bobbed his head and pattered away.

It was time to make progress, Cord decided. He leaned forward confidentially, although he took no pains to lower his voice.

"You're wondering why I'm looking for pirates," he said earnestly. "I wouldn't have come here otherwise. The fact is, Connor, I'm a writer. Publisher back on Ursina gave me a contract and a big advance to write a tape about space piracy. Gotta have historical perspective about planet-bound pirates to give it a scholarly aura, a lot of local color and lurid description. So I've got to talk to at least one pirate, right?"

"It sounds as if you do," Roi concurred. "Well, do you see anyone here who looks like one?"

Cord gazed around the room. He let his eyes unfocus slightly. "They all look like cutthroats to me. Guess I wouldn't know a pirate unless he announced himself. Oh, well, I'll try on another world. The publisher gave me expense money, too; chartering a ship isn't cheap."

"You're not traveling on a passenger ship or a freighter?" Roi was surprised.

"I came on a freighter," Cord said. True. "But maybe I'd find it easier to get close to pirates by traveling with a tramp pilot. You know, someone who'll go anywhere and do anything for pay."

"I have heard the term before," Connor said wryly. "How did you happen to begin on Komonor?"

"There's a lot of piracy around here, so they say.

And the friend of a friend arranged an interview with the local authorities—to wit, Duke Ashek. He seems like a forceful type—why doesn't he clean out the pirates?"

"He has other matters on his mind," Roi responded absentmindedly. His attention seemed to be elsewhere. "Look, where were you planning to go from here?"

"Back to my hotel. Need to get some sleep."

"No, I meant, when you find your tramp pilot, where are you going?"

"Wherever he suggests. It wouldn't be hard to get in touch with the Litheen pirates, but I'm not really interested in them. Too political. And the Seti appear to be well organized—they're almost like a multi-planetary corporation. I want desperadoes led by a bandit chieftain, not a board of directors and an accountant. At least, my readers want that."

Connor was amused. "And what is the happy medium between the patriotic rebels and the businessmen?"

"The Ael. They should be perfect."

"Perfect is not a term I'd have thought to apply myself," Connor mused. "You've done your research, I'll grant. Well! Tonight you won't make any more progress, not with half a bottle of that good drink in you. Why not start fresh tomorrow?"

"I have a deadline to meet," Cord replied, letting his voice go fuzzy. "Maybe I should stay . . ."

"Now what's the use of that? Another night will make no difference—in fact, so you won't lose the time at all, in the morning I'll introduce you to some captains and pilots who may be able to give you a lead. Isn't that easier than sitting here and maybe being robbed on your way home?"

"Yes—thank you. Shouldn't have drunk so much— just worrying about the contract. If I do a good job, this could be my lucky break," Cord explained, letting himself be steered toward the door.

They had gone a block or so when Cord, maintaining his pretense of drunkenness, said, "I don't think this is the way to my hotel."

"What hotel are you staying in?"

"The Crown."

"I do beg your pardon," Connor exclaimed. "And here I was, thinking you must be at one of the port hotels, to be close to your work."

"Too much like hotels on every other civilized world. I wanted something with local atmosphere—exotic background always comes in handy for a writer."

"I see. The fastest way to the Crown should be through that alley. It connects with Imperial Way, which leads into town."

Cord assessed the black mouth of the passage before them and braced for trouble. Connor Roi was a little too good to be true, though he did not seem like the usual cutthroat. Cord noticed that the pilot approached the alley with some caution, but his mind gave no indication that he anticipated trouble. He was merely wary by nature. Cord wished he could throw off his masquerade of alcoholic fog. With every muscle tensed for action, it was hard to appear rubbery. He settled for keeping his shields down to catch the first hint of danger.

They were a dozen paces into the noisome alleyway when Cord sensed two minds, waiting with fierce expectation. Two more minds gave off a slightly different shade of the same emotion.

Footsteps followed them into the alley. They belonged to the second pair of minds, Cord realized. The other two were ahead—in a doorway, perhaps. His companion had stiffened when the steps turned into the alley.

"Connor," he whispered, "I think we're in for a fight."

The pilot glanced at him quickly. "You noticed? We could outrun them, maybe."

"They've got friends ahead."

The footsteps began to run.

"Damn!" Roi swore.

They both swung around to meet the oncoming attack.

"Out of the way, you fool," one of them snarled to Cord, pushing him aside. "We're not interested in you. Get out of here."

Connor Roi had ducked as the first man rushed him and thrown himself against his opponent's knees. The attacker flew over Roi's shoulder to sprawl on the ground. The second man aimed a vicious kick at Connor's head. While the man was still off-balance on one leg, Cord slammed into him and sent him smashing into a wall. Roi got to his feet, only to be tackled by the first man again. They rolled in the dirt, next to the second man, who lay groaning.

The reinforcements at the head of the alley were running to the rescue. Cord drew his dart pistol, an Electra V, and loosed a barrage of knockout darts.

The approaching figures flinched but did not stop. Anesthetic darts often did not take effect at once, particularly if the target was wearing heavy garments. The smaller of the two went down first, he seemed to stumble, and then went boneless. He would be out.

The second of the two Cord had shot was still on his feet. He was pulling a handgun from under his jacket. His movements were slowing, but it would be suicide to wait for him to collapse. A bolt from his cutter would be deadly. Moving with the speed he'd learned in childhood, Cord kicked the gun from the man's nerveless fingers and sent it skidding. Then he followed up by swinging his closed fist in a sideways arc; it connected with the man's chin and snapped his head back. The man staggered and fell. Since learning the Terran art of boxing, Cord had become quite intrigued by it. He expected the blow would keep the man unconscious until the drug took effect.

Connor Roi stood up. His adversary lay motionless. A quick check for psychic energy told Cord what he already suspected—the man was dead. Cord bent to examine him.

"We'd better get away," Connor said, pulling at his arm.

Little light reflected into the alley, but it was sufficient for Cord's Mehiran eyes to see the marks of strangulation on the neck. He also noted that the dead man—and the other three, too—were Komonori. He allowed Roi to pull him down the alleyway.

"We have to get away now. They attacked us, but we haven't any witnesses. And the police are not sympathetic even to innocent victims. At best, we'd both be inconvenienced. At worst, we could fester in jail until they got around to trying us."

Cord nodded. He did not care to come to the local authorities' attention in any case. He let Roi lead him out into the lights of Imperial Way.

It was a wide, well-lighted thoroughfare lined with shops, all closed now for the night. There was no one to watch their hasty emergence—Komonor's law-abiding citizens went early to bed.

"Thank you for helping me," Connor said. "If you hadn't, they would have had me. They weren't interested in you; you could have left."

True. But Connor might provide him with a lead to the ones he was seeking. And he had been seen leaving with Connor. If Connor Roi had been beaten or killed Cord would be the prime suspect. The denizens of Port Row would not take kindly to him after that.

Cord shrugged and said, "I don't like uneven fights." He sensed the pilot's bafflement and curiosity.

"There was no need for me to escort you home," Connor pointed out wryly. "You can take care of yourself."

"I am new to writing," Cord explained, "but I've been fighting since I was a child. I grew up in a tough district."

"Ah, then, that explains it."

They strode along the street, their steps crunching in the newly fallen snow. Roi wore a short jacket over his jumpsuit and appeared not to notice the cold. Perhaps he was used to it. Cord pulled up the close-fitting hood of his coat and still wished he were indoors.

The Crown rose up before them, the tallest building in the block. Five stories in height, its white, blocklike form seemed eerily buoyant, as if it were made of ice and mist. Its carved stonework and infrequent, narrow windows increased its resemblance to an ice grotto. The lights around the arched main entrance looked like icicles lighted from within by a pale glow.

"Come in and have a drink, Connor. Warm up before you start out."

"I will, with pleasure." Connor slapped Cord on the shoulder. "We seem to have walked off that ice wine we drank earlier."

The Crown catered to visiting Komonori rather than to tourists, so it was not as cosmopolitan as the port hotels. On the other hand, Cord enjoyed its greater luxury and more personal service, and its very alienness was an attraction.

At this late hour, most of the guests had retired; the hotel was extremely quiet except for some low noise coming from the restaurant lounge. Cord removed his coat and draped it over a muscular arm; Connor unfastened his jacket. The lounge had very few people in it: one couple murmuring low over their drinks, three businessmen arguing finances. Cord and the pilot had a large section of the lounge to themselves.

They chose a small table near the wall. The table, the walls, and the floor were of pinkish, veined stone that made Cord think of the flesh of a pale-skinned woman. Perhaps tonight he would ask the attendant to send one of the slave girls to his room.

A Komonori waiter approached them. Neither Connor nor Cord felt any desire for a cold beverage; the waiter suggested a hot drink that was unfamiliar to Cord but met with Connor's approval.

The waiter did not return with their drinks; instead a woman brought them. She wore a low-cut uniform of silky red and black that revealed excellent cleavage and shapely buttocks. As she served the drinks, she smiled warmly at them. Then she stood expectantly at Cord's side while he sampled the drink. It tasted like the one he'd drunk at the duke's palace, though it was differently spiced.

Cord nodded his approval. "Bring us another round when we've finished."

The woman acknowledged his order and walked away. Cord watched her go; his expression hadn't changed, but Connor knew what was on his mind.

"I see you have an eye for the ladies."

"I most certainly do." Cord lifted his glass in the air. "And I drink to them all."

Connor didn't reply, so Cord looked around the dimly lit lounge. A fire burned in a great glass-and-metal cylinder in the lounge's center. Cord, who was unfamiliar with the custom of lighting fires indoors, found it welcome. The flickering light danced; except for it, the room was almost unlit.

"That was no ordinary attempted robbery," Cord finally commented.

"I imagine it was more in the nature of attempted murder." Connor laughed. "I probably offended someone. Though I'm not sure what other offers I declined besides yours."

"Then they will be after you again as soon as they wake up—the three that are going to wake up, that is."

"Oh, not they," Connor said knowingly. "They will report back to whoever sent them, and a fresh team will be dispatched to find me." He threw back his head and finished the last of his drink.

"Will they know where to look?" Cord asked. He admired Roi's nonchalance. The first time someone had tried to kill him, he'd been stunned and angry. But then, maybe it wasn't the first time for Connor.

"My lodgings are known. I don't think I'll go back there tonight. My ship is safe. I'll sleep on her, and tomorrow I'll find a job to take me offplanet. Even if I have to invent one, and lift with an empty hold."

"You're welcome to my room—I have a suite with plenty of sleeping space. Any one of the pieces of furniture could be turned into a bed. And in the morning ... well, I was going to charter a pilot and ship. Why shouldn't it be you?"

"And help you look for pirates, huh? For a holotape—"

Connor broke off as the waitress approached with fresh drinks. "Put these on my bill," said Cord. "Room 20J."

"Is there anything else you'd like on your bill?" the waitress asked suggestively. "Me, perhaps?"

Cord smiled and raised his eyebrows at Connor. The pilot shook his head negatively. "I've had enough excitement for one night."

"Sorry," Cord told the woman. "Another time, perhaps."

She walked away, and Cord turned back to Connor. "How about it? You don't plan on staying on Komonor."

Connor sipped his drink thoughtfully. "Why not?" he said after a moment. "I came here with a load of liquors and spices. I sold them successfully, but I haven't been able to get a decent outbound cargo. Your offer is a handy replacement. Not only that, for the sake of my health, offworld travel is required."

"And the pirates?"

"Ah, the pirates. Before we lift, I'll check with a few old friends. They should be able to give us a lead."

"We have a deal then?" Cord lifted his glass.

Connor clicked his glass against Cord's. "We do indeed!"

Chapter 3

Last night's snow was turning to gray slush under this morning's bright sun. Cord, standing at one of the suite's tall, narrow windows, felt that spring was coming. Also, room service had arrived with breakfast, another hopeful sign.

The waiter finished setting out the dishes as Connor Roi came out of the lavatory, freshly showered and debearded, though his clothing was creased from having been slept in. The plainness of his garments contrasted with the splendor of the Crown, but the man himself was at ease in his surroundings, Cord saw. Cord himself was wearing a tunic and trouser set of velvety brown trimmed with gold embroidery. Its easy cut concealed a number of weapons.

"Hungry?" Cord asked, nodding dismissal to the servant.

"Ravenous," Connor replied, taking a seat at the table.

The best thing Cord knew of Komonor was that its people gave breakfast its full importance. Spread before them this morning were soft rolls and crisp sheets of bread, three kinds of preserved fruit, pickled meat, toasted cheese, a granular, sweet beverage, and another of heated fruit juice.

"I've been thinking," Connor said, covering a sheet of bread with a green fruit preserve. "Would you like to leave immediately?"

Cord, chewing a mouthful of pickled meat, did not reply at once. Connor Roi hurried on.

"I am not anxious to stay on Komonor half a day longer than necessary, myself. If it's not convenient for you to go right away, there's no more to be said."

Considering the events of the previous evening, Cord thought it would have been strange if Connor had not been in a hurry to get away from Komonor.

"The sooner the better," he said. "I want to get my research done and get back to more civilized parts to write my book. Can you get clearance to lift so soon?"

"Since I'm carrying no freight, yes. No customs red tape to unravel. No doubt your papers are in order?"

"Yes."

"And your bags?" Connor asked. "Can you pack quickly?"

"I don't have much; perhaps two small bags."

"Good." Connor dug into the meal enthusiastically. "I'll take you to the ship, and while you're getting settled in I'll nose around for information. We should be off long before midday."

Cord nodded and then gave all his attention over to eating.

Roi's ship, *Rose of Flame*, was what one might expect of a tramp freighter. She was small, with good cargo facilities but no luxuries for her crew or passengers. Roi manned her by himself, no hard job on an old, small craft.

"It's the great ships with all the latest equipment that need the most supervision. The more systems you have, the more can go wrong," Connor explained. He was very proud of *Rose*.

And the ship's condition showed it. Her hull was as scarred and dull as any, but within she was carefully maintained. Plain but neat, like Connor himself. Such was not always the case with small freighters, Cord knew. He'd been on enough to recognize the difference.

Connor left him to stow his luggage in the second cabin, saying, "I've got to check out with the port master. It won't take long."

"Want me to come along?"

"No, stay here. The port's security is all right. There won't be a repetition of last night. Not here."

Connor was gone for so long that Cord began to wonder whether some mischance had befallen him. Cord's gear—a worn but originally expensive set of rhinosaur-hide cases—were secured against free-fall conditions and also against snooping. He had also done some investigating of his own.

The *Rose of Flame* contained several places for cargo storage other than the hold. They were not large or in obvious locations. Who would look for half a cubic meter of space in the galley, behind the robo-chef? Or under the deck plates in the control room? Still, the spaces were empty. If Connor was in the habit of smuggling he was at least not doing so on this trip. And possibly he wasn't even guilty of cheating customs. Perhaps the storage compartments were only precautionary: places to keep valuables when the pilot did not trust his passengers. After all, Cord had taken measures to ensure that no one (including Connor) would discover the tools of his own trade in his largest piece of luggage.

Cord took the time to study the *Rose*. She consisted of the cargo hold, lifepod, galley, head, two cabins, and the control room. It would be interesting to see what Rio's quarters looked like. However, the door was locked, and Cord did not care to start off a promising partnership on the wrong foot. Among spacers, one's cabin was off limits except to close friends, and then only upon invitation. It was a necessary convention on a ship like the *Rose*, where a crewman's only privacy was in his cabin.

The passenger accommodation was probably identical in conformation: a bunk with storage cabinets above, a pull-down table and seat, closet, intership screen-computer link.

When Connor returned, he found Cord reading a disk of news articles about piracy.

"There's a lot of activity in this sector," Cord remarked, switching off the screen.

"That's because there aren't many highly developed worlds out here. If this were a busy sector, full of technologically advanced civilizations, pirates wouldn't stand a chance. They'd be hunted down—or else they'd go out of business."

"In a sector like this, I suppose it's easier for them to hide, too."

"Evidently so," said Connor. "Ready to lift?"

"Yes, whenever you are."

"Why are we standing here, then? Let's go. Come on up to the control room, if you like."

"Thanks."

It was the first time Cord had ever been in the pilot's domain at launch. He was fascinated. Roi made no mystery of it, and the whole procedure lacked the tension Cord had expected. They strapped in. Connor checked a number of gauges and dials, talking all the while, and then spoke to the port control.

It was gibberish to Cord. Then port control's voice said, "You may lift."

"Lifting," Connor confirmed, pulling back a lever.

Cord remembered the first time he had seen a launch. Then the ship had seemed to rise in slow motion. It always surprised him to find that it felt entirely different on the ship. It didn't feel slow or graceful: it was raw power gripping your bones.

*   *   *

The gray-blue-and-white globe of Komonor was a moon in their aft screen when Cord asked, "Where do we start?"

"I favor Oranekko. Have you ever heard of it? It's a nonhuman world orbiting a red star about a hundred parsecs from here. Primitive, but it has plenty of natural landing areas, and attracts a low class of beings. If I were looking for a place where pirates might put in to meet with underworld merchants, it's there I'd look first."

"Is that what you heard while you were out this morning?" Cord asked innocently.

Connor Roi gave him a sharp look.

"After I'd spoken with the port master, I had a chat with some old friends. They talked more freely to me than they would have if you were present, taking down their names and memorizing their faces. Some of these old spacers keep themselves mighty private. Publicity is the last thing they like."

"Good! You did find out something. After all," Cord went on, "I can always be tantalizingly inexact about sources of information. The hints I give can be vague enough to refer to anyone—or no one."

Cord had found that it was useful to pose as a writer when he needed a disguise. The public was ready to believe almost anything of a writer; they knew little enough about literary matters so his own failings were not readily apparent. Besides, it gave him an excuse to inquire into all manner of things.

He looked up Oranekko and made notes to give his cover story verisimilitude. It sounded like a perfect pirates' den, though the computer atlas made no mention of illegal goings-on. The planet was chill and rocky, with exposed bedrock in some areas which provided landing for small craft. The indigenous inhabitants were few but tough enough to hold their own. They traded rare minerals to offworlders in exchange for whatever bits of technology appealed to them. Oranekko was not a world likely to be overrun by prospectors—bare survival was too much work. It was cheaper to buy from the Oranekki. One main town housed the offworld population and the visiting spacers. It was said to shelter about five thousand. Cord decided he was well prepared for whatever Oranekko had to offer.

It was a pity that, in the end, he never got there at all.

Two weeks out of Komonor, Connor said, "We're within two light-years of a space station I know. Would you mind a detour? We might learn something of interest there. Also I would like my guidance system checked by a professional. It seemed all right when we left Komonor, but now I don't quite like its responses to routine tests. The station has top facilities."

"It's fine with me," Cord replied. His fingers continued the intricate braid he had begun. Slowly it was becoming an ancestor bag, a receptacle for a memento of great significance in his life.

On his home world of Mehira, mementoes were of great importance. Mehirans worshiped their ancestors and cherished objects which helped to keep memories of the dead fresh. To preserve the relics, they were kept in special pouches. The knots and twists formed a variant of written Mehiran, recording information about the family and the memento stored in the bag. Occasionally, similar ones were made for other purposes. In this one, Cord planned to keep Julia McKay's scalp.

"What's that?" Connor asked.

"It will be a pouch. Knotwork is ... a traditional craft on my world." Cord did not explain further. He could not tell any non-Mehiran about ancestor worship because inevitably that involved revealing Mehiran empathic ability. He also preferred not to tell anyone that whatever else he might be doing, his main interest was in tracking a woman who had killed again and again. Julia McKay was his secret, and he hugged his knowledge to himself. It was the only stable thing in his ever-changing universe.

Out of reflex, he probed his companion's feelings. Since leaving Mehira, he had made it a point to use his empathic sense regularly and to take no one on faith.

Connor's emotions screamed at him

Nervousness. A desperate need to conceal something. Hurry. Hurry.

Not for the first time, Cord wished he could sense thoughts as well as emotions.

I could, of course. . . .

"How long will it take to reach your space station?" he inquired.

"At this factor, we'll be there in four ship-hours."

"Good," Cord said, and smiled. After a while, he folded up his knotting and went to his cabin. Deliberately, he took out his equipment case and opened it. He removed a flat box attached to a harness. Cord moved without haste, shedding his orange-and-brown tunic. It was, perhaps, a trifle dressy for travel on a free freighter. He smiled once more, this time with genuine pleasure. It was good to have money to spend on fine clothing, the best food and drink. He strapped on the device, then added a shoulder-holstered needle gun of his own design before putting on his shirt. Around his waist was looped a leather-and-knotted pouch. He slipped a long, slender knife into his boottop. Both weapons were special in one important way: they were constructed entirely of a high-density plastic whose outstanding characteristic was its transparency to detector rays. He closed and locked his suitcase, and then studied his reflection in the cabin's mirror.

Neither gun nor blade was apparent. Most of his garments had been cut by a high-priced tailor to avoid showing bulges. The psi machine around his lean waist was equally inconspicuous. Satisfied, Cord locked the cabin and rejoined Connor in the control room. As he passed the pilot, Cord stumbled and reached out to catch himself. In doing so, his fingers made contact with Roi's shoulder.

"Sorry," he apologized. "I tripped over my own feet." Cord uttered the words without listening to them himself. His attention was focused on the thoughts received through the brief touch:

. . . hope Hafed approves . . . I'm a joy girl if he's a writer . . . Hafed doesn't mind intuition . . . keep him long enough to check his story . . . if he's real, no one the wiser . . . if he's police . . . Hafed's problem . . .

So Connor Roi was planning some treachery, having seen through Cord's act. Well, he himself had thought Roi too good to be true. However, no immediate violence against him was intended, he gathered. Good. Once he was in the space station, he would be in a stronger defensive position.

The screen protected their eyes from the glare of the blue-white star. Even from the edge of the system it was huge. The space station circled it at a discreet distance.

"Nothing modern," Roi said. "The station itself is Terran Space Force surplus. It's the personnel who make Kappa Station exceptional."

The man was making conversation, but Cord felt the reverberation of apprehension in his mind.

The giant wheel hung in the viewscreen. The sight of it combined with Roi's emanations of unease to chill Cord to the heart. He shook off the unaccustomed sensation of dread.

Roi was radioing the station.

"Kappa, this is Connor Roi of the *Rose of Flame*. I require unscheduled repair. May I dock?"

"Permission to dock granted," a voice crackled back after a pause which was due to more than transmission lag, Cord thought.

"I've been lucky. If the automatic guidance system weren't acting funny, I wouldn't be here now. I'm chartered—my passenger is a writer looking for information on piracy."

"Is that so? Too bad we can't oblige."

Something lurked behind those words. Well, Cord expected to find out what—and soon.

Rose of Flame slid toward one of many protuberances around the hub of the wheel. Connor Roi was bringing the ship in manually, not trusting the guidance system. As they approached, Access C-4 swelled from seeming no more than a nub to a tube larger in diameter than the *Rose*. Meanwhile the station's size had become apparent. It grew larger so that they could not see the whole of it in the screen. It contained more area than many asteroid mining complexes.

"Do they get enough business to support this?" Cord inquired.

Connor was humming to himself as he eased the ship straight into the cylinder which gaped before them.

"They do well enough. The owner got the station cheap at a government surplus auction. It was already assembled, so he only had to move it here."

Rose of Flame nosed into the tube. Mechanical arms uncoiled to grapple her. Sparing a look at the aft viewscreen, Cord saw a sphincter door close behind them.

Connor was switching off the control panel, all its colored lights winking out one by one. When they were all dark, a bell chimed.

"There's atmosphere in the hangar now," Connor said. "Come on."

Cord followed him, alert for trouble.

They walked out of the ship's lock onto a catwalk extruded by the station's interior. Below was a dizzying fall to the bottom of the cylinder which housed the *Rose of Flame*. A door before them slid open and closed again behind them, momentarily shutting them into a small airlock. Cord's nerves tensed; this was too much like a trap. His mind groped for Connor Roi's and found no panic there. Roi had no doubts or fears. Cord forced himself to relax.

The airlock opened, admitting them to a corridor. It was empty.

"This way," Roi said. "We'd best see Hafed. We'll get rooms here and enjoy ourselves a little while the techs work on the *Rose*."

"Enjoy ourselves? Here?"

"Ah, Cord, not only is this the best service station in this sector, it's also a gambling den, bordello, and nightclub. A spacer can relax in perfect safety on Station Kappa. You can't even do that on a lot of these half-civilized planets. Here no one wakes up minus his credits, catches a disease, or is arrested."

"How comforting," Cord said wryly. Though it had been too long since he had cuddled a woman, he dismissed fantasies of scented skin and hair. Roi had mentioned the name Hafed several times, once openly a few moments ago and earlier in his thoughts. Hafed was the owner or manager—or chief brigand. Station Kappa might be all Roi claimed as a repair center and red-light district rolled into one, but that wasn't all of it. If nothing else was going on, why was Connor worried?

So far, the station looked normal: plastic-coated floors and walls, variously colored in neutral tones. It was distinguished from the interior of many planetside buildings only by the airtight section hatches and a certain lack of vertical orientation. If the station's artificial gravity were changed, the inhabitants might walk on the ceiling exactly as they now walked on the "floors." A small pneumatic train of open carts ran around the wheel's periphery; it transported personnel and visitors between living quarters, work areas, and amusement areas.

Roi and Cord bypassed the train because the offices were located near the *Rose of Flame*'s berth. Connor led the way to a door marked "Station Manager" without hesitation. The panel swung open, admitting them.

There was a waiting room, less utilitarian than the hall. It was furnished in black and smoldering red, and the angular plastic furniture was embedded with opalescent flakes. Perhaps it was the work of a master interior designer, but the result was low-class.

"Hafed's a great businessman and good fellow," Roi muttered, "but he has no taste at all."

They stood in the room for only a moment when a door opened opposite them and a woman entered. She left the door ajar and stood next to it.

"Please go into Captain Hafed's office," she said.

Cord's attention was arrested. She was by far the most beautiful woman he had ever seen, and he thought he'd encountered some remarkable ones. Long honey-colored hair, violet eyes, flawless features, graceful movement, dulcet voice. She was so perfect she seemed inhuman.

She *was* inhuman. The discovery jarred him. He had opened himself to check the receptionist's emotional signals, and there was nothing. It wasn't even the wrongness or incompleteness he had found in Julia McKay. This woman had no more psychic emanation than if she were a three-day-old corpse. She seated herself at a screen and began to work. With a last, curious look at sleek haunch and thigh, Cord detached his attention and went into Hafed's office.

Here the furnishings dulled to orange. The chairs and cushions were plumply stuffed, but hard.

"Hello, Connor." The man at the desk was blocky, with a square, expressionless face. The orange business coverall he wore missed matching the walls by one shade. In this case, one shade was way too much.

The effect was worse than unpleasing: it was unsettling.

"Captain Hafed, this is Rait, my passenger. He's doing a tape on piracy in this region. This is Captain John Hafed, the owner and commander of Station Kappa."

Cord and Hafed studied each other curiously. Cord dropped his shield but felt only cool detachment. He feigned heartiness and said, "It's a pleasure to meet you, captain. Connor tells me this place is something quite out of the ordinary."

"Does he." Hafed's eyes, black as the impenetrable material the Terrans used to shield spaceports, did not change. "Perhaps you will write an article about Kappa."

Hafed's voice was so uninflected that Cord was not sure whether the sentence was a statement, an invitation, or a question, but his psychic emanations flared.

"If you'll permit me," Cord replied. "Of course, I need to get my pirate project out of the way first."

"Of course. In the meantime you will both join me for dinner at nineteen hundred hours, station time. Seventeen will assign you rooms."

Hafed pressed a button on his desk, and the receptionist came in.

"Rooms for them," the captain said.

The receptionist nodded once, glanced in their direction to make sure they were prepared to follow, and then walked out.

"Thanks, John," Connor called over his shoulder. "See you at dinner."

"Goodbye, Captain Hafed," Cord added. The captain nodded and turned away. Their host possessed all the charm of a rock. And his secretary was remarkable, too. Cord wondered whether he could have heard her name wrong. He spoke Multi-Lang very fluently now, but names were always difficult because they came from so many different dialects.

She gave them each a plastic disk—room keys—and a tri-d diagram of the wheel to assist in finding their rooms. "Thanks, Seventeen," Connor said. "Let's be off, Cord. We're in D section."

He led the way down a mauve-colored corridor while Cord studied the multicolored map. C was offices and docking for smaller ships; D was the entertainment and residential section. A was warehousing and workshops; B and E were docking facilities for "great ships." He wanted to have a look at those areas. Later tonight, perhaps.

He handed the map back to Connor, who refused it. "I don't need it, but you might want it later. For entertainment, drinking, gambling, women."

"Is Seventeen off limits? I found her quite interesting."

"Didn't you realize she's an android?" Connor was surprised. "I admit it's hard to tell—androids are getting better every day."

"So she's a human-appearing robot," Cord mused. "I didn't guess. Robots aren't common on my homeworld."

Connor turned a corner, and the corridor's colors changed to an iridescent purple. They passed three other humans; two wore orange coveralls similar to the captain's, and Cord wondered if that was an official uniform. The third human was a woman whose costume consisted of tinkling beads—a joy girl perhaps?

"Is that a robot too?" Cord whispered.

"I hope not," said Connor. "They're not supposed to be as realistic as that. Most people think you should be able to tell the real from the plastic."

"What is the advantage of using a robot rather than a humanoid?" Cord answered his own question. "Security? A robot is honest and incorruptible—assuming its circuits can't be tampered with."

Connor laughed. "That is the official explanation, sure enough. But you're too innocent to live, Cord, my friend."

Cord was annoyed. He did not think he was especially naive: he'd outgrown innocence long since.

"What's the unofficial explanation?" he inquired.

"He sleeps with her," Connor retorted.

"With a robot?"

"Android. XB-17's an android. It's called 'connecting.' People who connect with androids usually keep quiet about it; it's not socially acceptable. Most connectors are people who have a fixation on someone they can't get—celebrities, for instance. You can have an android built to look, act, even talk like the original."

Intrigued, Cord asked, "Who is XB-17 patterned after?"

Connor shook his head. "That's the sickest thing of all. She isn't a model of anyone. Seventeen's a standard receptionist unit. And it's rumored that she isn't even programmed to respond when John humps her. Some people like it that way. The less human contact involved, the better."

They stopped in the middle of a corridor. "Here's your room. Mine is across the hall, but I'm going to look up some friends first. Care to come along and see the entertainment area? Something for every taste, they say."

A broad smile split Cord's face. He clapped Roi on

the back. "Best offer I've had so far. To hell with pirates."

One or two passing people turned at that statement but kept on walking. Connor shushed him. "Better not talk about pirates. Leave that to me."

"You can have the pirates—if I can have the women."

"Pretty horny, aren't you?" said Connor. "We haven't been in space that long." They rounded another corridor, still iridescent purple. The people here must be travelers; very few wore orange coveralls.

"It's not that," said Cord. "Where I come from, making love is a compliment, a pleasure that everyone is expected to participate in."

"Just don't compliment me." At the end of the corridor was a three-car transport; they hopped in, and the tube took them quickly to the entertainment area. Here the colors were even more garish; purple clashed with red, pink with orange.

Cord cautiously lowered his shields, but the disordered assault of so many minds intent on pleasure almost overwhelmed him. He winced and quickly raised his shields. At least he could tell that the crowd was engaged in a genuine orgy of erotic emotions.

They hopped out. "I'll leave you here," said Connor. "When you've had your fun, go back to your room, but don't forget about dinner with the captain. Don't worry about a change of clothes or any of that. Every room has an assortment of costumes and toiletries. Good luck with the ladies."

Cord watched Connor Roi walk away from the entertainment area. He had half a mind to follow, but a comely lass had suddenly taken hold of his right arm and was caressing the soft down that covered his muscles.

She was dark-haired and dark-skinned and more than friendly. She draped herself against his thigh and smiled. He appraised her tiny sparkling orange bandeau and slit orange shorts and liked what he saw.

"Who are you?" he inquired.

"I'm here to serve you. What would you like?"

"You."

She dimpled and laughed. "Very clever. But first you can buy me a drink or two."

She led him through the portal to the entertainment area. The arched opening was hung with multicolored beads which tinkled and sensuously caressed them as they passed through. Inside was a writhing mass of people, mostly humans, a few humanoids along the fringes. People stood up along the curving bars or danced in the center, under flashing lights.

The woman ordered an unfamiliar drink for them both. When the small purple glasses arrived, she clinked hers against his in salute. "I'm Mallie. What are you?"

"Isn't that supposed to be, 'Who are you?' "

She giggled. "Yes, but I haven't seen your kind before."

"You're asking that and you haven't even seen all of me," Cord said in mock sadness.

"Oh, what are you hiding?" She looked him over thoughtfully, from his pointed swiveling ears to his broad shoulders, from his soft tawny fur to his tail.

She started to reach for him, but Cord twisted away; he didn't want her to accidentally feel his gun. "I can show you in a more, um, intimate place. Your room, perhaps?"

Mallie nodded. "Before we leave, you have to give the 'tender your room key; that way he can charge for the drinks and me."

"I should have guessed from your orange outfit that you work for Station Kappa." Cord fished out the key from his pouch and handed it to her.

"Oh, sorry, is this your first time?" She quickly amended that. "Your first time here?"

Cord nodded, amused. She threaded her arm though his and looked up. "I'll just have to teach you the ropes."

Cord pocketed his key and led her away, his tail twitching in anticipation. "And I'll just have to teach you some new tricks. . . ."

Of the trackers Duke Ashek had hired, Yevren thought Cord was the most likely to succeed. Too, Cord had Connor Roi as pilot, and that decided the matter. Discreet questioning at Port Control elicited Roi's stated destination. Accordingly, Yevren gave instructions to his own pilot.

Oranekko's spaceport was rated as Level 3—full fueling and some repair facilities, subspace communications, an adequate field but no automatic guidance system. And no *Rose of Flame*, either. That much was clear by the time Yevren and his pilot reported to port control.

Yevren left the pilot to deal with the payment of port fees—and bribes—and went to stare out the wall-sized window at the field. He was not familiar with spacecraft, but he had studied pictures of the *Rose*. None of the six or eight ships in port could be Connor Roi's, no matter how carefully camouflaged.

Roi had let it be known that he was bound for Oranekko. Yevren had made it a point to lag behind, lest the sight of a Komonori craft arouse their suspicions. Though the *Queen* bore neither Komonori nor Ashek's ducal sign, being intended for inconspicuous work, Yevren was not prepared to swear it was unknown to the spacer's underworld.

There were two possibilities. One, that the *Rose of Flame* had met with a deep-space or subspace accident, which was unlikely by reason of Roi's skill and the proverbial reliability of old ships of the *Rose*'s class. The second, and by far the more likely, was that Roi had never intended to go to Oranekko. So for whatever purpose he had let it be known he was bound for that world, his intent had been criminal. The ducal police had long suspected Connor of having at least one foot in the underworld.

Tanet, the pilot, joined him and said, low-voiced, "I had a little chat with the port master about recent arrivals and departures. *Rose of Flame* hasn't been here."

"No," Yevren agreed, turning away from the window. "We've been tricked. Come. I want to find the subspace communications center."

After dispatching a spacegram to Duke Ashek, Yevren found lodgings for them. Having to admit his failure to Ashek awoke feelings he had hoped he had left behind him: shame, knowledge of his own inadequacy, and fear.

"I'm going out," he told Tanet abruptly.

"Shall I come with you?" the pilot asked. He was an earnest young man who intended to go far in the duke's service. That was how he had happened to be assigned to his present duty. "If it's a question of picking up port gossip, I could . . ."

"It isn't." Yevren smiled to soften the curtness of his words. "I want a stroll and perhaps a little entertainment. Go out yourself, if you wish."

"Oh . . . thank you, sir. Maybe I will."

Tanet's expression and tone told Yevren that the pilot had heard the rumors. No matter. It was not Tanet's place to approve or disapprove.

Anything was for sale, if one knew where to look, as Yevren did. He had learned when Duke Ashek had sent him away from Komonor for a year, to study at the police academy on Leka.

The brothel was discreet, and, he hoped, what he

wanted. He was mistaken. Oh, it catered to the most perverted tastes, it was true—but those were more peculiar, even, than his own. The women were cowed and pitiful, half starved, sick, some of them. Good enough for a clientele whose satisfaction came with killing. Many of the women looked as though they would welcome death, if only it wasn't too painful. What good was such submission to him?

He wanted proud, aloof, beautiful ladies who would resist until he had beaten and humiliated them. In his police work, he seldom had access to any but prostitutes, thieves, and traitors, but even their pain and fear pleased him. These malnourished, cringing girls gave him no pleasure. The timid creature he eventually chose was half sobbing even before he stripped her of her gaudy rags. She lay beneath him unmoving as his fingers dug into her shoulders and breasts. She should be dressed in silken gauze and jewels; she should try to push him away. He fantasized that her back would arch as she tried to buck him off. She would try to bite, and he would bite her nipples until she cried out. If he had her back on Komonor, he would spread-eagle her, exposing her most private parts. Then a small flame, held close, but not close enough to burn the flesh, only to heat it a little, until she was moaning with fear and the stimulation of warmth.

The girl under him neither struggled nor whimpered, but the memory of other soft bodies was sufficient. He remembered arresting and searching a fifteen-year-old suspected rebel; how her bare buttocks recoiled from the dirty, frosty brick wall and how the blood steamed on her slender thighs. There was a woman whose plump limbs parodied orgasm as he ignited tiny bits of fluff on her naked back. His breath came harshly as he filled the prostitute.

The release was only physical. He was as tense and irritable afterward as he had been on arrival, but he could not honestly blame the girl. She knew she had not completely satisfied him and now waited passively for the anticipated beating. Yevren could detect the shadows of earlier mistreatment on her skin. She had been through it all before, and she was afraid.

She reminded him of the women—kitchen girls, sluts, and slaves—who had made it possible for him to survive early childhood. They'd given him scraps of food and cast-off clothing, showed him warm, safe places to sleep, from before he could remember until he was ten, when Ashek, himself newly of age, inherited the dukedom. Suddenly everything in Yevren's life had changed. There was enough to eat, warm clothing, and no more curses or blows. An occasional scolding or admonition to make his noble patron proud of him, when he did not do his lessons perfectly. Such had only spurred him on to greater efforts, since there was nothing he wanted more than to please his lord. Over twenty years had passed since Duke Ashek had taken him in, and he was still the best and brightest part of Yevren's existence.

Abruptly he rolled off the whore and sat up, feeling her shrink back as he did so. Without looking at her, he said in his most neutral voice, "You were too submissive. I like a woman with spirit." Of course, if she *had* shown fight, she might now be dead or broken and bleeding on the dingy mattress. She still faced that end, if he complained to the management. . . . He finished dressing, reached automatically to see if his braid was smooth, then remembered he had had to cut it off, as part of his disguise. His hair was now close-cropped, so he ran a hand over it instead, and added, "I won't mention it."

Chapter 4

As soon as he saw it, Cord knew that Hafed's taste had not been allowed free rein in the dining room. He had seen enough to know that if the emerald-green walls and floor were startling, they were at least not vulgar. Turquoise chairs and tables were covered in a soft printed fabric, and gold and ivory material was draped over mock cornices. Thank goodness, the staff was not dressed in orange here; they wore only orange emblems.

Captain John Hafed and Connor Roi were already seated when Cord arrived. Hafed, he noticed, did not look any more jovial than he had in the afternoon, though he had had the good taste to change into an official uniform of a dark fabric with the same orange emblem. Connor seemed slightly depressed, although he made an effort at his usual cheerful insouciance when he sighted Cord.

"Have a Maze Runner's Delight," the pilot urged, swishing the contents of his glass. The liquid was lavender, with an oily sheen.

"I'd better stick to ice wine."

Hafed was not drinking anything. Neither did he talk much. The questions he asked were short and to the point. Cord felt that he was being interrogated, but could not determine for what purpose. Hafed was a master at concealing his emotions; a by-product, perhaps, of boffing an android? His inquiries were those that any normally curious person might pose to a writer.

The difference was that Hafed was not curious, not idly inquisitive, anyway. There was a driving purpose behind those opaque black eyes and ice-cold mind, a singleness of purpose, and not the strange alien trace that had tainted Julia McKay.

Cord answered all questions with an appearance of candor. Any hint of evasion would alarm Hafed, and Cord was extremely interested in finding out what the other was hiding. Apart from his rather strange sexual preferences.

The dinner was good. The other people looked and acted like the usual space-station crowd. And still, something was wrong. Cord could sense it hanging over the room like a miasma: watchfulness and tension.

They sat and talked long after they had finished eating. Hafed drank a nonalcoholic roasted grain beverage. Connor swilled his terrifyingly colorful drinks. Cord sipped wine. He could not leave without arousing Hafed's suspicions still more. The captain would wonder what he was up to.

Connor Roi slurred, "Better go to bed. Maze Runners sneak up on you fast. . . ." He pulled himself to his feet and swayed gently, blinking his eyes.

"Connor, you fool, you drink too much," Hafed stated. "Here, I'll help you back to your room."

You might say those words to a good friend—but you'd say them affectionately. Uttered in Hafed's dead voice, they were like a cold shower. Roi sobered noticeably.

"I'm all right, John. I—"

Hafed cut him off. "Come on. Good night, Rait."

Cord watched them go. Roi's tendency to weave was subdued by the captain, who plowed straight toward the exit.

He sat a little longer, finishing his glass of wine, before taking his own leave. No one paid him any attention. When he did stroll out, he was reasonably sure no one would notice where he went.

It was still too early for reconnaissance. He returned to his own room to wait and to check his map once more.

Four o'clock in the morning, station time. Cord slipped out of his room and made his way toward the warehouse section. The corridors were empty: those who had to report for duty in the morning were sleeping now. Those who were on duty were not roaming the halls.

He got into one of the tube cars and pressed the code sequence for A Section. The station seemed to require surprising amounts of warehouse space, even considering the size of the wheel. Also, it was remote from the living areas and the offices. The station map indicated few means of access, which might mean nothing or everything.

He left the tube car two stops before A Section; once inside it, there were no tube-car platforms. He was in an area meant for docking great ships. The big freighters and passenger ships did not enter stalls. They were too large. Instead, they nosed up against the station's side and were tethered—very much like a boat moored at a dock.

The yellow corridor in A Section looked well used, although it was empty at present. Cord took a moment to orient himself. This was the main hallway, and it ran along one side of the wheel—the "top," as if the station were lying flat on a surface. The tube train ran along the outer rim, where the great ships docked.

There was more room in Station Kappa than could be accounted for by the number of personnel. Kappa did not advertise as a trading station, not even for independent freighters, so what did they use it for? It would be interesting to see exactly what was in the warehouse. Cord took a transtube "down" to the nearest tube station, where he entered a car headed in the direction of the storage areas.

If he met anyone he was prepared to give a display of advanced intoxication to explain his presence. *I wush jush looking for m' room,* he thought wryly.

So far, so good. The transtube stopped and he stepped out into what seemed like an ordinary yellow corridor until he noticed the sign posted by the door opposite.

"Personnel access only. *No* cargo to be taken out this entrance. Freight *must* be routed through Cargo Door A-120."

Well, he was personnel, and he had no freight with him, so this door was meant for him. Boldly Cord pressed the door switch. It slid open, which made him more than usually cautious. He worried when things went too smoothly.

The warehouse was large, but not as large as it showed on the station map. Cord was certain of it. In the dimly lighted space, he could make out both ends of the chamber. He headed left. According to the map, in that direction lay the major section of the warehousing area.

Cord passed stacks of crates, all secured by lines or nets in case the gravity generator failed. The goods looked innocent: their labels indicated contents appropriate to a space station. He wasted little further time examining them, but walked on, keeping to the shadows as much as he could.

Ahead, he could see a barricade of boxes . . . and a wall.

Which was odd, because the map showed the warehouse was three times as long as the distance he had come. Cord turned to follow the wall. He came to a gap between packing cases, and melted back behind them as a door slid open.

"Milk concentrate—10,000-liter equivalent—Product of St. George—Shipper: Smith & Daughters; Consignee: Kappa Station" stated the label at eye level.

Men had come through the open door, their voices echoing in the vast spaces.

"I can think of better places to be, myself. Come on, let's lock up." He heard a click and then two men in orange passed by.

Cord lost sight of them among the piles, but their footsteps retreated. They were going toward the door through which he had entered.

"Hurry up," he heard. "There's a lot to be unloaded, and Hafed likes it done fast."

"Don't worry, this will be quick. It's mostly two-legged cargo tonight. Not much hardware at all. Only some rare-metal ingots, pharmaceuticals, some textiles, and some registered mail. Passenger ships don't want to bother with bulky stuff like farm machinery."

"Neither do we," said his partner.

The first one laughed. "It may be hell to shift, but there's a market for it. Hafed says there's a market for everything. He should know."

They went through the door; it clicked behind them.

Cord came out of hiding and swiftly approached the second door. Fishing in his pouch, he came up with a metal apparatus with many protusions. After a few minutes of trying different combinations, the lock clicked open. He activated the switch, and the door slid open to let him pass.

The room beyond looked very much like the one he was in: high-ceilinged, dim, stacked with boxes and bales with only passages left for access. With his eyes and ears alert for any sign, Cord edged toward the door, paused momentarily, and darted through. He threw himself behind a large, corded bundle.

Its label he could not read at all: it was in some language other than Multi-Lang. The squiggles and geometric forms in half a dozen brilliant, disharmonious colors betokened a tongue far removed from those with which Cord was familiar. The bale also exuded a rich, alien scent.

He eased his way from one bundle to the next,

always working toward the far end of the room. Most of the activity centered there. Men and women in orange coveralls were pushing pallets into place. The goods did not concern Cord particularly; no doubt they were as the spacer had said—ingots, cloth, drugs. His own interest was in the "two-legged cargo."

This clandestine warehouse was of the same size as the official one, which meant that the third section was used for something else. His progress was slow; he could not risk being cornered by the hurrying personnel. Once he crouched behind great ceramic barrels, eavesdropping on a conversation. He recognized the tones of one of the speakers. It was Hafed.

"I want the ship out of here fast," the emotionless voice said. "This time, see that it goes into a sun, if you can. It stirs the authorities up when they find a derelict. When nothing is found, who can say what happened? There are many dangers for vessels, and some are lost every year."

"We're working as fast as we can, captain," a second voice replied. "Processing the crew and passengers always takes time, though."

"You didn't lose any?"

"No. We caught the crew off guard. They were asleep before they realized they had a problem. The rest were the usual mixed bag. They're all right, or will be once the gas wears off."

Hafed grunted. "Good. The Liff will pay well for spacers. Anyone else of interest?"

"Nobody who isn't salable, if that's what you mean, captain."

"No, that isn't what I mean. I've never had any difficulty disposing of human or humanoid cargo. Someone always buys, for specialists, paramours, sacrifices, experimental subjects—there's always a demand. I mean—were there any diplomats or nobility on board? Any billionaires? Celebrities? People like that are worth more in ransom than on the slave block."

"I didn't recognize any of the names on the passenger list, sir."

Cord felt the psychic shrug with which Hafed accepted the statement. The station owner went on to ask about details of the ship's manifest. Cord listened with half his attention, having discovered that he could see the goings-on beyond a pair of open double doors.

A procession of men and women shuffled by, expressions dazed, guarded by spacers with drawn weapons. It seemed a needless precaution. The prisoners were obviously drugged.

"Get them bedded down," Hafed was saying. "And get everyone who's not on guard duty out of this section. If they want entertainment, they can pay for it in the brothel. And make sure that guard detail understand their orders. They aren't there for an orgy. If the merchandise is damaged, the profit goes down. You can let the drugs wear off. I expect an Aestian merchant ship in a day or so."

"Yes, captain."

Hafed stumped away. Cord listened for the lighter tread of the woman Hafed had been talking to. She continued to prowl the area, for what reason, Cord could not guess. Once he caught sight of her bending to read a shipping label on a box. He wished she would go elsewhere. He couldn't make a move while she was there. Or he could end up as merchandise, himself.

He gave it some thought. Tonight's expedition had told him a great deal. Hafed was a slave trader and clearinghouse for pirates' loot—if not the instigator of hijackings—and the prisoners were evidently kept in the third "warehouse" section. Also, Cord now knew that a ship would soon arrive to take them away. However, they were not his assignment. His mission was to locate the woman Edwina. There was no point in wandering around the warehouse—at least, not without information.

There was no sound from beyond the double doors. The spacers were apparently busy with the captives, or had dispersed to other parts of the station. The woman was still poking around the crates, now with her back to him. Cord saw that she was making notes on a clipboard.

She was wearing a sidearm, but at present she was intent on her work. Cord regretted the absence of his anesthetic darts, and shrugged mentally. He would make do with what he had.

With one last glance in the direction of the door, Cord came out of his hiding place, stalking the woman. He would enjoy wrestling with her—but there would be none of that. Not now, anyway. He drew out his gun and held it steady. When he was right behind her, he said gently, "Excuse me . . ."

She jerked urpright and swiveled to face him. Her eyes widened, her hand snaked down to draw her weapon. She froze as he continued.

"I wouldn't. You couldn't shoot me before the explosive darts in this made a cavern in your midriff. Do as you're told and answer a few questions for me, and you will survive. Well?"

She nodded.

"Good. First, we are going to close that connecting door so we can have some privacy. Keep your hands well away from your belt, turn around, and walk toward the door. Casually."

She complied. Cord kept close behind her. If anyone was in the other area, it would seem that he was only following her. No one was visible, however, and the third section was lower-ceilinged than the one in which they stood. Cord deduced that the prisoners' cells or holding areas were upstairs. A circular ramp led upward in one corner, which seemed to confirm his guess.

Cord flicked the switch to close the door. His prisoner stood woodenly as the panels met.

"Raise your hands over your head and lean against the door. Feet apart." Cord removed her handgun and searched her efficiently. She had wide hips and shoulders. It would be very easy to forget what he was doing. . . . She seemed not to be armed, apart from the cutter. Well, appearances could be misleading, and he would not swear she had no other weapon, not without stripping her and examining her skin. That would be fun but not practical. Cord concentrated on the job at hand while working, but no matter how single-minded he might be, he preferred not to introduce a distraction which would challenge even his dedication. He would assume she was dangerous.

"Over here—behind these boxes," he said, gesturing with the gun—but not so wide a gesture as to leave her stomach uncovered.

She moved to the boxes.

"You may as well sit," he added. "I intend to."

She lowered herself onto a crate, never taking her eyes off Cord. He seated himself on a bundle with his back against the wall. The projectile gun's muzzle never deviated from her torso.

"What's your name?" he asked.

"Susan Clay de Torre."

She was tall and lavishly molded; she looked as if she would be bouncy in bed and good in a fight. Her skin was delicately pale, her eyes a rich brown, a combination Cord found intriguing. The woman's hair was yellow, worn short, spacer-style, but dusted with gold powder in concession to fashion.

"Rank?"

"Rank?" she repeated, cautiously.

"On Hafed's pirate ship. What are you—captain, first mate?" It was safe to assume it *was* a ship in Hafed's employ, considering the way he'd issued orders.

Cord could feel her increasing doubt and fear. No doubt she had hoped that he had seen and heard less than he had.

"Susan, we are in a locked cargo compartment. No one else is within earshot. To spare me the bother, and you the pain, of my beating it out of you, I suggest you answer. Also, I am in a hurry, so be quick and honest."

"I'm Hafed's first mate," she replied. She managed not to stutter or speak too fast, an effort to retain her dignity that Cord silently applauded.

It was a good thing she had not defied him. He hated to apply torture. It pained him mentally as much as it hurt the victim physically.

"How many guards are watching the prisoners?"

She delayed a second too long.

"How many?" he rasped.

"Four," she said, and Cord sensed from her psychic emanations that she had blurted out the truth.

"I would hate to break such pretty fingers or blacken such soft skin," he purred. "I suggest your stop stalling. Now, how many prisoners are there?"

"One hundred and eight passengers and eight crew."

"How are they guarded?"

"They're in individual cells. There's a guard at the end of the passage, two more in a room outside, and one at the door leading out of the warehouse."

"Which is in the next hold?" He nodded toward the next section.

"Yes."

"Who has the keys to the cells?"

"One of the two men in the outer room," she answered.

"You say there are a hundred and sixteen prisoners. Are there none left from your last raid?" He wanted to ask it casually, so it would not seem important. If Susan Clay de Torre saw that it was his major objective, she might be tempted to lie.

"No, they're already gone. Captain Hafed doesn't like to keep them around any longer than necessary."

"The current lot is to be shipped out on an Aestian ship. Was it the same ship that picked up the last captives?"

"No." She swallowed, and her eyes flickered to his face. "Do—do you want to know what vessel took them?"

"Yes."

"It was the *Orion's Sword* out of Salash."

"And where did the *Orion's Sword* take them?"

"It was bound for Irru."

"And did the cargo include a woman taken from the Komonori ducal yacht?"

"That's right," the woman replied.

Cord knew she was worried and nervous. Anyone would be. What bothered him was that she was growing more and more tense. He had held many men and women at gunpoint; when they were not shot at once, they tended to become calmer. The exception was when they were planning something.

Years of training had honed Cord's skill. While questioning the first officer, his ears and nose still channeled information to his brain. There had been no sign of danger.

Now a sibilant whisper reached him—the preliminary to the opening of a door. The door connecting with the slave pen: if it had been the farther one, even his ears could not have detected it.

The woman had not heard it, though he suspected she was waiting for it—for someone to come looking for her. Before the door slid open, Cord had melted back among the crates so that his prisoner could see him but whoever was approaching would not.

The first mate stared at him, puzzled; she was going to speak, Cord thought, seeing her lips part. He shook his head and made a warning movement with the projectile gun. Her teeth clenched on her lower lip. Under her coverall, her breasts rose and fell more quickly.

"De Torre?" a deep voice said.

Cord pronounced the words without speaking them: *Call him over here.* Susan de Torre hesitated, opening her mouth. *Call him,* Cord repeated.

"I'm over here, Captain Hafed." Her voice shook only slightly, not enough that the other would notice, Cord thought.

"What the hell are you doing, hanging around . . ." Hafed's sentence ended as he came around the pile of boxes to face Cord.

"Hands up, please, captain."

Hafed obeyed. He made no display of surprise or anger, only watched Cord with those black impassive eyes.

Cord made Susan de Torre lie face down on the floor while he searched the station's captain. Hafed was armed with a short-tubed cuttergun, a vicious-looking weapon. Cord appropriated it. It might be useful.

With the two of them as his prisoners, it should not be difficult to get access to any part of the station—and more to the point, to get a ship away. Now that he knew where Duke Ashek's woman was, there was no point in remaining on the station. He would notify the authorities that Station Kappa was a pirate base once he was well away from it.

"Lie on the floor," he ordered. "Pardon me—the deck—Captain Hafed." And he would find something with which to tie them up.

Chapter 5

"I don't think that will be necessary, Cord, my friend," said the voice of Connor Roi behind him. "Would you drop that pistol, please?"

Cord let the projectile gun fall. He cursed Roi inwardly and cursed himself for not having kept his shields open. If he had, he would have sensed the man's approach. He had grown lazy, he decided. Too seldom was there a challenge now. Consequently, he had been taken by a ruse which should never have deceived him. To gain time, he turned and said amicably, "So you weren't drunk after all."

"Me, drunk? On Komonor you saw me put down a petty nobleman's ransom in ice wine. Compared to that, a Maze Runner's cocktail is a child's drink, the next thing to its mother's milk.

"You must be wrong, John," he said to Hafed. "This can't be a bounty hunter. Not a dangerous one, anyway."

"His first name is the same as the bounty hunter's," Hafed said. "You said he claimed to know the duke. And he's here. So it doesn't matter a howl in vacuum whether he's Cord the Hunter or not. He's dangerous. You were right to bring him here."

"You wouldn't be thinking of . . . ah . . . removing him permanently, now?"

Hafed made a grunt that might have been meant as a laugh.

73

"When I can get him out of the way and make money at the same time by selling him on some world where he won't escape easily? Don't be a fool, Roi. Clasp your hands behind your head," he told Cord.

Roi was at his back with a weapon; Hafed was directly in front, and Susan Clay de Torre was waiting in the background. The odds were better at the moment than they were likely to be again.

Cord's tail tip curled around the pommel of the knife in his boot. He was raising his arms, pretending to comply with Hafed's order, when he suddenly twisted around. The tail-held knife slashed up, across the captain's groin, while Cord's right elbow smashed Roi's throat. Hafed's bellow, vocal and mental, reassured him. But the blow to Connor Roi's neck only sent him reeling back; he still held the gun. It was a projectile weapon—either explosive or anesthetic darts. He did not intend to find out which. Springing at Roi, Cord slapped the wavering gun aside and rammed his fist into the gasping pilot's solar plexus. Cord felt Connor Roi's consciousness wink out as he fell. Cord picked up the gun. The woman next; he turned to do whatever was necessary.

Only moments had elapsed. Scarlet gushed from Hafed's wound as he made frantic, scrabbling efforts to apply pressure. The woman, frozen for one critical second, looked from Roi to Cord and then bounded toward the exit.

Cord's hand snapped up. Automatically he squeezed off two shots. Instead of a double explosion, he heard a whooshing sound. Susan Clay de Torre ran two or three steps before her legs gave way. She collapsed and lay motionless, but she was not dead. So these were anesthetic after all.

Hafed had stopped moving; there was a surprising amount of blood pooled under him. The sliced artery had been fatal; Hafed was no longer a problem. De

Torre was going to sleep for a good long while, and Connor Roi was unconscious. Cord took the precaution of pumping an anesthetic dart into him, too. Now he should have time to take care of other matters.

First, he retrieved his knife and his own projectile gun. He checked the one he'd taken from Roi. It still contained nine darts. More than enough, he thought.

He went into the next room. No sound came to him. Cord went up the spiral ramp quietly, prepared for opposition. If he understood the layout correctly, the ramp would bring him to the outer room.

Near the top, he halted, pressed against the inner wall. There was no conversation. Dropping the mental barriers that insulated him from humans' undisciplined emotions, Cord "listened" for the guards. Their psychic activity was low: one might be dozing and the other seemed to be concentrating on something. By the quality of the man's focused attention, Cord surmised he was reading.

Slowly he continued his progress. Now he could see a corner of the room. A pair of legs wearing short space boots were visible. They were stretched out and crossed at the ankles; they obviously belonged to the sleeper. Cord took aim and fired. The dart caught the napping guard in the thigh.

"Huh?"

The sting had wakened him, but Cord was not worried. The man would not be alert long enough to discover that dart.

"What's the matter?" the other spacer asked. His emanations remained calm; probably he had not even glanced away from the viewer.

"Don' know—nothing, I guess. . . ." The words were slurring.

Cord stepped out of the curve of the ramp. The drugged spacer was too far gone to speak or notice. The bookish pirate was sitting with his back to Cord, but started to look over his shoulder as he saw Cord's reflection in the viewer's screen. They had had it too easy too long: it did not seem to occur to the man that this was anything but a surprise inspection by Hafed or the first mate. Cord shot him before the man realized that anything was wrong. His body hit the floor with a heavy, meaty thump. Since the room offered no cover, Cord pressed himself against the wall close by the door leading to the cells and waited. The panel hissed open as a tall, burly spacer from the prison section came to investigate the noise.

"Ric? What are you do—?"

He got no further. Cord planted a dart in his shoulder as accurately as any medtech. But one human in six does not succumb immediately to the standard anesthetic charge, and this was the one. He snapped around to face Cord as he felt the prick of the needle and leaped with the force of a steel spring. Cord got off one more shot and flung his dart gun aside, rather than have it turned upon himself.

The man had not thought of drawing his own sidearm. Instead, he fell on Cord, crushing him in a rib-breaking grip.

Cord was pinned, unable to move his arms or tail. The breath was knocked out of him, and, horrified, he realized he could not expand his chest to take in air. The spacer's weight and deathlike grip made it impossible to breathe. In a few moments, light and dark spots danced in his eyes. He did not have much longer.

With a wrenching effort, Cord twisted his head to one side and bit down. The jugular vein was there; with luck, he might bite through it.

He tasted blood. The man bellowed an obscenity and released his grip. Cord pushed himself away and scrambled to his feet, gasping heavily. To combat the dizziness, he went into the fourth stance of Ba-Reet-Su and silently chanted a few lines from a contemplative hymn. Everything seemed to slow down.

The spacer's progress was slow and studied, as in an underwater dance. His hand balled into a fist and rose slowly in an uppercut curve. Cord sank into a crouch, grabbed one of the spacer's ankles, and stood up. Thrown off balance, the man landed jarringly on his back. He rolled onto his side and tried to rise. Cord kicked him in the stomach. The man finally passed out, less from the kick than from the drug. Cord made a mental note to remember for future use how long the anesthetic required to take effect on some people.

He remained cautious. After drawing his knife (still bloody, he saw—careless of him to put it away unwiped), he knelt beside the spacer. The human's emanations proclaimed him unconscious. Somewhat reassured, Cord took his weapon, a cutter, and then transferred his attention to the other two.

The second one he searched, the reader, proved to have the key. Armed with those, he entered the prison section.

A long aisle stretched before him, lined on either side by closed cells. They were small, barely long enough for the prisoner to lie down. Each door had a window of dura-plas giving a view of the occupant. The first two cells on the left side contained women. One was asleep on the pallet; the other sat huddled but looked up, startled, when Cord peered in. She looked down again, quickly, as if not seeing would make her invisible to her jailer.

He checked several cells on the other side of the passage. Males were on the right. He continued checking both sides at random, until he spotted a uniform. That cell door he opened.

The woman surged to her feet. The well-cut magenta-and-blue uniform clung to her, but it was her steely eyes Cord noticed. The high color in her cheeks betokened ire and spirit.

"What is the meaning of this?" The words crackled

with authority. She did not come forward, however, which was hardly surprising, as Cord was still carrying the cuttergun.

Not that he was pointing it at her. He merely held it negligently, to suggest that it would look in her direction if she gave trouble. He wanted no further fights tonight, espcially not before he had a chance to explain.

"Captain?" By the amount of trim on her uniform and her air of command, it seemed a reasonable hypothesis.

"Yes, I'm Captain Nakowa. What do you want?" The voice was still sharp, the emotions behind it spiked with fear and suspicion.

"Captain Nakowa, this is a rescue. I am Cord the Hunter. You may have heard of me. I want you—and your crew—to assist me." He stepped back from the door, and she warily followed. Cord rapidly glanced in the next half-dozen cells on either side and opened those that held ship's crew.

"Now," Cord said, when the eight were assembled in the corridor, "I don't know how many of the station personnel are part of this, so we'll assume that everyone is. You'll go to the control section, take it over, and send a distress call, detailing the operations here. Call Komonor—Duke Ashek will be pleased to send a ship and men to clean up Station Kappa. I'd like to lock up the whole pirate crew, but that would be overly ambitious. From the control room you can maintain or cut life support to any part of this station. I suspect you can also lock the inter-section doors, so that each is isolated. That would probably be a wise precaution. Right now, help me get these into cells. You, you, and you,"—Cord indicated crewmen. "There are two more out in the hold. Get them in here, too."

"What about the passengers?" someone asked.

"Leave them where they are for the moment."

The captain spoke sharply. "And while you're ordering us around, what do *you* intend to do?"

Cord smiled icily.

"I am going to take a certain pilot and his ship and leave. Please present my compliments to Duke Ashek, and tell him I am continuing my mission."

He handed her the cuttergun. "I have no wish to run a space station—it's all yours. Just make sure there's no interference when I leave in the *Rose of Flame*."

Cord turned and walked away. He found Connor Roi still unconscious. Cord slung his prisoner over his shoulder and made for Section C-4. If anyone in the corridor noticed them at all, they would think no more than that Roi was being helped back to his room or his ship by a less-drunken friend. And anyone who had seen Connor's performance in the restaurant earlier would have no doubts at all. Roi was lighter than Cord had expected.

Cord used Connor Roi's limp hand to open the palm lock sealing of the *Rose of Flame*. Once inside, he took the pilot to his own cabin, threw him on the bunk, and methodically began to remove hypo-sprays and drugs from his first-aid kit.

Cord found what he wanted and checked for the correct dosage, guessing at Roi's weight. The stimulant would be most effective—and fastest—injected near the heart. Cord tore Roi's shirt open . . .

. . . and stared, paralyzed with surprise.

Ashek folded and refolded the flimsy spacegram sheet. Kenek waited, too wise to ask for details. But because it did concern his heir, Ashek offered the information: "Yevren is concerned that Cord and his pilot did not arrive on Oranekko. He requests that I initiate certain inquiries. Quite unnecessary, of course, since we heard from Station Kappa. I have already sent my reply. By now Yevren is probably en route to

Kappa to pick up the trail."

Now that Kenek had been briefed, he should have withdrawn. Instead he ventured, "Father?"

Ashek looked up, surprised and not pleased with his son. "Yes, Kenek?"

"Senek is very friendly with one of the emperor's granddaughters. And he has become friendly with her retinue and with other members of the imperial circle. If it were M'Sen . . ."

"If it were M'Sen, it would not matter, because he is a fool and it would mean nothing beyond his usual indiscretion. But, after you, Senek is my heir. Do you think he is ingratiating himself with the emperor for cause? Or is he infiltrating their camp on our behalf?"

Kenek forgot himself and began to snort in derision. He turned it into a cough. "He has not favored me with any information about the emperor's plans." The word "me" was faintly accented. The implied question was clear: Has he told *you* anything?

Ashek replied with a question. "What do you suggest I do about your brother?"

Kenek's handsome, cold face clouded. "You might send him off on some pressing errand, sir—to help Yevren, perhaps. Or ignore what he's doing. He doesn't know about Edwina, so perhaps if he were told what's happening, he would stand by us. Or he might have an accident."

"Which would you advise? Bearing in mind that if he knew more, he might use it to cement his position with the emperor. If you died, he would be the next duke."

"If our line survives, Father," Kenek said softly.

"I note your concern, Kenek. If, as you say, our line survives." It was patently a dismissal, and this time, Kenek heeded it.

Ashek sat back to wonder just what he would do. If Yevren did not accomplish his mission quickly, the duke would certainly have to choose one of the alternatives.

Chapter 6

Connor Roi sat in the pilot's seat aboard *Rose of Flame*. A shot of stimulant had wakened him and cups of black coffee from the galley kept him going. Cord watched unsympathetically.

"Ah, Cord, I don't know that I'm in the best condition to pilot a ship. Maybe we should wait a little—"

"If we wait long enough, Duke Ashek's men will arrive," Cord snapped. "Then I would have to find a new pilot. The duke wanted the pirates kept for him to dispose of. As Hafed's source of information, you would qualify, wouldn't you? Do you want to find out how the duke proposes to deal with Hafed's merry men? And women?"

Connor Roi's face whitened, and the pilot swallowed. Cord had given no clue before that he knew Roi's secret. Now it was plain that Connor was in an agony of suspense—did Cord know or not?

Cord sighed. He preferred to travel with a pilot whose mind was on the job.

"Connor Roi, I know what you are. Or what you aren't, at least. But we can discuss that later. Right now, I want to get on with my assignment. Will you pilot me—or would you rather speak with Duke Ashek?"

"No, perhaps not," Roi agreed. "Where are we off to?"

"Irru."

Connor Roi, in the midst of running through his checklist, turned to stare at him.

"That forsaken hole? The pit of this end of the galaxy?"

"It's not in the Komonori Empire. That should be an attraction. Remember, Connor, I am all that stands between you and Duke Ashek's justice."

Roi's face went blank and he returned to methodically preparing for takeoff.

Once they were away from Station Kappa, Cord asked, "Now I would like to hear why you are passing as a man."

Connor Roi, who had been very subdued since their departure from the space station, looked up from the instrument panel. "I don't look like a woman, do I?"

Catching the pain in Roi's mind, though the voice was perfectly level, Cord did not answer directly. Besides, he liked Connor—whatever sex the pilot was.

"You don't try," he said. "If you made any effort at all to dress like a woman, I wouldn't have thought you were anything else."

Connor Roi grinned wryly, showing strong white teeth. "I'm flat-chested and hipless. I'm sterile. Nothing I wear can change that. I might as well be a man."

"You don't have a beard," Cord pointed out, "or a hairy chest."

"It would be better if I did, maybe. Fortunately for me, spacers are a private lot. They will not undress in public, which has been the saving of me."

Cord reached out and patted her shoulder. "I'm sorry. I wasn't prying intentionally. How did you happen to take up piloting?"

"How is it I'm a freak, you mean?" Connor did not sound either bitter or offended. She shrugged. "I was born on Litheen—one of Komonor's subject worlds. When I was eleven, I got a dose of T-radiation. My family didn't have the money to send me for treatment. My mother even asked her Komonori employer for help—and if you'd ever lived on a Komonori world, Cord, you'd understand how much courage that took. He refused. He said I'd be as useful to him one way as the other, because my value was in my intelligence. I was a plain little girl," Connor added parenthetically. "It hasn't been too bad, some ways. I've avoided certain problems, at least. When I was seventeen, I signed as ship's boy on as unspaceworthy a freighter as I've ever seen—without official permission, of course. My father was dead by then, and my mother was safe enough. Her Komonori employer was indulgent. I expect he'd taken her to bed, when she was younger, and she'd been a loyal worker."

"Then what?" Cord asked curiously, paying homage to a saga stranger than his own.

"I stayed with the ship until I had some experience, then began looking for a better one. I'd had a good technical education, so I caught on fast. I served on several ships, working my way up, and became first mate on . . . well, on a ship that picked up its cargoes in the oddest places. We made two or three good hauls, out of which my share was sufficient to buy the *Rose*. I'd learned to pilot already, of course. Since then, I've carried anything and anyone who could pay. I've passed as a man ever since leaving Litheen. You're the first who's guessed."

"I didn't guess. I opened your shirt to give you an injection to counteract the anesthetic. Then it was obvious. You simply aren't constructed the same way, breasts or no."

"I wish you hadn't found out."

"I'm glad I did," Cord replied. "I forced you to blast from Station Kappa, but I doubt I could hold you prisoner and make you take me where I want to go. One or the other, perhaps, not both. I have to sleep sooner or later. I'm willing to treat your part in Hafed's piracy as a misunderstanding—if you'll cooperate. Once you've gotten me to Irru—and off again—you're welcome to go wherever you wish. Is that fair?"

Roi's eyebrows went up with a trace of past insouciance. "Exceedingly—depending on what 'cooperation' entails." The color rose in her cheeks. " 'Entails' was perhaps not the word I meant."

Cord laughed delightedly as his appendage twitched. "I've never had to coerce my sexual partners, and I don't intend to start now. But perhaps the trip would be less boring if we had something to do."

"Something to screw, you mean," Connor said bitterly.

Cord could feel her emotions churning: hatred, revulsion, and desire. He would have to break through her wall of reserve first.

"There's no rush," he said softly. "But you might enjoy it."

"I doubt it," she muttered, hands working at the ship's console.

Cord stood up. "When the ship's on autopilot, meet me in the galley."

"You're always eating," Roi commented.

"It's my second favorite thing to do. . . ."

In the galley, Cord amused himself by setting containers of food and drink in the air and watching them bob gently in free fall. Eating well in zero G was difficult. Once in hyperspace, Connor could put the ship into a spin which would simulate gravity—since the *Rose* was too old to possess gravity generators—but she considered it risky to do so while accelerating under ion drive. It introduced an additional variable into navigational calculations. Meanwhile, Cord waited impatiently for the ship to enter hyperspace. Connor eventually floated in and hoisted herself over the counter and into a confining seat. She ate a green energy pill and watched Cord juggle the food containers.

"I'll take you wherever you want to go," Roi announced, "not being in love with lost causes—to wit, Hafed and the Ael."

"How do you come to be working with the Ael?" he asked casually, seemingly concentrating on his juggling. "I would have thought you'd join the Litheen raiders."

Connor Roi laughed. "It's not so surprising. I avoid my own people for fear of meeting one who knows me. And Hafed paid well for the snippets of information I brought about ships and cargoes. I grew up poor—I don't wish to live that way. I grew up under Komonori rule. I don't want to die that way—which is what will surely happen to a Litheen freedom fighter. All I want from life is to be free, not poor, and to fly my *Rose of Flame*."

"How long before we land on Irru?"

"We must spend the rest of a standard day on ion drive. Once we're in hyper, we can cross hundreds of parsecs in hours. But no ship can safely come out of hyperspace inside a system, so we will spend several more days entering Irru's solar system while on ion drive."

Cord made a face.

"The *Rose of Flame* possesses an old but reliable navigational system—which," Connor remarked, "works best when untouched by human hands. Her destructor field will deal with small space rubbish. Larger debris will trigger warning sensors and give me time for evasive action."

"I suppose you've become quite adept at evasive action," Cord said, meaning it several ways.

Connor's eyes grew dark and luminous. Disturbed, she threw herself out of the seat and left the galley area. Cord remained seated, his hands now at rest, but his mind busy. Apart from checking gauges and monitors at intervals, Connor would not have much to do now that the *Rose* was on course. Cord would have to find a way to overcome her wariness. Perhaps if he treated her more offhandedly, she would relax.

Later on in the standard day, they met again in the galley. Connor hauled out a heavy 3-D jigsaw puzzle and studiously played with the pieces. Cord had brought along a special-model cuttergun and had dismantled it; the pieces were spread over the small table in front of him. He busied himself with polishing each piece and studying it.

They worked in silence, until Cord started telling Connor about one particularly bizarre job he'd been hired for on Califax. It involved searching for a rich man's pet—which turned out to be one of the planet's most dangerous fauna. Trying to catch it and survive the experience had made the job a comedy of errors. Connor was laughing by the time Cord finished the tale.

In return, she regaled him with spacer exploits. Cord tried to top her with yet another outlandish tale. Just when he felt she was warming up to him, Connor smiled and said, "Now that I've told you about myself, will you tell me why a gentleman of your enterprise would want to go to Irru?"

"The last prisoners to sample Captain Hafed's hospitality went to Irru."

"Oh. And you sent for Duke Ashek to take over Kappa. So you *are* working for him?"

"Yes. Does it bother you that I'm working for a Komonori?"

"A bit," Connor replied, after a pause. "I don't like Komonori—though their money is as good as any, as long as they've got no hold on you. And Ashek's the best of a bad lot, by all accounts. The old Komonori emperor hates the sight of him, they say."

"Then what can you tell me about Hafed's last prisoners? And about Irru?"

"Not much," Connor admitted. "I wasn't involved in that affair. I've already told you about Irru."

Cord continued to methodically construct the now polished cuttergun. He snapped the last part into place. "You haven't told me about Irru in detail. I want to know everything—its government, climate, techno-level, whom to bribe . . ."

"You'd better use the screen," Roi said. "The computer has every inhabited world in this sector in its memory banks. It can tell you better than I can."

With this, she turned back to her game. Taking it as dismissal, Cord put away the gun and released himself from the seat.

"Use the one in my cabin; it's a newer model than the one in yours."

Cord laughed and rotated in midair. The offer was casually made, but a spacer permitted only good friends in his—or her—cabin. He pulled himself up the hand-holds and went through the circular hatch to topside. Connor's computer terminal *was* newer and slightly more deluxe—though not by much. Cord punched in instructions for information about Irru.

A succession of multicolored graphs showed Irru's location, first from deep space, then within its sector, its star system, its solar system. A three-dimensional line drawing of Irru and its continents rotated in front of his weary eyes. Then the readout began printing. Cord wished that the pilot had a more advanced model—one that would recite the facts aloud, to give his tired eyes a rest. But he persevered.

Chapter 7

Irru was an example of what happens to a planet which passes from feudalism to industrialization overnight. A trading company had discovered the world's stores of minerals. They brought in prefabricated factories and set up hydro-electric projects to power them, training several hundred bright young Ir to maintain them. The Ir mined and smelted half a dozen valuable ores for a fraction of the cost of labor on civilized worlds. On a planet where most people eked out a grim survival from subsistence farming, with perhaps a little left over to sell, the trinkets with which the company paid their Ir technicians and overseers were riches compared to the ingots of unusable metal. To the Ir, the esoteric ore was no good for knives, plows, and jewelry. So a fraction of the population lived in luxury; most existed on the brink of starvation. Seventy percent were illiterate and without any kind of medical care. On Irru, life was cheap. Literally.

While he was committing the important facts to memory, Cord sat on Connor Roi's small cot, anchoring himself with one hand. By the end of the tape, his vision was blurry and Cord was on the verge of sleep. He leaned to one side, and before he knew it, he was asleep.

The dream was of Julia McKay. Her long auburn hair sparkled with flecks of red-gold. Her fathomless dark eyes glistened. Her full body lay over his, and the tips of her heavy breasts brushed his chest. Her eyes closed and she groaned with passion, her body moving rhythmically against his. Then her mouth opened, revealing sharp little fangs. A pink tongue darted out and traced hot, wet circles around his right nipple. He could not resist being aroused, and he strained upward, struggling to fill her. She leaned back, moaning with ecstasy, her body continually moving over his. An orgasmic explosion ripped through his body as Julia reached her own heights of rapture, but still she rode him. He tried to buck her off, to no avail. Though he struggled terribly, something was holding him down. Julia knew he was trapped. Smiling, she lowered her fangs to his throat and ripped—

With a mighty effort, Cord sat up. A broken strap dangled from the cot. Momentarily confused, he sat there, clearing his head. He realized the ship's engines sounded different.

Connor Roi walked into the cubicle and stopped when she saw what Cord had done. "You—you were sleeping," she stammered. "So I just strapped you in. We just went into—"

"Hyperspace," Cord finished.

"Yes. I didn't want you to get hurt in the transition." She solicitously touched his shoulder. "Are you all right?"

He pulled her down next to him. "A very bad dream. I'm sorry about the strap."

She plucked at it nervously. "No matter." She started to rise, but Cord grabbed her arm. "Don't."

He slowly stroked her smooth skin. She shivered. "Don't leave me alone. I need you."

He embraced her slowly, carefully, as if she were a fragile flower. Tentatively she returned the embrace. They lay entwined for a long time. Cord touched Connor's mind: she was apprehensive yet concerned.

As they lay there, quietly listening to each other's heartbeat and feeling the heat of their bodies, Connor's mood changed.

Cord began to stroke her back and arms, and she relaxed even further. Eventually she returned his caresses, and he was able to unfasten her shirt and then her trousers. His rough but experienced tongue worked erotic patterns over her chest. It was true that she didn't have breasts to speak of, but she had pert little nipples that now pushed outward. His tongue trailed down over her smooth skin and danced between her thighs. By now the reserved pilot had shed her inhibitions, and Cord could tell she was ready and eager. Though her body was awkward with lack of practice—almost virginal—she responded willingly.

Up till now Connor's eyes had been closed. She opened them as Cord was about to ease into her—and shied away in surprise.

"I've never seen anything like that," she murmured.

"Standard equipment for my race," he assured her. "It will be all right; trust me."

Conversation lapsed as Cord concentrated on giving her pleasure. He had had better sex, he reflected, but this presented the thrill of challenge, at least. Connor Roi was as shy and elusive as some rare wild creature. Her unfeminine body did not bother him; in an experience of women spanning countless light-years and a dozen or more worlds, he had come to appreciate many kinds of beauty.

Afterward she seemed content to lie in his strong arms. Cord sensed she was at peace with herself and the universe, a state which he guessed was uncommon for Roi.

Connor Roi disentangled herself from Cord and modestly pulled on her breeches and shirt. She turned to the computer terminal, which Cord had left on, and pressed the proper button to close it down.

"Learn everything you need to know?"

"Well, I would like to know more about the slave trade. How does it pay?"

"Not badly," the pilot admitted.

"I mean, the economics of it. How did Hafed sell the people he captured?"

"Well, Hafed doesn't—didn't—sell directly to the public. He sold to hand-picked entrepreneurs who transported the merchandise to wherever they could sell it most profitably. On Irru, for example, it wouldn't pay to offer common laborers. Irru has cheap labor to spare. Unskilled workers go best on uninhabited planets that are just being developed. A company can more easily afford to buy men to dig ditches and level ground for spaceports than to hire them. Employees have to be paid, be covered by insurance, and then often leave after only a short time."

"And what sort of slaves do the Ir buy?" Cord asked.

"Technicians and scientists, probably. The ten percent of the population that are wealthy and understand the advantages of technology want to modernize. There's also some call for exotic humanoids," Connor Roi added, grinning. "Among the elite on such worlds, there is often some competition to acquire the most alien lover who is still able to ... ah ... give satisfaction."

"Which category did Duke Ashek's concubine fall into, I wonder?"

"Now that, I could not say, never having seen the lady. Hafed was angry, though: he expected to make more money on her. He mentioned being surprised at Ashek's taste. I don't know what he meant."

"She's no beauty," Cord answered. "Not if her holopix are truthful. But there is something unusual about her face."

"What?"

"I don't know." In some way he could not describe, Edwina was—different. So were her psychic signals, if the ring was any indication. He wondered again whether she was the one he sought. She could be Julia McKay. She might have undergone surgery on Brunan, either before he cornered her or after he lost her. After all, alterations were Brunan's specialty.

Connor read and worked on 3-D jigsaw puzzles between instrument checks and equipment inspections. Cord worked on his weapons.

"Do you never do anything else for relaxation?" Connor finally asked.

"Not when I'm hunting."

But when they entered orbit around Irru, Cord packed away his knives and dart pistols and rifles and went to stare into the viewscreen.

Muscular arms folded across his broad chest, he studied the golden-orange curve of the world. As their ship passed over the surface, the expanse shaded to deep green.

"There are several large deserts," Roi said. "We've been over one. Most of the towns are in the temperate latitudes. We will land at the largest, since the best port facilities are there. If that is satisfactory to you?"

"Would the *Orion's Sword* have come down there?"

"Probably. Kirino is where the big money is."

"Then it's fine."

Station Kappa was in turmoil. Yevren's courier ship and pilot had brought him quickly, while the cleaning-up operation was still in progress. Dressed in his police uniform, he strode authoritatively through the cargo hold. It would not do to be mistaken for one of the station crew by the Komonori police now in command of Kappa.

From space, nothing appeared to have changed at the station: if a ship approached and requested docking, it would be granted permission. Once its crew were aboard Kappa, the police would find out whether they were innocent, or pirate conspirators. At present it was assumed that all the station personnel were implicated and that any ship which put in at Kappa would be, too.

So Connor Roi had known that Kappa was a pirate stronghold, Yevren thought. Roi was too free and easy with the law. He was said to have come from Litheen, too, another reason to put an end to his freebooting ways. He should be serving his rightful master on Litheen, not roaming at will and flouting the emperor's law.

Yevren stared at the groups of prisoners assembled in the hold. These, he understood, were the incorrigibles. Many of the station personnel had cooperated with the police, but these refused to give information. Some showed signs of questioning, but their interrogators had been far too gentle. A mistake which would be remedied now that he was here. . . .

There was a woman leaning against the wall, arms folded on her chest. Her hair was golden rather than merely yellow or tawny. Her skin was as pale as . . . as pale as milk, Yevren decided. He approached her and said, "What's your personnel classification?"

"Maintenance," she answered, looking him straight in the eyes.

"Not according to two of the prisoners who've been helpful," the constable beside him said. "They say she's a big catch—one of Hafed's top people."

Yevren looked her over carefully, noting the way her uniform pulled taut over the breast and hip. "If you're an officer, why not admit it?" he suggested. "It's nothing to be ashamed of." When she made no response, he added, "But maybe you only earned your alleged rank by letting Hafed ride you."

Blood suffusing her face, the woman snarled out an

obscenity, hand darting to draw a weapon the police had already taken from her. She froze, realizing she had betrayed herself. Then she cursed him for a rotting eunuch, a pervert who had crept into the Komonori sewer, and half a dozen other things, each filthier than the last. She had a fine command of invective. Yevren waved back the policeman who moved to silence her.

"I'll question this one myself," he said. It was difficult to suppress his grin. Oh, she was proud—now.

Yevren straddled a red-and-silver plastic chair, and planned. Now that he knew where Cord and Roi were likely to be found (not to mention Edwina), he was anxious to be on his way. The courier ship he had requisitioned was faster than the *Rose of Flame*. He would be on Irru before they were, even if he postponed his departure until he had caught some sleep. But then again, he could sleep on the scout. The past day had been . . . eventful.

Susan Clay de Torre lay near his left foot, unconscious or pretending to be, curled into a fetal ball. As he had expected, she had been good. When he returned to Komonor, perhaps he would visit her in prison, to see if his influence endured. Of course, she wasn't very interesting, now that she cringed at his every movement. She wasn't beautiful, either, and never would be again—not without some extensive plastic surgery. She was blind in one eye, and all of her toes were smashed. The cuts, bruises, and broken ribs would heal, as would the burns in her palms and between her thighs. He licked his dry lips, feeling tired and sweaty. The memory of so much pleasure took his breath. Now that he had fulfilled the double goal of easing his tension and acquiring the necessary information, it was back to business. He nudged her with the toe of his boot. "Wake up, Susan." He stood up.

Instantly her remaining eye opened and focused on his hands. "Sir?" she whispered through cracked, bloody lips. A tear trickled down her right cheek.

Yevren ignored her, went to the door, and summoned the policeman waiting outside. "Take her away," Yevren ordered. The constable saluted and asked, "Any special treatment, sir?" Yevren glanced at the woman lying motionless except for her shallow, racking breaths.

"Make sure she doesn't die," he said pleasantly. "I may wish to question her again, on Komonor."

Chapter 8

A quarter-rotation later, as Roi and he left the port, Cord knew he had made the right choice. Inside the port, all was as it would be on hundreds of worlds: clean, orderly, efficient. Once through the heavily guarded gate, the city sprawled around them like an old harlot. The street was roughly paved but dirty, though only a narrow aisle down the center was really visible. The sides were thronged with people—peddlers selling food, drugs, souvenirs; pimps; pickpockets; prostitutes; others less definable, willing to do anything, anything at all, for a price. And not a very high one, either.

"Honored sirs, I can supply companions—girls or boys, whichever you prefer. Clean, talented, beautiful. I won't lie to you, they aren't virgins—virgins come expensive—but fresh, definitely fresh. Almost untouched. There are some who would try to take advantage of you because you are strangers, but I guarantee—"

"Go away," Cord said, cutting off the words with knifelike precision.

The pander, a ratlike little man who had seemed ready to attach himself to them until they gave in, sheared off abruptly.

"I told you it was a benighted place," Roi muttered. "There's nothing lower than a pimp."

"Nothing at all?" Cord looked at her inquiringly.

"Well, maybe slavers. Where do you plan to start looking?"

"Where do you think? The slave market."

The city roiled around them. On their way to Good Bargain Square, they saw, by Roi's count, eighteen beggars, a corpse, a knifing, half a dozen more panders, and rogues too numerous to mention. The smell of dust, sweat, strange food, and misery ceased to be noticeable after a while.

Cord occasionally opened his mind to receive the psychic output of the crowd, but there was nothing there to interest or alarm him. He felt the same urges and unhappiness as in any large group of humans and humanoids. A little more desperation and fear, perhaps; life was precarious on Irru.

The emotional atmosphere changed as they approached their destination. Mehirans, being empaths, kept their psychic emanations under control. To be exposed to others' anguish was painful, so care was taken not to broadcast negative emotions—both by eliminating as many causes of unhappiness as possible and by suppressing feelings of hurt and anger. Mehira had developed a peaceful culture, devoid of aggression (devoid of interest, too, Cord sometimes thought). When the Terran traders arrived, the Mehiran Council, fearing the aliens' strength, enacted strict controls on trade and communication with the spaceport. Cord had never broken the vow of secrecy he and his family had taken, though he felt no loyalty to the Council and little for Mehira. The ability to sense what the people around him felt was a useful tool, however. It gave him an edge.

At first, the uninhibited play of violent emotion around him had been distressing. Now he was hardened to it, although he preferred to screen out the background "noise," opening his mind to it at intervals to check for danger. He hardly noticed normal psychic output.

As they drew near to Good Bargain Square, the psychic clamor increased so much that Cord gave extra attention to screening it out. It was as if a thousand voices cried aloud their hatred, fear, rage, and humiliation. Cord's stomach knotted.

On all sides of the plaza were fenced areas, the courtyards of buildings behind. In these cages, men and women were on display. Others, less attractive merchandise or with more specialized skills, remained in the warehouses. Those in the yards were luxury goods to beguile the customers to make other, more expensive purchases.

The captives' misery lay like a fog on the square or rose like dust from the hard-packed ground of the cages. Here an enclosure held women destined to be concubines—tall, petite, slim, or buxom, with hair and skin of every imaginable pigmentation, all of them beautiful. None of them, however, had tails. There were men, well muscled, with faces either handsome or rugged. Someone for every taste.

Another enclosure contained more unusual specimens—entertainers, servants, a handful of aliens valued for unusual appearance. A chalkboard outside their area advertised:

Cosmetologist/hairdresser—100 Ki
Musician—plays 4 instruments—attractive—250 Ki
Cook, Ir and exotic cuisine—300 Ki or best offer
Inquire at desk for specialty merchandise.

Another sign read:

Omri's for technical workers. We have electrical techs, one computech, a physician, many clericals.

And high up on the face of one of the buildings, in gaudy red and black, a flashing sign proclaimed:

Gia, Broker. Simplify your buying. Listings from all major, most minor dealers. On world or off. Offices around the corner.

Cord made a circuit of the square, observing. There were four major slave dealers, all of whom had display areas, but there were many other sellers as well. These kept booths in the center of the plaza with listings of their merchandise. Some had only a few to sell, while others sold in bulk lots. Slaves were big business on Irru.

An antiquated hauler, so primitive it ran on wheels rather than on an air cushion, crawled past, its cargo area filled with chained laborers. Nearby, a hard-faced woman dressed in shimmering purple and yellow-orange with turquoise beading studied male slaves through the wire fence.

"Physique isn't enough. He's got to be able to do the household accounts, too. I need a steward, not merely a toy," she told the dealer brusquely. "That one looks intelligent. The blond. Call him over here."

Connor Roi was gazing at the women offered by Dependable Zita. There were many; some of them eyed her in return, hopefully. She turned away.

"This is sickening. And it looks like a devil of a job, finding one woman here. If she is still here."

"I've taken harder jobs," Cord replied, after a long look around. "This shouldn't be too difficult. I've located what I need."

"Have you, now?" Connor asked, falling into step beside him.

Cord threaded his way through the crowd, sidestepping vendors selling snacks and drinks, avoiding the occasional slave being led away, elbowing his way past businessmen and whoremongers and those who were simply windowshopping. He left the square via a narrow lane called Suet Street.

They were not yet out of hearing of the square when Cord halted. The little street was lined with solid-looking, if dirty, buildings of rough gray stone. A metal plaque over the arched entrance of the one on their left proclaimed it to be Felicity House. A wooden sign, hung beneath, added, "Office to let. Inquire at the blue door." Another listed the occupants.

Cord looked it over, passed under the arch, and started up the stairs leading off the lobby. Roi followed him without a word. They climbed steadily up the spiraling stair until they reached the third floor. Cord strode down the corridor and opened a red-and-black door.

The office inside was as squalid as the rest of the building: the bright-lacquered door was the freshest, cleanest thing about it. The room was ill-lit with the dim incandescent bulbs which were high technology on Irru, and the faded upholstery and wooden floor both looked as though they needed cleaning. The man who rose to greet them was richly dressed, however, and an obviously valuable crystal flask and goblets stood on the massive silver tray.

He was shrewd-faced, middle-aged, and thickset, with sharp blue eyes and gray hair in ringlets to his shoulders. His blue gown reached to mid-calf, revealing a pair of expensive brown boots beneath.

"How may I serve you, gentlemen?"

"I'm looking for a slave," Cord said.

"I'm a broker of slaves. I can probably help you."

"So I thought. Your name and business are prominently displayed in Good Bargain Square, Master Gia."

"They are, indeed. The price of those signs keeps me a poor man. Relatively speaking," Gia added with a deprecatory smile. "Please be seated and tell me your business. A glass of wine? You say you want a slave. What kind?"

"The woman I'm looking for is called Edwina, and was stolen from Duke Ashek of Komonor."

"Where they come from is no affair of mine. My concern is only where they go," Gia replied, pouring out three glasses of pinkish liquid from the crystal bottle. "A client comes to me and says he needs—for example—a weapons-systems analyst or a flamenco dancer. I locate one and take a finder's fee. That's all."

"You don't initiate slaver raids yourself?" Cord asked, careful not to sound condemnatory.

"That would be both dangerous and expensive." Gia smiled. "And what need? Every day, somewhere in the galaxy a few hundred people are abducted by pirates or sold by their own governments. I am seldom unable to fill a request."

"Good," Cord said. "Then you should be able to find the woman I'm looking for."

"A particular woman who has already been sold, in all probability," Gia pointed out. "Tracing is somewhat out of our line."

"But not impossible for one with your contacts. Naturally, I would expect to reward you for the information. Shall we say, the same fee you would have received for locating her for her purchaser?"

"Naturally, I will try," Gia answered. "Some research will be required. And I will need to know as much as possible about the woman—Edwina, you called her?"

Cord produced the holopix Ashek had given him and passed it to Gia.

"What are her skills and talents?" the broker inquired, studying the picture.

"None that I know of." Except, perhaps, a flair for killing. If she were Julia McKay.

"Planet of origin?"

"Unknown."

"When was she brought here—assuming she was?"

"My source was the pirate crew that captured her. It was within the last sixty standard days."

"That is something. Help yourself to more wine while I check my records, gentlemen."

Gia opened a wooden cabinet in the corner, revealing a small but newish computer.

"Female, human, unskilled, transactions in the last two months," Gia muttered to himself. "Bear in mind that she may be dead."

"Even that information would have some value. Not as much as if she were alive, of course."

"What are the chances she's dead?" asked Roi.

"For an unskilled woman not pretty enough to be valuable as a concubine?" Gia stated the facts brutally. "Such end up in hard, dirty jobs or as cheap whores. The life expectancy is not long—on the other hand, it hasn't been long since she was bought. Duke Ashek may get his woman back—if he still wants her, well broken in as she is likely to be, or scarred or pregnant."

"Two out of three can be remedied." Cord shrugged. What Ashek did with her after Cord restored Edwina to her original owner was no business of Cord's.

"You keep good records," Roi observed with a cutting edge to his voice.

"Of course. Sometimes fond relatives or friends want to ransom the unfortunate victims of pirate raids. As is the case with your employer."

Roi did not reply, and Cord saw no reason to explain that Ashek would certainly refuse to ransom his own property, however much money he spent in getting it back.

"Here," Gia said, scanning the list on the screen. "This may be your girl. The date and statistics are right. She sold for ninety Ki."

"Well?"

"Would you like to make an offer to her owner?"

Cord calculated the amount of expense money left and nodded.

"Go ahead." It might be cheaper to buy her out than to steal her.

"It will take some time," Gia told them, pressing a button on his desk.

Cord's muscles tensed as a curtain at the side of the room rustled and a burly, dull-faced young man entered. He bowed to Gia and waited as the broker scribbled a note.

"Go to this address and speak to the master. Ask if he will sell the woman he bought recently. Offer two hundred Ki, and bring back his counteroffer. And don't linger along the way."

The servant bowed again and went out the way he had come. "Are there no screen communications in Kirino?" Connor asked, having watched the performance curiously.

"Oh, yes. The spaceport has screens, and so do the offworld companies—the mines and smelters. But they are too expensive for most of us Ir. Slaves are slower, of course, but there is seldom much need for haste. Except in long-distance communication, and for important matters we can buy screen time from one of the offworld traders."

"I noticed that you gave your servant a note with the address but gave him the message verbally," Cord remarked. "Why?"

Gia smiled. "A written message to Merchant Ch—to the merchant would have been useless. He can't read. I chose not to speak the merchant's name and direction aloud because information is my stock in trade; if I broadcast it to my clients, how can I stay in business?"

"Your servant could have read him the note."

"The boy is able to read names, numbers, and sim-

ple directions. It was neither necessary nor profitable
to teach him more. I almost despaired of teaching him
that much," Gia added, "but it is useful to have a
slave who can read prices and recognize one's clients'
names. It is a bad practice to let them read other
things, however. Either they will waste time reading
for entertainment or they will get seditious notions.
No, no. Give me a strong stupid slave every time. Or a
pretty one. May I offer you more wine? And some
tidbits to go with it?"

The servant was long gone—no use now in trying to
follow him to discover the merchant's address. But if
they accepted Gia's offer, the slave broker might leave
the room long enough for Cord to take a look at his
desk and its contents. Cord accepted with the verbal
flourishes the Ir expected.

"Good!" Gia pushed the call button on the desk
twice, and a voluptuous brunette came from behind
the curtain. Breast, thigh, and rump pressed against
the clinging blue silk which covered her without concealing much from bosom to ankle. Her shoulders
seemed to beg to be pressed into a bed. When she
bowed, Cord waited expectantly for her breasts to
surge out of the strapless gown. They didn't.

"Refreshments, Ati," Gia ordered.

She bowed again, and disappeared through the
curtain, leaving a faint scent of spice and woman.

After she had served them and retired once again,
Gia said, "I see you admire my Ati. Perhaps you are
interested in something similar? I have contacts with
the best suppliers of recreational slaves. If you gentlemen spend much time in space, you can hardly make
a better investment than a concubine. Some spacers
prefer a simple, primitive lass who is overawed by the
ship and equipment, and so won't meddle or try to
jump ship at the first planetfall. On the other hand,
some prefer slaves from technological cultures who

can double as crew. There are conditioning processes to guarantee the slave will not attempt sabotage or escape. Such treatment is expensive but well worth it, as resale value remains high. If I can oblige you in such a way ..." The suggestion was delicate. No high-pressure selling for Gia.

"I prefer androids, myself," Roi said.

"And you, sir?"

Not wishing to offend the slave broker, who might still be of use, Cord chose a diplomatic lie.

"As you can see, I am not human. Having sex with human females comes close to being a perversion for me. However, if you happen to know of a woman of my own race, we might do business." If Gia had access to a Mehiran woman, Cord *would* purchase her, by all his ancestors. Otherwise, why should he pay for what he could get for free?

"I shall certainly check," Gia said, turning to his computer, but without much confidence.

Cord's credit account proved to be safe; no Mehirans, male or female, were listed in Gia's data bank, although there was one tailed being of a lizardlike species. Its sex was unknown.

Not having Cord's patience, Connor Roi was beginning to fidget by the time the messenger returned.

"Well?" Gia demanded to his servant.

"Sir, Master Ch—the merchant will not sell. He says all his wine would turn sour or be spilled from the casks if he let her go."

"Enough. Go to your quarters." When the boy had gone, Gia made a disparaging gesture.

"It is possible Duke Ashek is destined to be disappointed. Still, we might tender another offer."

"Do so," Cord responded. "His grace would be surprised indeed if I took one refusal seriously. This merchant may reconsider for more money. Or maybe money is not the right inducement. Are there offworld goods he could not easily acquire? Another slave for whom he would trade this one? See what you can do for us, Master Gia. If the man will not bargain for any amount of money, find out what he will take. It will be worth your while." With a nod which was not quite the courteous bow of Ir society, Cord took his leave.

Chapter 9

"What now?" Connor Roi inquired, as they went out into the street. It was growing hot, and the city was growing correspondingly more smelly. Powdery dust puffed up from Suet Street (unpaved, like most of the side streets) and made Roi sneeze.

"Since the easy way has failed, I'll have to kidnap her." Cord strode on in silence.

"All by yourself, man?"

Cord's tail lashed. "Who's to help me?"

"I am, by damn!" Connor exclaimed, slapping her thigh. "Besides, you need me to get you—and the woman—off Irru. How would you get her away without my help?"

With considerable difficulty, Cord admitted to himself. But to Connor Roi he said, "I might have had to hijack a ship and soothe the hurt feelings with money later. But if you'll help me, so much the better. You won't lose by it."

"Trust a great nobleman like Duke Ashek to be free with money." Roi grinned. "Do you have a plan?"

"Not yet. When I've looked over the house, something will occur. Meanwhile, Gia will continue to try to earn his commission—which should keep him from tipping off the merchant about us. I hope."

"How are we going to find out who the woman's owner is?"

Cord laughed. "It should not be too hard to discover.

We know his name begins with 'Ch' and that he sells wine."

"Irru must have thousands of grog shops," Connor protested.

Cord shook his head. "The runner was out only long enough to have gone somewhere inside the city. I've seen no sign of motorized transport as private vehicles or mass transit—certainly no jethoppers—so wherever he went, we can assume it was within walking distance. Also, the merchant must be a man of wealth, not simply a tavernkeeper. Most of the drinking houses I've seen do not suggest sufficient profits to buy a ninety-Ki servant. Plain drudges can be bought for thirty or forty. Besides, whatever the risks to his wine, a common tapster would not refuse a generous offer. He might try to raise it, but he wouldn't refuse it outright.

"You're sharp," said Roi admiringly. "I must watch your technique."

In a city as primitive as Kirino, it was too much to hope for a city directory. Instead, there were other methods of learning what Cord wanted to know.

"Let's go in there," Cord suggested, seeing a brightly painted representation of a wine pot and a heaping platter of food hung over a door. The street was poor and dirty, but full of people; and through the establishment's open windows came the sound of many voices. The tavern was obviously a lively and prosperous place.

Inside, rough tables accommodated the customers— petty merchants, vendors interested in resting in cool, dim surroundings, entrepreneurs of varying degrees of success and honesty. Cord sized it up as working-class and decent, not a place to attract the criminal element. A door at the back opened on an interior courtyard. He glimpsed a cook shed where a wiry middle-aged woman, probably a slave, was busy grilling meats and vegetables.

"What's for you, friends?" the innkeeper, a paunchy, balding man, greeted them, giving their table a swipe with the corner of a gray rag. It left the table little cleaner, but the surface had been reasonably clean to start with. One could expect no better on a world where ninety percent of the population were without running water.

"A jug of your house wine," Cord said.

They took seats at a long table with several other drinkers. They attracted a certain amount of attention as strangers and non-Ir. It was not a tavern which saw many spacers or tourists.

"Spacers, are you?" one of their fellow drinkers asked.

"Freighter pilot—and owner," Roi said. "Connor Roi is my name."

"Rait is mine," Cord said. Irru was the butt end of the universe, all right; all the same, he wouldn't chance someone, even here, having heard of Cord the Hunter.

When the man had brought their wine and they had sampled it, Cord ventured a comment. It is only on very sophisticated worlds that conversation (and friendship) are rushed into.

"This is good wine. Is it a local product?"

"The Three Hills dew-petal wine? It is," the tailor sitting next to Roi said. "It is good, and the better for being cheap."

"Last spring was cool," a woman commented. "Good weather for dew petals."

"It might sell offplanet. We could take a few cases—or barrels—with us when we lift," Cord remarked to Roi. "Unless we ship some other cargo. No point in lifting empty."

Roi caught on fast.

"I have no argument. If we couldn't sell it, we'd

have it for our own use." He drained his wine cup and thumped the drained jug on the table, the Ir signal for service. "The pitcher's as empty as my hold."

"Where can we buy a quantity of this?" Cord asked when the proprietor bustled out with a new flask. "Are there wine merchants who ship offworld? Naturally, it would have to be packed correctly."

"There are several," the tavernkeep told them, and mentioned names.

"Wasn't there one we heard of, called . . . called . . . what was his name, Rait? It began with a 'Ch.' "

"Chaar? He sells wine wholesale, true. I don't know if he trades offworld—maybe he couldn't pack it to suit you. But he does a big local business. The cheapest wines and spirits, mostly."

"We might let him bid, anyway," Roi said. "Where can we find these wine sellers?"

"Just stroll down Gourd Street," someone said, laughing, "and you'll trip over vintners and brewers."

By the time Cord and Roi took their leave, they knew a great deal more about Kirino and about Chaar. Chaar was rich, lived in a palace, and had risen from squalid beginnings. In his youth he had lived by scavenging, and retained the determination and cunning by which he had risen.

It was growing late in the afternoon, and that was fine by Cord. There was something he wanted to check out. Their drinking companions had supplied directions to Gourd Street. Cord wanted to go there at once.

"It will be dark, then, before we get back to the port," Roi remonstrated.

Cord raised his eyebrows quizzically.

"This isn't a good place to be after nightfall," Roi explained. "Anyone out alone stands a good chance of being robbed—or shanghaied into slavery. I told you my opinion of Irru."

"Do you think we're in any danger?" Cord gave him a feral grin.

Seeing it, Connor Roi laughed.

"Come to think of it, no. We did do a good job on those police bullies back on Komonori."

"Police—so they weren't ruffians with a score to settle with you?"

"Well, no. But you didn't ask before you joined in, and there wasn't time to tell you, was there?"

"Not that you would have, anyway," Cord commented.

"And me about to be arrested by Duke Ashek's police? Of course not. Can you imagine what they'd have done to me in the cells?"

"Why were they after you?" Cord asked.

"It might have been any of several little affairs. Nothing of interest to a gentleman."

"Only to the police?"

"Exactly." Roi smiled.

Merchant Chaar's house had once been a great man's residence. It faced inward to its courtyard, showing its back to the outer world. In the old days it had been surrounded by gardens and open land on three sides, with the river flowing by the fourth. Since then, the city had crowded near. Small factories and warehouses jostled it, and their effluvium tainted the river. Chaar found its decaying halls, cellars, and galleries suitable for the storage and sale of his wines as well as for his and his dependents' and slaves' habitation. The painted traceries filling the window openings might be faded or touched up in garish colors, but the possession of this corpse of a palace made Chaar a leader among the merchants of Kirino. Even those whose businesses stretched farther and whose credit ran to multiple figures respected him, though not so much for his princely dwelling as for his acumen.

So much Cord knew from tavern gossip. Now, lounging on a wharf in sight of Chaar House, Cord let Roi ask the questions. The pilot spoke to a boatman painting a small craft moored there.

"A fine boat you have," Roi observed.

"I like her," the sailor replied without looking up from his brush.

"Fast?"

"The fastest on this river or any other," was the retort. "As anybody but a stranger would know."

"Well, that's what we are," Connor agreed. "My partner and I are offworlders. We're looking to start a trading business here. We plan to buy dew-petal wine, ingots of rare metals, and anything else that might sell off Irru. There's a profit to be made for anyone who's willing to work hard. We are interested in finding warehouse space—on the river—for choice—and in making contacts with suppliers and freight handlers like yourself.

The boatman's manner thawed a little.

"There are places to be had. There's a warehouse at the Fish Reach Docks, south of here."

"We would want to have office space either on the premises or nearby. What about that great building over there? I see they have a wharf. Does the owner use the entire place, or does he rent out space in it?"

"Chaar? Not him. It'd take him down a peg to let anyone else use his house, even if he had any room left over, which I'll bet he don't. Merchant Chaar does a big business in wine: it comes downriver and goes into Master C's cellars to come out again in bottles. Not watered, though, I will say that much for Chaar. He's a hard man to beat in a deal, but he gives good value. He keeps a big household, too: his apprentices, house guards, a double dozen slaves and servants, and his family. Not all the slaves work on the wharf or in the cellars, mind you. Some work lying down. Chaar is so rich he could keep a different wench for every night if he could get it up that often. Which I don't guess he can, even with all his charms and spells and omen readers. The Great Thief be praised, I can still keep my wife awake nights. Or some sweet little dockside doxy, when I'm upriver."

The light was almost gone. The boatman wished them a good night, packed away his paint and brush, and departed, bound for dinner and his wife.

Cord and Roi strolled up Water Lane to the street which ran in front of Chaar House. It was deserted.

Just as he had hoped.

"All right, Connor. Let's get back to the port."

"Did we learn anything?" Roi asked as they made their way back toward the heart of the city—the port.

"Yes, we did. We found out that there's no one in the street around Chaar's house at this time of day."

"Is that good?"

"Perfect," Cord replied. "I have everything I need on the *Rose*. Late tomorrow afternoon I'll get Edwina out."

"What can I do?"

"You'll wait in the street, a block or so away. Once I get Edwina, we'll rendezvous with you and head for the *Rose of Flame*. You can lift her without much delay, can't you?"

"I can get her off the ground on five minutes' notice, if I'm fueled," Connor replied. "Which is a thing that I can attend to in the morning. But do you have a plan, Cord, my lad? I'm thinking it won't do much good to walk up to the door and knock."

"That's exactly what I plan to do. And they will let me in."

Chapter 10

A day later, Cord trudged down the darkening street. At sunset it had emptied of passersby as workshops and wharves closed for the night. Those who lived on their business premises were starting the evening meal, their shopfronts shuttered or curtained.

To the east, the sky was dark. West, behind the square mass of Chaar's mansion, it glowed topaz and amethyst. Irru was beginning to have a pollution problem.

Casually Cord glanced up at Chaar House. It was the most imposing building in the street. In the middle of the front, an arch led into the central court. Lights shone in the windows of the two upper stories— the ground floor had no windows, typical of old semifortified manors on Irru. The entrance to the residential part of the palace was in the courtyard.

Cord could not resist a quick look at his chronometer, although he knew he was exactly on schedule. As he looked up again, a column of black rose over Chaar House like the head and neck of some monster. Cord stood immobile for a second, staring as the smoke spread wider. Then he broke into a run, hurling himself through the gateway.

A steward came in answer to the tattoo beat upon the entrance gong, his face scandalized at such rudeness. A gentle person touched the gong once, not too hard. To hit it more than once, or loudly, suggested

that the servants were poorly trained—or that the
house could not afford them at all. Or that the caller
was drunk, of course. In any case, a social solecism.

The man's expression changed as he saw that Cord
was neither drunk nor an Ir, and was obviously agitated.

"Fire," Cord panted. "Look—the roof—"

The steward's eyes followed his gesture and snapped
open wide as he saw the black clouds blotting out the
brilliance of the sky.

"Fire!" the slave screamed. He ran back into the
house without shutting the door. Cord followed him
in.

The hall was spacious but bare. A stairway rose
along the far wall, curving and widening so that the
foot faced the door. A corridor on the right led to
other rooms; a door on the left must connect with the
commercial premises. The door possessed a stout lock,
sealing the offices and shop at night. Cord dismissed
it from his mind. He was not interested in robbing the
merchant. Not of money or wine, at least.

"Fire!" Cord shouted. His warning was almost
unnecessary—the steward was spreading the alarm
and panic quite effectively all by himself.

The family and apprentices had been at dinner.
They surged out of the corridor into the hall. Cord,
standing with seeming hesitation by the still open
door, identified a spare, wide-shouldered man in silk,
a napkin tucked into his collar, as the merchant. The
apprentices revolved around him; he seemed the only
one with any presence of mind.

"Joru—get the apprentices out and count them,"
Chaar called. "Ayet—the girl's upstairs. You let her
out while I unlock the cellars and start the servants
moving out the casks."

"Master Chaar ... the house is burning ... the
roof's already going ..." the man stammered.

"Damn you," Chaar returned, "then you get the wine out and I'll go myself."

"No," moaned an aging, overdressed woman with an accent one degree more refined than Chaar's. Madame Chaar, presumably.

Cord stepped forward.

"Sir, I spotted the smoke and came to alert your household. I'll go upstairs, if someone's up there. I've had some firefighting experience. And it may not be too bad yet. I only saw smoke, no flames." He had no fear of Chaar's being able to identify him later. His tail was concealed in baggy trousers, he was wearing a shaggy wig, and he had darkened his golden skin. "Tell me where to go, and then get your lady out."

"Top floor, the barred door at the back. Bring her out and you won't lose by it," Chaar shouted as Cord sprinted up the stairs.

"Why, oh why, didn't she say anything?" Cord heard Madame Chaar lament.

If only the panic continued. If only no one realized there was no real danger. Having seen Chaar in action, Cord revised his opinion of the man. It was easy and common to think of the merchant class as fat buffoons, cowardly and ignoble. It was also a mistake, Cord now realized. A man who had clawed his way up from scavenging must be shrewd and ready to take risks. If anyone saw through the deception it would be Chaar.

In truth, he would not have needed the merchant's instructions to find Edwina. His sixth sense open to receive her psychic output, he could locate her with no further knowledge of the mansion. He raced along the corridor. There was no smoke and no risk, but he did not care to linger. If Chaar realized that the roiling smoke was not increasing, and that the only flames were confined to a very small area on the roof, where Cord had planted a basin filled with flammables guaranteed to send tongues of flame leaping up, he was in trouble. It wouldn't occur to anyone that he was attempting a kidnapping; everyone would suspect him of emptying the house to burglarize it.

The upper corridor was narrow and hot—not surprising on a warm day, so close under the roof. Servants' or slaves' quarters did not need to be comfortable.

There was only the one barred door, and only one presence behind it. Probably all the other servants had been in the kitchen eating their own supper or serving the family. Cord pulled out a cuttergun, threw the bar aside, and pulled the door open.

The woman sitting on the bed rose. She was not frightened, Cord sensed.

"Come on," he rasped. "The house is on fire."

"No, really?" she inquired. Her face was serious, but her voice—and her emotions—bore an overtone of polite amusement. Nevertheless, she came forward.

Cord's heart pounded. He held the gun at ready. Was she Julia McKay? The voice was unfamiliar—but vocal cords could be altered as easily as faces, changing timbre and pitch. Only one thing could not be disguised. Psychically he reached out. It had been so long since he had felt Julia's mind, and even when they had been together, her essence had been—elusive.

Strange. This woman was strange, with an alienness that almost repelled him. She did not belong here—but she was not Julia. The woman Edwina was different, but she still had human emotions. Julia's psyche was as black and deep and cold as space.

"Come on," he repeated, more gently, putting away the gun. He was not going to kill her, as he had expected to do, but he was not going to take the chance of telling Edwina she was being rescued. She might prefer Chaar to Ashek—who knew? She might raise an alarm if he told her the truth. Unfortunately, he suspected, she was not going to come trustingly, without asking questions and hearing answers.

"Where?" she asked, proving his point.

Cord, touching her mind, decided she did not believe in the fire.

"Away from here. I'll tell you later."

Alarm flared in her; he could feel it. She began to draw back. There was no time to persuade her.

"Don't be afraid," Cord said, and took her arm. He was careful not to squeeze tightly. He did not wish to terrify her into screaming or fighting. Violent action increased the speed with which the drug concealed in a needle ring on his finger took effect, but offsetting the gain was the fact that adrenaline tended to decrease its efficiency. Edwina did not even feel the sting of the needle.

In the act of pulling back, she stopped, as though she could not remember what she had been doing. Cord caught her as she began to slump, lifting her without difficulty. Unconscious, she could betray him neither intentionally nor inadvertently. It added verisimilitude, too: the rescue of a slave girl overcome by smoke.

Trusting instinct, he did not retrace his steps. He had come up the main stairway—the front staircase. Cord felt certain the slaves did not ordinarily go up and down that way. If he continued, he should find the service stairs. When he found them, he started down as swiftly as he could with such a dead weight in his arms.

The flight emerged, as he had anticipated, at the rear of the house, by the kitchen. He went through the pantry and scullery. There was a back door, he knew, opening from the kitchen onto the narrow alley at the side of the house. The previous evening he had watched while a kitchen boy came out to dump refuse into the river.

The kitchen stood abandoned, a pot bubbling on the fire, a tray of tarts growing cold on a work table. A pot of meat drippings had been spilled in the commotion; grease was congealing on the stone floor. Cord stepped around it and pulled the door open.

No one was in the alley. Naturally not. It was narrow. In a real fire, there would be danger from falling debris. He thought he heard an Irruvian voice shout, "Hey there!" but the last word was chopped off and Cord disregarded it. He made for the nearest wharf. It was almost dark, but he could make out the lights of a launch tied up there. Its paint was dingy and it carried no ornamentation, but it was motor-driven, unlike the sail- and oar-powered craft which were common on Irru. Still, offworld influence was making itself felt—power boats were not unusual enough to cause comment. It was peculiar that powered land vehicles were almost unknown. On the other hand, the lanes and streets of Kirino were ill suited to motorized transport.

Roi was casting off as Cord crossed the gangplank.

A frame covered with canvas provided shelter on the deck. Cord carried the woman inside and placed her on the pile of blankets that passed as a bed. He had left rope and a kerchief in the "cabin"; he used them to bind her hands and feet and to gag her. He didn't want any trouble if she woke up too soon. That was the trouble with drugs. There was no way of guessing how they would react with any one person's body chemistry. And Edwina was far too valuable to be allowed to get away.

As he came out on deck, the boat was already in the main channel and gathering speed. Its engine made little noise. Behind them, the oily smoke over Chaar House was beginning to thin.

"Did it go all right?" Connor Roi asked.

"I'm here, and so is the girl. The hard part was

getting the smoke bombs in place last night." It had
taken some time for Cord to assemble the bombs and
the brazier of burnables. Then he had returned to
Chaar House and scaled it with his climbing hooks
and rope. It had required three trips to get everything
up.

The east had been tinged with light when he coiled
his rope and started back to the port. The smoke
bombs—equipped with timers, and fire basin—had all
gone off according to schedule.

"We'll make Port Landing in half an hour," Roi told
him. "Fifteen minutes to get through the gate and
onboard. We'll lift in an hour."

Cord nodded. He would be glad to get back to a
civilized world. Especially with his reward from Ashek.

Out in the street, a crowd milled and chattered,
staring up at the smoke pouring from the roof of
Chaar House. Yevren hung back in the shadows of the
narrow alley that ran by the house from the street to
the river, about halfway between the two. He had
observed certain preparations earlier which led him
to believe that such a vantage place would give him a
view those in the street would lack. As he leaned
against the brick, arms crossed on his chest, brisk
footsteps sounded in the alley, coming from the street
end.

This was unexpected. Yevren flattened himself
against the wall, hugging the shadows. As he did so,
an awkward form emerged from a doorway at the
river end of the passage and ran toward the river. A
broad-shouldered man standing in front of Yevren
turned and saw the runner and his burden. He called
out, "Hey, there!" and dashed after the fleeing figure.

Without hesitation, Yevren sprang after him, clasp-
ing his fists and swinging them like a club. The sav-
age blow caught Cord's pursuer on the back of the

head and felled him instantly. Yevren paused to kick him in the gut, silencing the man completely. Then he ran lightly toward the river himself. His own transport, a one-man floater, part of the *Queen*'s standard equipment, was parked in the shadow of the warehouse next to Chaar's delapidated palace. It was almost in sight of a riverboat Yevren had seen cruising up the river earlier.

Now he saw the boat pulling away from Chaar's wharf. He found his floater, mounted it, and set off in the direction of the spaceport. Even going by way of the crooked, narrow streets, he could make better time than the boat could. He no longer needed to keep Cord in sight. There was nowhere but the port the bounty hunter could go with Edwina.

A sort of customs inspection was necessary for those arriving in Irru. Though the Ir themselves did not care and did not have a sufficiently centralized government to enact or enforce import laws, the offworld companies with large holdings on Irru did care. Advanced weapons which might be used in a coup, drugs which would demoralize the workers, and certain other items were banned by the firms that managed the spaceport. But what the visitor took from Irru when he left—that was his business. When Cord stalked into the port, Edwina lying unconscious over his shoulder, the company guard did not even look up from the form he was filling out.

"Souvenir?" he asked.

"Yes," Cord retorted.

The guard waved him through. Connor Roi trailed behind.

"Hurry," Roi urged. "I want to lift out of here."

"Do you think the port authority would stop us if Chaar complained?"

"It's possible," Connor replied, walking faster. "The

companies run Irru, all right, but only because the Ir let them. If Chaar puts pressure on his fellow merchants to pressure the companies, then the companies would hand us over."

Cord nodded thoughtfully. "Yes, but why worry? By the time Chaar tightens the screws, you'll be running guns to Litheen and I'll be looking for a new employer."

Connor Roi was still laughing as he locked the hatch.

"Get her strapped in, Cord. The *Rose* is going to flame."

Later, when they had made the transition to artificial gravity and Cord went to unstrap his captive, he found her awake. The drug was efficient, leaving no aftereffects. Edwina was studying her surroundings with a carefully expressionless face.

"Do you feel all right?" Cord inquired, freeing her hands and feet. He had strapped her in, so she was virtually a prisoner: safer for all of them, in the event she was inclined to resist. Now that the touchy part was past, he would give her a little freedom and see how she reacted. "Would you like something to drink?"

She shook her head.

"I'm fine, thank you."

He was surprised that she did not exclaim over her rescue or ask questions, but he sensed a wariness in her. Well, he was not in the habit of volunteering information, himself.

Roi entered the cabin. "I've set the course for Etir," she said. "If you have no objection, Cord, my lad, I'd like to part company with you there. I'm not anx—" Roi caught the faint, warning headshake Cord gave her, and saw that Edwina was conscious.

"Oh, hello," Connor added. "I hope you're not too shaken up."

"No," Edwina responded. She was looking at Connor very intently.

"Well, I'll be in the control room if you need me," Connor said to Cord, quickly. The pilot nodded and smiled at Edwina and left the room.

The woman sat up, crossing her legs beneath her, her flowing black robe concealing the lines of her body. Cord sat on the built-in seat. Neither of them spoke. Cord had intended to let her ask the questions, and he remained silent to give her an opportunity. When it became clear she was not going to break the silence, he didn't, either. To offer information would be to give her the advantage. He did not choose to cast himself in the role of an underling reporting to his master.

The situation was disconcerting. Many people had traveled in his custody, either for their own safety or at another's pleasure. Some begged for their freedom, offered him money, their bodies, land, titles, anything. Others were sullen, resisting passively. A few tried suicide. Edwina did not fit into any of those patterns.

She was not even paying attention to him. Her eyes seemed to look inward. Cord liked to know what his prisoners were feeling. It made them easier to anticipate and control. Yet although he was open to her psychic emanations, he could not claim to know what they meant. He found traces of apprehension and traces of amusement, but nothing to give any indication of what he could expect from her. Either she was very cool and professional or she knew something he didn't.

However, she was not Julia McKay. It was a disappointment, in a way. If she had been . . .

If she had been Julia McKay, she would not be here, because she would not have left Chaar's house alive. And he would now be free, able to live his life without the abscess of hate that was in him.

What was one more setback? Next time he would find Julia. Right now, he had to find a way to deal with this woman. Casually he removed the alien ring from his pocket, not letting her see what it was—in case she happened to be paying any attention at all.

"I have something of yours, I think," he remarked, tossing it toward her.

She caught it neatly, one-handed. His action surprised a flash of interest from her. She looked down at the silvery band in her palm.

"Thank you. I didn't expect to see it again." She slipped the massive ring onto her ring finger.

It fitted her. Cord's eyes did not see the transformation, but he knew it must have occurred. One moment the ring was too large for his own middle finger or thumb; the next, it went around Edwina's finger as if made for it.

Did I ever try it on? he wondered. He could not remember. Perhaps not, since it had obviously been too big. If he had, would it have shrunk for him?

"That's an interesting ring," he said.

"Yes, isn't it. Unfortunately, it doesn't do anything."

This time, Cord caught an undertone of real bitterness and anger in her mind. Still she asked no questions. Cord had hoped she would want to know how he had gotten the ring. If she was curious, she hid it well. Edwina sat silent and motionless as a statue.

"Duke Ashek let me take it. Sometimes it's helpful to have some belonging of the person I'm looking for. The duke will be pleased to have you back safely."

The woman really looked at him for the first time. "What did you say your name is?"

"I didn't. I am called Cord." *Or Cord the Hunter, or any of a dozen common nouns, none of them complimentary*.

"I'm Edwina.

Cord was amused by her sudden apparent change of attitude and quaint formality—was she going to try to cultivate him for her own purposes?

Her underlying emotions were unchanged. But now that she was opening up it would do no harm to flatter her a little.

"You were very calm, back at Chaar's house. Most people would panic if they thought they were trapped in a burning building."

"It's no credit to me," she replied. "I didn't think it was on fire."

"Why not? Everyone else did. My special effects were pretty good."

"I'm sure they were," Edwina assured him. "I couldn't see them. But I knew Chaar House wasn't on fire."

"How?"

She gave him another of those unnerving, probing looks.

"Intuition."

He accepted the explanation. He often acted on hunches, himself.

"Was all of it really on my behalf?" Edwina inquired. "And how many were involved?"

"Only Connor Roi—the pilot—and myself." Cord felt he would gain nothing by pointing out that the operation had been less on her behalf than on Ashek's.

"It was very impressive."

"Considerably more so than I would have preferred," Cord replied. "I would have bought you from Chaar if he had been willing to sell."

"It may have made it more difficult for you, but it was much less trying for me. By the time those slave-trading bastards brought me here—there, to Irru, I mean—it was very clear to me that unless I made myself valuable, I was going to end up working in a mine—or worse."

Having seen the barred windows of certain houses of pleasure, the kind that catered to the sickest tastes, Cord knew exactly what she meant. Such places had to get their stock in trade in slave markets. No prostitute, however desperate or degraded, would work in one.

"I understand," Cord said. Since she was neither beautiful nor skilled she would certainly have encountered the dangers she mentioned, but how she had avoided them was a mystery.

"And how did you avoid such a fate?" he inquired politely.

"I was in a pen . . ." Edwina began.

Chapter 11

She knew no one. That she was in a slave market Edwina was sure, though she had never seen one before. In fact, she'd never been outside Ashek's property since . . .

She shook her head. If she thought about that she would either cry or go mad. Instead, Edwina concentrated on the scenes around her. The building was like a small warehouse, open at one end. Both sides had built-in cages containing people.

Those in the cage with her belonged to a dozen or so more races or species and were of almost every age, from adolescent to elderly. Most were ragged and grubby. Not that she was giving herself airs: her own clothing was torn and the slavers were not interested in providing opportunities for washing.

The men and women in the pen across from hers were clean and well dressed. Edwina wondered how they had managed it. They were also extremely good-looking.

"Yes, they're the lucky ones," a middle-aged woman said. "At least while they're still young. When they are old, they'll end up here."

"I don't understand," Edwina said.

"No—you're new, aren't you? You can always tell newcomers by the way they stare at everything. Those" —she nodded toward the other enclosure—"will be bought by the rich, or at least the well-to-do. For pleasure," she added.

"Oh."

"While we will be sold to someone who wants drudges, because we don't have anything to offer. Sometimes if one person buys you, you can make yourself useful enough that he'll keep you. But most of us in this pen will be bought by companies or in groups, and never get close enough to our owners to ... to ..."

"Ingratiate ourselves?"

"Yeah. Now do you understand?"

"Yes," Edwina replied. It was an aspect she had not imagined before. In retrospect, she supposed she had been lucky with Ashek.

She continued to study the slave market, trying to think of something to do, some way of improving her chances—if not of freedom, then at least of better treatment.

I'm smart. That should be an advantage. I'm educated. But there are things for which a degree in archaeology does not prepare one.

Out on the street, his garments shimmering harshly, in the sun, a man was approaching the pen.

"He'll be buying," Edwina's informant stated. "Look at the slave trader with him. I can tell you without even hearing what he's saying: 'Only the strongest slaves here, excellency. Smart enough to do their work, not so smart they will make trouble. I can offer you the best prices because I have more coming in any day, and the pens are full.'"

The imitation was so lifelike that Edwina almost laughed before she remembered that for them, it was a matter of life and death.

"Now, girl, watch the others. They're like kittens or puppies looking for homes. The smart ones here will do their best to attract the merchant's attention. Those who recognize him, anyhow. That's Merchant Chaar. He's comparatively decent. He used to come to dinner at my last master's house. We always laughed about his peculiar ways—there he was, a rich, important merchant, and as superstitious as some of the offworld primitives."

"Superstitious," Edwina repeated.

Her companion took it as a question.

"He has his horoscope cast before every business deal, they say. He won't buy a slave with certain physical traits—some people think eyebrows that meet over the nose are a sign of a were-being. You know, nonsense like that. Chaar believes it. He goes to wise women and alchemists or anyone who claims to have powers."

Edwina's breath came a little faster. Now she knew of a way out.

Chaar stopped in front of the cage, and Edwina moved closer.

". . . half a dozen strong dock hands," he was saying to the slave merchant. "No, none of your package deals. I like to handpick my workers."

Others besides Edwina had moved forward. Nearly all were men, laborers by their look. The slaves' grapevine was efficient. A deep-chested man with great arms and shoulders and a thick neck brushed past Edwina and elbowed his way close to the wire screen.

Light burst behind Edwina's eyelids. Before her imprisonment by Ashek, she had felt the sensation six times in her life. Since, it had come as many times in as many months. When she had recovered from the now increasingly familiar shock, she heard the husky man saying, "Take me, Merchant Chaar. Look at my muscles. If you want strength, I'm the one for you."

"He seems all right," Chaar commented to the pen owner. "Got initiative, too. I like that."

Edwina thrust herself forward without stopping to

weigh the consequences further. This might be her one chance.

"Merchant Chaar, I wouldn't buy him if I were you. He'll be a bad investment."

Faces turned to stare at her. The big slave was outraged that she would spoil his chance when she was not even a possible rival. The rest of the slaves were startled at anyone daring to say such a thing in front of the slave master. The slaver was furious, but an interested Chaar intervened.

"Why do you say that?" he asked, before anyone else spoke.

"He's going to die soon. Before the next cool season, I think. My vision does not pinpoint it closer than that. I see him carrying a bale. He drops it and falls to his knees beside it. He clutches his chest and gasps. Then he topples over in the dust. An overseer commands two slaves to drag him away. That was the end of my seeing."

She crossed her arms on her chest and looked straight at Chaar. She was aware that some of the captives in the pen were shrinking away from her and making furtive gestures—some sort of attempt to avert the evil eye, no doubt.

"Are you a witch?" Chaar asked. He did not shrink away, but he did finger a plain crystal pendant around his neck.

"No. I do have second sight, however. Would it be useful for you?"

"How much?" Chaar demanded of the slave merchant.

"And you managed to fool him?"

"Yes—and no. Three times I've had premonitions that came true. . . ."

"Not overwhelming evidence of prescience," Cord said cautiously.

Edwina leaned forward, her face desperate. "Three times *that I know of!* But often . . . the visions . . . are of strangers! If you passed a girl on the street and suddenly imagined you saw two gasoline trucks colliding and bursting into flame—what would you tell her? How could you say anything? Was she in one of them? One of her relatives or a friend? She wouldn't believe you. And if she did, she couldn't do anything to prevent it. She'd live in fear until it did happen, days or months later—I wouldn't know for sure. Coincidence? Maybe. A guilt trip? Definitely."

"You really can see the future?" Cord was startled and a bit confused by her strange language. He had never before encountered anyone who made such a claim, except for a few obvious charlatans who earned a living pretending to read the future in bowls of water or in mirrors. But those had all done so for money. They had bedecked themselves in exotic finery and pretended to divine oracles.

"You make it sound simple," she said, flushing. "But it's not like catching sight of a newspaper headline. The things I see don't always make much sense. I can't tell you what the stock market is going to do, or whether there's going to be a war. I might 'see' a financier shoot himself, and not know why, or even that he was a financier. My impressions are vivid, but they aren't always very useful."

Though he had no idea what the "stock market" was, Cord was impressed. Even with its drawbacks, Edwina possessed a valuable ability. No wonder Duke Ashek wanted her back.

"Do all your people have similar powers?"

She looked at him blankly for a moment.

"Oh—no, of course not. I'm human. Or Terran, I guess I should say. My grandmother claimed she had the Sight."

"Terran—but Ashek said you spoke no known language when he . . . found you." Ashek had also said she was a liar, Cord remembered. On the other hand, he was not inclined to take anything Ashek said at face value, either.

Edwina laughed wryly.

"It would be more correct to say I didn't speak any tongue currently spoken. English as I know it seems to have died out. Or maybe it's such an obscure little dialect only a scholar would recognize it."

"*Where do you come from?*"

"I told you, Terra. It's *when* I come from that's important."

Chapter 12

The picnic was not turning out as Edwina had expected. In spite of bright sun with a few puffy white clouds, in spite of the solitude of the old gravel pit on Fitts Field Road, things were not working. On the way they had had trouble finding a store with ice, and then when they arrived, it had taken an hour to get the fire going. Now Frieda and Jim were exchanging curt, cutting retorts and Peter had gone off to take pictures. Peter had a very low tolerance for adversity and friction.

At least going off alone was a less embarrassing way of releasing tension than making a scene, which her old roommate and her roommate's boyfriend were determinedly creating. Jim made another sarcastic remark about Frieda's city-girl ways.

Edwina walked away from the rutted dirt road where they had parked the station wagon, down to the gravel pit. She could still hear bickering voices behind her—but she could pretend she did not. She looked around with a professional eye. It was too bad there were no traces of habitation by Indians. She could have immersed herself in her specialty as thoroughly as Peter did in his. She walked a little way along the pit's edge. The gravel pit had not been used for years; with willows and birch grown up around it, and reeds along the water at its bottom, it might be only a small lake.

At the north end, the steep banks sloped down to a gravelly shore. She bent to pick up a stone to skip across the water, and a glint among the pebbles caught her attention.

A pull tab from a soft drink or beer can, she thought wryly, and reached for it. When her fingers closed on it, however, she felt a tingle of excitement. The object was strangely heavy.

It was a ring.

Edwina held it, feeling an unpleasant sensation of *déjà vu*. It was a moment before she identified the source of her uneasiness.

Shades of Tolkien. Here's the Ring, which must cast me as either Gollum or Bilbo.

And then it didn't seem so funny after all. A wedding band, a class ring, a bit of costume jewelry—none of those would have done more than make her wonder how it had come there. This was different.

For one thing, it was large: an inch and a half in diameter. Also its metal was peculiar, both silvery and lavender. Lines of script crawled—yes, *crawled* was the word—around it.

She slipped it onto her own finger, to get a clearer idea of the hand for which it must have been made.

"Maybe I can't do anything right." Frieda's voice rose sharply. "But I wouldn't do that macho act if I were you, Jim. At least I can cross a rope bridge without upchucking."

This is awful. Edwina's fist closed on the ring as her stomach tightened up with tension. She hated emotional scenes. Then something seemed to twist, throwing her off balance.

For one panicky moment she thought she had lost her balance and was falling. But a moment later, she was standing again. Or still standing.

There was no gravel underfoot, but instead a smooth, hard surface, and no sunlight, only a cool pale glow.

She gazed at the blue-glazed floor and walls around her and began to be afraid.

"So the ring transported you to Komonor from Terra," Cord mused, more to himself than to Edwina. "And virtually instantaneously at that." If the ring was a matter transmitter, it would be valuable indeed.

The woman chuckled. "Not instantly," she said. "When I left Earth—Terra—we had visited the moon a few times. Now I'm told Terra has had interstellar travel for several centuries. Don't you see? I've moved in time as well as in space."

"If the ring is responsible," Cord ventured, "Why haven't you used it to go back?"

"I tried! Again and again, until Ashek's people discovered me. Nothing worked."

"Perhaps you have not adequately duplicated the circumstances. What variables have you considered?" The possibility of traveling in time and space fascinated Cord. It would give the ring's user almost boundless power. *I could go back and prevent my parents' murder. Or I could be the greatest bounty hunter in the galaxy, by going back in time to pick up a criminal's trail at the scene of the crime.*

"I've assumed that the ring responded to my desire to be somewhere else," Edwina replied slowly. "I don't know what else to try. What else could affect it?"

"I can think of two of three possibilities."

"You accept it very easily, Cord. Ashek thought I was lying or crazy." Her psychic output had gradually relaxed. Cord interpreted it to mean she was warming to him.

"I'm interested in the ring's powers. And I know a little more about such things than the duke does, I think. Tell me, Edwina, how badly do you want to go back to Duke Ashek?"

"Not at all." Her face was set, mirroring the determination in her mind.

"Then perhaps we might reach an agreement of our own."

"What did you have in mind?" she inquired, loosening the neck of her enveloping black robe. It exposed a V-shaped patch of pale skin.

"I want to learn how the ring works. Help me find out and I won't take you back to Komonor."

"Reword that. Promise you won't hand me over to Ashek or any agent of his. It will give me a feeling of security." By now the dark gown was open to the waist. Cord caught a tempting glimpse of pale breasts.

"As you wish," Cord agreed. "I won't return you to Ashek or hand you over to anyone who might."

"Good enough."

Edwina tugged at the gown, and it fell away from her shoulders, leaving her completely bare from the waist up. Cord reached for her.

"Finally!" Edwina murmured, pulling him down beside her on the bunk. "Playing wise woman is all very well, but it's fatal to a sex life. No man wants to go to bed with a woman who predicts things.

"What nice ears you have," she added, "just like a cat's. . . ." As he pulled off his trousers, revealing his tail, she gasped, but it may have been pleasure rather than surprise, as his lips and tongue found her erogenous zones.

Loving Edwina was like embracing a hurricane. She writhed and twisted beneath him, twined around him, and was in general so exciting that Cord had to exert great control to hold back.

He taught her every Mehiran love technique except those she was unable to do by reason of lacking a tail. His own tail was busy around her soft body, keeping her alternately aroused and fulfilled after this third orgasm reduced him to only one erect member.

"I needed that," she murmured sleepily at last.

"What you need is a regiment, sweetling."

"You'll do for starters, Cord."

A pity to break the mood of postcoital bliss, but there were things which had to be discussed. "We need to plan," Cord said. "Connor Roi and I will be splitting up when we get to Etir. It will be best if Roi doesn't know that my plans have changed. Originally I planned to find a passenger ship bound for Komonor. We will let Connor think I still intend to do so."

"What will we do instead?" Edwina asked, lying beside him, one arm under her head.

"I'd like to find someplace remote where we can study the ring. There must be laboratory facilities, too—it will be necessary to analyze it carefully."

Edwina twisted the strange ring around her finger, her face sad. "It would be nice to go home."

"Some of us," Cord said, a catch in his voice, "can never go home."

Cord had expected some difficulty in keeping the truth from Connor—that he was going to break faith with Ashek. Not that Connor would have cared, but the pilot might (reasonably enough) want a share of whatever profit came from the ring. Cord wouldn't have minded cutting Connor in on any money, but he was not anxious to reveal the possibility of time travel to a third person.

The pilot was sharp; and although Edwina understood the necessity for letting Connor Roi think she was a prisoner being returned to her master, Cord doubted she was actress enough to maintain the pretense long. To keep the two apart as much as possible, Cord kept Edwina locked in his cabin. He wondered if Roi would think it strange—after all, there was no place Edwina could escape to, since she could neither get off the *Rose of Flame* nor pilot it.

However, as it happened, when Cord returned to the control room, Connor said, after glancing past Cord's shoulder to make sure Edwina wasn't with him, "Ah, I see you've left her in your cabin. Locked in, I trust?"

"Yes," Cord admitted, relieved he need not introduce the subject himself.

"I was meaning to ask if you'd restrict her to your cabin," the pilot said. "It's almost impossible for anyone to do serious damage in here, but still . . ."

". . . there's no point in giving her the opportunity to try," Cord concluded. "That's what I thought."

"And besides, Cord, she makes me uncomfortable," Roi admitted. "I feel as if she could see through me. Which is probably only my guilt speaking, as it goes against the grain with me to hand anyone over to the Komonori."

"You aren't responsible," Cord answered. "I am."

"True, but it wouldn't make any difference if I had the strength of my convictions."

"Be glad you don't." Cord grinned. It took a weight from him to find it so easy to keep them separated, but he didn't know whether to be glad or irritated that Connor showed no sign of jealousy.

"He has Cord the Hunter and Edwina under observation," Ashek told his eldest son. He had no desire to discuss the matter further with his heir.

"Father," Kenek ventured, "earlier—before we, ah, lost Edwina—we talked about hiring a scientist and letting him study the ring. Maybe it would be best to do that *now*." Now that riots had broken out in the duke's own capital. Now that the militia had killed hundreds, trying to restore order—and failed. Now that the emperor had taken notice, and sent Ashek a sardonic little note questioning the duke's ability to rule. The common people presented no real threat,

Ashek thought. It was the *agents provocateurs* of the emperor, and the lesser nobility he was inciting to defy the duke: the counts, the barons, and even the landed gentry could all expect some advantage from the fall of a ducal house. A hunting cat may bring down a buck, but the jackals feed, too.

"We no longer have that option," the duke replied. Kenek stared at him, perplexed. "I no longer have the ring," Ashek explained. "Cord has it. I had hoped that if he had both the ring and the woman, he might solve the mystery for us. Then Yevren would step in and bring it—and Edwina—back."

Kenek seemed amazed, a reaction the duke found all too easy to understand. It must seem a reckless action. But the ring had been useless, as it was. There had been a chance that a new mind, a non-Komonori intellect, might approach the problem differently.

"But could Yevren be trusted with such a thing?" Kenek's protest was moderate indeed. It was a challenge the duke could meet without a qualm.

"There is no one else I would trust it to," he answered. "Yevren is loyal to me; I would stake my life on it."

"You *are* staking your life on it," Kenek retorted. "And mine, and Annen's and Senek's and M'Sen's. Well, perhaps not Senek's and M'Sen's," he corrected himself.

Ashek nodded. Senek was in the emperor's good graces, and M'Sen was too silly to be a threat to anyone.

"My one mistake, Kenek, was in not letting Yevren extract the secret from Edwina his way. When he brings her back—with the ring—I will certainly permit him to do so, if Cord has not spared us the trouble. By the way, I've promised Yevren one of the emperor's granddaughters as a reward. I think that if this affair goes our way, you also will be well advised to marry one of them. The second eldest, I suggest. She's the most popular with the people. The oldest is too devout. You will naturally keep my promise to Yevren. Give him his choice of the others. He has sworn to be as loyal to you as he has been to me."

Kenek said, white-lipped, "Sir, you are talking as though .. as though you didn't expect to ... to be duke much longer."

Ashek smiled his cold smile. "Why, I've sometimes thought you were growing impatient to take my place. It's very natural. I used to pray to the gods every day that my father's dissipations would catch up with him."

"I don't want to succeed to your position under the present conditions," Kenek answered frankly.

This time Ashek laughed, a rare thing for him. "Good. I wondered whether you had been frightened into the emperor's camp."

"No chance of that, Father. Not with Senek poisoning the emperor's mind against me. But what are we going to do?"

"Wait. We will wait for Yevren to come back with the ring. In the meantime, I have arranged for accidents to happen to certain persons." Ashek named a count, three barons, and a great merchant, all of whom had in some way promoted rebellion. "As a lesson to the other rebels."

"And who else but you, my lord father, could teach them so well. . . ."

Kenek bowed and left the duke alone with his wintry smile and chilly thoughts.

Chapter 13

"Good luck to you, Cord," Connor Roi said as they stood in the concourse of Etir's main port. The pilot smiled shyly at Edwina. Roi had never overcome an instinctive wariness of her, even in the confines of the *Rose of Flame*.

"I hope your enterprises go well," Cord replied. "Be careful." He never knew what to say at partings. He had already handed over a pouch of flame beryls in payment for Connor's help. At least Duke Ashek's wrath at Cord's defection was not likely to fall on Connor—Roi's past activities made the pilot sure to shun Komonor.

"No hard feelings, I hope?" Roi ventured to say to Edwina. Cord stifled a smile. Connor was not yet used to the realities of working with a tracker, one of which was delivering human cargo to places they did not wish to go. He himself could not remember the last time he had been embarrassed by his trade or had felt pity for his quarry.

Edwina smiled. "I don't mind going back to Duke Ashek. My stay in Irru showed me how fortunate I was." She extended her hand.

Roi took it hesitantly and gave it a quick shake.

"Goodbye." Connor clapped Cord on the shoulder and walked away before either of them could speak again.

Which was just as well, because an unexpected

surge of raw emotion broke over Cord, in spite of his defenses. He turned to Edwina.

She was watching Connor's back retreat into the crowd, a frozen expression on her face—and he realized she was the source of the shock wave.

"What's the matter?" he asked harshly. He had to repeat the question before she responded.

"Nothing." Her eyes were opaque with shock.

He had not revealed his sixth sense to her, so he could not tell her that he *knew* she was lying.

"I can see you're upset," he rasped.

She occupied herself with shaking out the elaborately tucked and pleated sleeves of her tunic before replying.

"I always thought there was something strange about your pilot. I just realized Connor is a woman."

They spent the rest of the day in a shabby port hotel which offered the advantage of computer terminals in every room. It catered mostly to spacers. The place was comfortable enough in a run-down, old-fashioned way, though by Cord's standards it was rather ascetic.

However, the accommodations were of no interest. Cord was studying the computer atlas, looking for the right world. He had sufficient funds to take them almost anywhere, but how far they went was not as important as the facilities the world afforded.

"This one sounds good. Mte-4, it's called. It was a military staging area during the Indil-Waro Conflict. I've never heard of that one. Since the truce it's been opened up for colonization and is now a fairly active port for trade between Indil and Waro. The temperate zone is . . . well, temperate. Here's the attractive part: government installations, some still equipped, are available for sale or lease. Total planetary population: five hundred thousand. Most of them in one city. The only real town."

"Where is it?" Edwina asked. "Not that it makes any difference, since I've never heard of most of the stars you've mentioned."

"Mte and its five planets? It's about a hundred parsecs from the backside of nowhere, but it is on a regular passenger route."

"Will we go there?"

"It's a possibility. There are other places we could choose, though." He had compiled a list of half a dozen planets where they might stay out of sight and explore the ring's potential, but most had disadvantages of one sort or another: domed cities, infrequent visits by interstellar ships, or dangerous wildlife. He turned to Edwina. "Let's go out and find dinner. We'll think about this when we've eaten."

"And relaxed?" the woman suggested.

They ate in a small café, plain but with good food. Cord told Edwina about Mehira, and gave her a carefully edited account of why he had left. Edwina told him about the Terra she knew, but mostly she talked about those strange flashes of vision. Cord thought that they bothered her more than all the other things that had happened to her.

"I used to be able to ignore them," she said. "The first came when I was twelve. . . ." She paused to think. "That's less than one a year until—"

"You found yourself on Duke Ashek's world," Cord finished.

"Yes. Since then I've had six or eight. Maybe traveling in time increased my natural ability. I don't know. But I don't like it." She shivered, and in the soft glow from the tabletop, her face was unhappy.

"We'd better go back to our room," Cord said. "It's getting late, and we need sleep."

Only a handful of diners remained in the restaurant,

and the street was emptying. This was not the spacers' quarter or amusement district, where the workday never ended.

"This is the worst part of space travel," Cord remarked as they paid for their meal. "No matter where you make planetfall, it's never the same time as either the world you left or ship's time. It seems as if it should be early evening, but the night is half gone."

For a summer night, it was perhaps a little cool. Edwina wrapped herself in the great scarf she had only carried when they started out. Cord had grown accustomed to a variety of climates since leaving Mehira, so he ignored the chill breeze, merely angling his ears back so the wind did not rush into them.

In such deserted surroundings, Cord let down his mental defenses. With many humans around, he preferred to keep them firmly in place unless actually checking their psychic emanations. But except for himself and Edwina he could could sense no other person awake in the vicinity. Edwina's mind was at rest and thus posed no source of discomfort to him. It was at times like this he most missed Mehira. There he could have gone unshielded without encountering the unguarded emotions of those around him. Empaths, even if they cannot feel something pleasant, prefer not to broadcast negative feelings.

The attack was so swift that if Cord had not been braced for it, he would have been overpowered, even with his skill. As it was, he felt their psychic energy change indefinably as they tensed for the attack. He pushed Edwina to one side and filled the mouth of the alley with fire. He continued to rake his weapon back and forth. With no cover in this street, he was taking no chances.

Several cutter beams had flared briefly in the alley when first he opened fire, but they'd been shot off at random as their owners died. None had come near

Edwina, crouched low and out of the line of fire, or himself. And no one was firing now.

Cord approached the alley cautiously, although he could sense no presence there. The narrowness of the alley, the lack of cover for the attackers, and the fact that he'd been carrying a cutter, rather than a dart pistol or other projectile gun, had saved them. With most high-velocity weapons, you still need to hit the target somewhere. But the ray of a cuttergun would slice apart almost anything it touched.

The narrow space between the buildings was a slaughterhouse. In the dark, even with his keen Mehiran night sight, Cord could not tell how many bodies there were. Before him was a tangle of severed arms, legs, and torsos.

He stepped farther in, examining the corpses as well as he could. The men and women here were not dressed as spacers, but Cord was certain they were all ships' crew. Something about the way their hair was cut, about the jewelry they wore, suggested spacers making an effort to disguise themselves. It was not worth the effort to search the disgusting mess for their identification.

He sensed that Edwina had come to the alley mouth, but did not warn her back. In gloom like this, the human's eyes could probably see nothing but a heap. Cord doubted she would care to investigate further.

Something moved immediately behind him, something close to the ground. But nothing could be alive there—that was all Cord could think as he whirled around.

He jumped back as the pearly beam of a cutter scored a smoking line in the wall in front of him.

A surviving spacer, buried under severed body parts, struggled desperately to kill him. But a quick-thinking Edwina had whipped her long white scarf around the man's gun hand, throwing off his aim.

The cuttergun waved wildly in the air. Before the injured spacer could slice free of the cloth, Cord threw himself into the heap of bodies and immobilized him.

When Cord wrested the cuttergun from his hand, the spacer gave up. Keeping his own weapon trained on the man's chest, Cord flung the other out of reach. Then he took his emergency light from its place on his belt and shone it at the spacer. Cord would not ordinarily have risked showing a light, but if the noise of the fight had attracted no attention, the pin-sized beam of light was not going to bring anyone running. And he needed to see the man who had no psychic emanation at all.

Everyone—everyone human or humanoid, anyway, and all the alien species Cord had ever met—had some mental signal. With most it was possible to interpret their psychic output as emotion. Cord could tell how others felt, even if they did not speak the same language. Even Julia McKay, the most frighteningly alien mind Cord had encountered, gave off a signal, though her emotions were not interpretable. Not by him, anyway.

But this spacer was the exception. If Cord relied on his empathic sense alone, he would have sworn only he and Edwina were in the alley. And yet there was life in the blue eyes that stared into the light. The pupils contracted in reaction, and the man pulled his cowl farther over his pale smooth skin.

A robot? Cord wondered. It was his understanding that robots could not harm people. It was simply not in their programming. Since he had a suspicious mind, he discounted the belief: an illicit factory somewhere might conceivably manufacture specially designed androids able to kill.

"Who are you?" Cord asked. "Why did you attack us?" Perhaps the answer would give him some clue.

"If I tell you, will you let me go?" the spacer asked.

"No."

"Then why should I give you anything?"

Cord smiled without any humor or kindness.

"You'll tell me because of what will happen to you if you don't," he said softly. "Your death can be quick or it can be very, very slow. You choose."

The spacer nodded, neither surprised nor frightened. He too was hardened to the realities of life and death. He sat up, and the cowl he wore fell back. Cord had the answer to the question he had not asked: the spacer's skull was hairless and metallic. Where his hairline should have been, the metal became flesh-colored plastic. There was a faint horizontal line across each cheek, where the prosthetic device met the man's own jaw. With his brain encased in a metal shell, it was not surprising Cord felt no psychic emanations. The energy Mehirans detected would travel through any substance except metal or stone.

The spacer said, "The Ae sent us to get you. You broke up the operation at Station Kappa. The Ae was real unhappy about that."

"The Ae? Then Hafed was not the leader?" No, of course not. Hafed hadn't the intelligence or connections necessary to the Ae, leader of a far-flung organization. Cord had not given any thought to the Ael pirates except as a lead to Edwina's whereabouts. Once he'd determined that she had passed through their hands to Irru, the Ael had ceased to exist for him.

The spacer laughed harshly.

"That android-humping pervert? Not likely. He wanted money, and the Ae was willing to overlook his habits. He made a good front at the station."

"The Ae must have a high opinion of me, to send six of you."

"It'd only take one to kill you. The Ae wants you alive."

"And now that you've failed?" Cord inquired. It was probably true. To be successful, raiders must inspire terror in their potential victims. Let it be seen that a single man could clean out one of their nests, and others might think of resisting.

"You've told me what I wanted to know," Cord stated. "You understand why I can't let you go free."

The spacer grinned. It made Cord think of skulls. The man's upper teeth were even and perfect: artificial, like his skull. The lower ones were yellowed and a little crooked.

"I know. If none of us survive, the Ae will never know where we found you—or if we found you at all. But it doesn't matter to me. I can't go to the Ae and tell him we failed, and where else could I go—a freak like me?"

"I'm sorry." Cold-blooded killing was the worst. Cord had never grown accustomed to it, although it was sometimes necessary.

"You will be," the spacer said. "You work for someone as bad as the Ae, I hear."

"What do you mean?"

The spacer, supporting himself on one elbow in that dank alley, chuckled huskily.

"This duke—what's his name—from Komonor. His mercenaries are asking for news of you."

"Why? About what?" A flash of alarm stabbed through Cord. Somehow the duke had found out about his defection—but so soon?

The man shook his head, and the light reflected eerily off the smooth metal.

"I don't know any more than that. A soldier of fortune—that's what he called himself; hired killer is more like it—spoke to us in a bar. My friend knew him from someplace, so the mercenary told him he was looking for you. He offered money for information. We played dumb. My friend just about split his guts laughing afterward. He didn't let on that we were after you, too."

"Why would Duke Ashek want me?"

"The killer was to make absolutely sure that you and the woman got back to Komonor. Sounds like this duke doesn't trust you."

Cord didn't answer. His mind was racing at the implications. Then he made his decision.

Cord had kept his cuttergun aimed more or less at the center of the spacer's chest. He continued to do so, but set down his light, making sure it was still shining in his prisoner's face.

With the thumb of his free hand, Cord pressed a certain stone in the heavy ring he wore upon the third finger. Smoothly, he pushed it against the spacer's neck.

"Listen," Cord said. "You have a few seconds before you lose consciousness. You can get away from the Ae if you want to. There are colonies that will take anyone who signs up. Go to one of them and you have a good chance of living. The kind I'm talking about won't care what you look like. But don't ever cross my path again. Or the Ae's."

The spacer's eyes closed and he fell back among the corpses. Cord rose and holstered his weapon. *Must remember to refill the ring*, he told himself.

"I'm glad you didn't kill him," Edwina said. "If he does report back to his boss, I suppose it won't do us any harm. We'll be long gone."

Cord handed her the scarf he had unwrapped from the man's gun arm.

"If he goes back to the Ael pirates, they'll know more about us than is healthy. I'm gambling that he'll be too scared not to break with them."

They walked through the alley.

"By the way," Cord said, "Thank you. You saved my life."

"Oh," Edwina murmured. "I had one of my flashes. I 'saw' him raising his gun a moment before he actually did. I was afraid warning you might startle him into firing sooner. Since he hadn't seen me, I pulled off my stole and used it like a whip, to lasso his arm as he raised it to aim at you."

"You have fast reactions. I'm indebted."

Edwina shrugged.

"It was for my own protection as much as yours." She looked up at him. "I didn't understand everything he told you, Cord. That the pirates are out to get you is understandable, I guess, but what's this about Ashek? We only got here—he can't know already that you aren't going to take me back to Komonor."

"No," Cord said slowly, "he can't. But he does. He must have assumed I would double-cross him, though I've never betrayed any of my employers—until now. If not for the powers of your ring, I would never have gone back on my bargain with the duke." Or, of course, if Edwina had turned out to be Julia. He added: "It's as though he was aware of the ring's power. But if so, why let me take it in the first place?"

Edwina shrugged. "He never paid any attention to my story of how I thought I'd gotten there."

"Well, then, why would he let you keep the ring if he thought it was valuable?"

"Let me keep it?" Edwina faltered. "He didn't."

"He said you kept it in your dressing table—I saw him take it from there."

"Ashek took it away from me almost as soon as I was discovered. If I had been permitted to retain it, it would have been with me when the pirates captured me."

Cord stared at her, then began to laugh.

"Duke Ashek is more underhanded than my usual clients," he observed. "He may have believed that I needed the ring to help find you, and he was sure that

I would not let you escape. Then he set his hunters on my trail to make certain *I* wouldn't escape—if I happened to get ideas about keeping it for myself. And you, of course."

"It fits," Edwina said. "It explains why Ashek dropped the subject of how I got into his private quarters. And now I know why he kept me as a concubine. It certainly wasn't for my irresistible beauty—he has a lovely Komonori mistress. But why bother with me at all, since he had the ring?"

"Perhaps he thought only you could make use of it. Or that through experiment he could learn how you did it. Even if we're wrong about his motives, he would never have allowed the pirates to kidnap you without taking action."

"Why not? Innate chivalry?"

"No. The duke rules with a strong hand. He would not want it seen that pirates could hijack his own yacht—and concubine—and get away with it. Besides, I have met men like him before. However little he might care about you, you are his property. What is his is important to him."

Edwina, wrapping her wide scarf around her shoulders again, discovered the bloodstain on one end. She quickly retied it so that the mark was out of sight.

As soon as they were back in their room, Cord began checking for ship departures. He found what he was looking for, made reservations in one name, and then located the listing for a ship scheduled for Komonor and requested reservations for that voyage also, but in his own name.

"If anyone checks, we'll be on the passenger list for the next ship to Komonor; they won't trouble to look any further," he said to Edwina, who was packing. Neither of them was carrying much. Edwina had the few changes of clothing he'd bought for her on their arrival, and he had the most necessary of his equipment.

The rest was in security storage on the world he had chosen as his center of operations.

"Our ship leaves in an eighth rotation. We'd better get going," Cord told her, once he had collected his few belongings.

As they left the room, he inserted credit tokens in the payment slot. He paid for the room for three more days; if their enemies were deceived even for a day, it would give Cord and Edwina a headstart.

Chapter 14

The vessel was the Vonarian luxury liner *Sen Ru*, with staterooms for a thousand. Her name meant "White Ship," and she was. Cord and Edwina, approaching in the last shuttle before the *Sen Ru* left orbit, saw her gleaming amid the blackness of space. She was so clean and sleek that she seemed made of ceramic.

"Expensive?" Edwina queried, gazing out the shuttle's port.

"Very. It's worth it."

From her glance, Cord knew she had understood what he meant. It was worth it to throw their pursuers, if any, off the trail. The hunters who came after them would look for them first on tramp freighters and colonial dormitory ships.

The *Sen Ru* was unquestionably the final word in elegance. There were no android servants, and the meals were prepared by real chefs, not by robotic kitchens. The passenger list seemed to consist entirely of the nobility of a dozen planets, billionaires, entertainment figures, and wealthy businesspeople. Cord was passing as one of the last category. His identity card showed him to be Fer Dain Mas, an importer. He had disguised himself slightly and Edwina a great deal.

During their brief stay on Etir, he had made her color her hair. It was now six distinct shades of green, beginning with moss green at root level and ending in leaf green at the tips. Her freckles had been bleached out. She also possessed several new outfits.

"I feel silly," she told him, studying her reflection.

Her dress was composed of what seemed like millions of tiny bubbles, no more substantial to the eye than a layer of frothing bath preparation. Every bubble was a different color.

"It may take getting used to, but it's an interesting effect," Cord maintained. "To be inconspicuous here, you must be conspicuous. If you dress too plainly, they'll assume you are a servant."

Cord himself was arrayed more lavishly than usual, and that took some doing. He was wearing a long, silky robe that was plum red until movement or a breath of air stirred it and the color shifted to pale green. With it, Cord wore wide bracelets and a matching jeweled collar, none of them merely decorative. The collar, of embossed gold set with a variety of precious stones and enameled, contained fifteen small tools for lock picking, surveillance, and repair—or modification—of almost any device he might encounter.

He looked like a self-made rich man, which was precisely the image he meant to project. It would keep the aristocrats on the *Sen Ru* away from him, and some of the old, established business caste as well. If there were any other upstarts aboard, they might try to get to know him, but a show of frank vulgarity should discourage them. Anyone with enough money to travel on a liner like this was almost certain to be trying to rise in status. A merchant with money did not need to make a bigger profit as much as he or she needed to acquire connections with "old money"— the titled, the mercantile families who were going to be titled, and the gentlefolk. So while the traders and factory owners around him were on their best behavior, trying to curry favor with their social betters, his conduct would be common enough to make them steer clear of him. *Still, I must not be such an outcast that they will remember me,* Cord told himself.

His plan worked, partly—as he admitted—because it was a large ship. It was not to anyone's advantage to get to know Edwina and himself, and since they did not put themselves forward, no one became friendly with them. He had not responded to the smiles of the women who had noted his wide shoulders; impossible to have a shipboard dalliance without revealing the fact that he was disguised. He regretted missing so many delightful opportunities, but business was business and pleasure . . . ah, pleasure was for other times, unless it could safely be worked in. And, of course, there was Edwina.

She was curled up in a form-fitting chair which was straining itself to its utmost to accommodate her posture. Still, her cross-legged position seemed to be comfortable for her. She was reading a pamphlet.

"Listen to this," she said, as Cord entered the room. She pitched her voice higher and began to read in an affected accent. " 'It is, of course, impossible to set down good manners for all classes and all species; what is courtesy on one world may be impudence on another. However, the author's study of many races and systems suggests to him that all humanoid civilizations can be divided into five systems: i.e., (1) Egalitarian, (2) Aristocratic, (3) Feudal, (4) Laissez-faire, and (5) Industrial/elitist. The polite person will make an effort to determine which system he is entering, and will adapt his behavior to the society. See chapters 2–6 for guidelines for each.' " She put down the pamphlet and sighed. "This is complicated. You'd have to be a sociologist to remember all this."

"That's why I suggested you stay here as much as possible."

Edwina groaned. "I can't spend the entire journey in this room. I'll go stir-crazy."

"I haven't heard that term before, but I understand your meaning." He ran a hand along her arm and then slipped it under her halter to cup a full breast. "I could keep you entertained."

"You're good," admitted Edwina, "but are you that good?"

Cord smiled. "Let's find out."

Cord spent some time in the gambling salon. The extensive gymnasium attracted him, but he felt it unwise to risk it. It is hard to maintain an appearance of sedentary habits while working out strenuously. While he had made no attempt at disguise beyond wearing clothing different from his usual and providing himself with a false name and background, it would be out of character for Fer Dain Mas to be too athletic.

The game was the Vonarian favorite, W*. Cord preferred it to the card games Terrans seemed to enjoy, partly because of the attractiveness of the game pieces. The smooth white disks were painted with symbols and geometrical designs which were somehow satisfying in themselves. The Vonarians had a knack for comfort and beauty. Cord fingered an oval bearing the likeness of a flowering branch before clicking it down beside another player's marker which bore a tree trunk.

"Tree," the dealer called, in his soft, accented Multi-Lang. "The hoard goes to the gentleman in blue." He bowed slightly to Cord.

In the next ship's deci-day the pile grew, diminished somewhat, and then mounded high. Cord played more for amusement than for gain, without risking great sums. He did not like to throw money away. It did his role of nouveau riche no harm. Miserliness in small matters was what everyone would expect of an upstart merchant like Fer Dain.

A woman stood near him, watching him win. Cord observed her because he always noticed lovely women, and also because if she stood any closer she would be inside his clothing. He could feel the warmth of her hip and thigh close beside him. A skirt of tiny silken pleats hung low on her hips; she was bare from the waist up, except for her thin white fur and heavy necklaces which obscured her firm breasts. The white down covered her right up to her jawline, then thinned out to leave her face bare. As were her nipples and aureolae. This Cord had established when she leaned forward to place her gaming piece. The hair on her head was actually longer, fluffier fur of the same color as the rest.

She had noticed him, too, he saw. Her orange eyes rested admiringly on his deep chest and broad shoulders—and his heap of credits. Here was a woman who had come to the casino only to find a man: she played for the lowest permissible stakes, and without the desperation of the real gambler. Others stared at the pieces, blind to everything else. A pair of four-armed Vonarian stewards were guiding out a man who was muttering. "Ten red, ten red, ten red, ten . . ." endlessly. But Cord's furry fellow gambler smiled at him when he won again.

She was his if he wished to leave the table. On sudden impulse, Cord scooped up his winnings, turned to her, and said, "Your place?"

She smiled wickedly, obviously understanding that his suite was already occupied. "Why not?"

So they strolled out together, to a ripple of envy and admiration—psychically audible to Cord, though he felt certain that his new acquaintance was aware of the effect she created. He wondered idly how much of the envy he sensed was due to his luck at the tables, and how much was tribute to his companion.

The corridors were dim and silent after the glitter and noise of the casino. The rich green of the carpets and walls absorbed light as well as sound; the Vonarian stewards flitted past them like ghosts.

"My name's Fer Dain Mas," Cord told her, letting her lead him. They were now in a section which was unfamiliar to him—his and Edwina's suite was in the other direction.

"Mine is H'La ta Kres ta La. H'La to my ... intimates."

H'La's accommodation was one of the least expensive aboard the *Sen Ru*—though even so, it had cost as much as a year's average wage on many worlds. The white, orange, and brown of the furnishings showed H'La and her alien eyes to good advantage, doubtless why she had specified the combination. The bed, enclosed on three sides, was almost cavelike.

H'La was not one to waste time on inessentials, Cord decided, watching her sweep the mounded pillows off the bed. Cord had intended to suggest ordering drinks while getting acquainted, but seeing how things were developing, he concluded it could wait. Having stripped the bed for action, H'La dropped her necklaces to the floor. (Costume jewelry, Cord judged; if she could afford that much solid gold and platinum, she would be staying in a suite of rooms like Cord's.) Her skirt followed, slithering down around her ankles, leaving her naked. The furred body had an alien attraction. H'La was not as rounded as a human or Mehiran, though there were curves in all the right places, but she was sleek and smoothly muscled.

"You look like a man for hot, hard riding," H'la breathed, flicking the closure of his robe with her foreclaw. Cord hoped she would keep her nails retracted. She seemed like the kind who would forget to be cautious or considerate in the heat of the moment. But a few scratches would be worth it, he thought as he threw off the garment. His organ was already out of its pouch, extended to full length. H'La gave a throaty little cry of pleasure at the sight and pulled him toward the alcove.

"Your skin is so bare," she murmured, letting herself fall back and pulling Cord down with her. "Still, you obviously have all the equipment—and you are not timid, like many human men, are you? Pleasure is for carnivores. Those who live on fruit and grain have not the energy for it."

Obviously there were no herbivores in H'La's family tree. Cord, who had grown up eating mostly vegetables and fish, hoped it would not handicap him too much.

Her orange eyes glowed with excitement, while the undulations of her lithe body almost dislodged him. With an acrobat's limber strength, she wrapped her legs around his thighs, moaning and lunging. Cord nuzzled her downy breasts, savoring her passion. He longed to probe her with his sixth sense as well as his body. Curious to discover what her emanations would be like, he opened his mind to her.

They came of different species, but lust was much the same, he found. H'La's passion was perhaps more fierce, but its essence was recognizable. She was losing herself in an ocean of sensation, and his own body responded, waves of need ready to crest, when he sensed the third presence.

He could not disentangle himself from her clinging limbs, but he rolled over. H'La, startled at the abrupt movement—and the cessation of some attentions which were of fundamental importance to her at the moment—loosened her grip. Cord swept her aside and sprang to his feet to confront the intruder.

The man was big: as tall as Cord and bulkier, but

his muscle was turning to loose fat. He was armed with a short, flexible truncheon. As he stood, surprised into immobility, Cord felt the man's emotions change from gloating complacency to near-panic. He had expected an easy job. Cord launched himself, landing a solid kick in the other's gut. The flabby man reeled back, staggering from the force of the blow, to smash into the jutting angle formed by the walls of the dressing room and bathroom. Then he toppled to the floor. He was human, not Vonarian, but he must be crew. His clothing and rough hands set him apart from the wealthy, pampered passengers of the *Sen Ru.*

"He's unconscious," H'La ventured, stress in her voice and anxiety in her mind.

Cord did not contradict her until he went forward to kneel by the spacer and feel for a pulse. It was unnecessary—for him, at least. He knew the man was dead. The psychic death scream was unmistakable. It would be stupid to let H'La see that he knew it at once, however. So Cord checked for a pulse in wrist and neck, put his palm over the crewman's heart, and pretended to be in some doubt. "I think he's dead," Cord said. He sounded surprised, and was. He hadn't kicked *that* hard. While seeming to look for signs of life, Cord conducted a surreptitious examination of the corpse. When the man had hit the metal wall, he had struck his head. The skull had fractured like an egg.

H'La crouched beside him without speaking. And no wonder.

"He was hiding in the dressing room, wasn't he?" Cord inquired. "Waiting until my attention was thoroughly . . . engaged."

He chose his words slowly, careful not to reveal his identity. He must not do or say anything Fer Dain

Mas, upstart businessman, would not. He had already acted out of character by his attack on the crewman.

H'La stared at him with her wide, brilliant eyes. The vertical pupils had contracted.

"Come now," Cord said dryly. "You must have arranged for him to be there. These cabins are impossible to break into." Not true, of course—not for an expert. But Cord doubted the corpse had entered by stealth. "What was your plan—to have your friend rob me and then threaten to tell my traveling companion I'd been with you unless I kept quiet about it?"

"He was no friend of mine," H'La declared. "I am always very honest with my customers. The owners of the *Sen* line do not permit on their ships courtesans who cheat their clients." The woman gave a little twitch of her furred shoulders, almost a shrug. "But you were not paying for my services, you see, Fer Dain. That one approached me earlier this evening and pointed you out. He offered me money if I would bring you here and hold your attention." She added, "After we had begun, I was sorry we were to be interrupted. One must be practical, however; there was money involved."

If it wasn't an apology, it was probably as close to one as such a proud, fierce being could come.

"Who was he? What did he want?"

H'La rose and went to the sleeping enclosure. She produced a brush from a drawer beneath the bed and began brushing the fur of her neck and shoulders before replying. "He said he was a temporary crewman taken on because one of the Vonarians had had an accident just before we left Etir. I don't know what he wanted."

"You didn't have any notion of his intentions when you agreed to his proposal?"

"I am impulsive," H'La explained. "Especially where credits are concerned. He said there was no danger to

me and that it would not come to the Vonarians'
attention. It seemed safe enough."

Cord was convinced that she was telling the truth.
Her emotional output was even and untroubled. To
H'La, her actions were quite reasonable. There was no
point in holding a grudge.

He did wonder whether the man had been one of
the Ae's creatures, or whether it was a simple attempt at robbery by a replacement spacer not as honest he should be. Cord tried to find out when the
crewman had made his deal with H'La—whether it
was after Cord's run of luck began or before. H'La did
not remember. She had not been paying attention.

"What are you going to do with the body?"
she inquired.

Cord's eyebrows rose. "Dear H'La, I am not going to
do a thing with it. Since you permitted the fellow to
attack me, I believe the carcass is your problem. You
might tell the Vonarians he came in—allegedly to
check the air circulation unit—and attacked you.
You kicked him, he fell back, and so forth. If you
bring my name into it, I will assuredly tell what
really happened, and then you'll never be permitted
to work on the *Sen* line again, will you?"

H'La accepted the justice of it without question.
"We were in the midst of interesting work, before,"
she said. "Shall we continue, now that we have finished this business?" She motioned gracefully toward
the rumpled bed.

Cord laughed. "I have made love in many places
and under many circumstances, but never in the presence of a corpse. It's an experience I can do without."
He picked up his clothing and started to dress. "As
soon as I leave you had better notify the authorities—
they might wonder if you let the body lie around for
any length of time." He smiled. "Tomorrow, come

and find me in the casino. Then we will have an uninterrupted session at your customary charges."

Cord did not mention the incident to Edwina, feeling that it would only disturb her. It worried him a little, too, since there was no way of telling whether it had been a coincidence or proof that the Ael were still on their trail.

However, as an antidote to anxiety, he kept his date with H'La the next day, and found it wonderfully restorative.

Chapter 15

They disembarked at Shaqin and Edwina looked around and said wryly. "Something tells me this is an industrial/elitist society."

Cord watched the uniformed, dull-faced factory workers walking home, past the gleaming displays in the shop windows.

"I believe you are right. Well, we won't be here long."

They need not even have left the port, but Edwina had wanted to see something of the planet. Since the ship for Mte-4 was not scheduled to depart until a full day after the *Sen Ru*'s arrival, there was ample time for a sightseeing and shopping tour of the port city. Shopping was a popular pastime for visitors to Shaqin.

"The price seems so low," Edwina said, admiring a filmy gown which seemed composed entirely of tiny tucks and almost invisible embroidery.

"Would you like it? As you say, it isn't expensive." Cord intended to show Edwina that he was her best friend. She had no one else to turn to, unless she went back to Duke Ashek, but he did not want her even to consider the possibility.

"Thanks, but I don't think it's very practical. Besides, I'd never be able to wear it without thinking that whoever made it was paid practically nothing."

"That's true," Cord agreed. "But if everyone's social conscience were as highly developed as yours, the seamstress would starve."

Edwina gave him a grin.

"Do you think so? We shouldn't let that happen."

They checked into their hotel laden with packages, most of them Edwina's. Not all clothing or jewelry, either, Cord mused. At her direction, they had also bought several small art objects and some textbook disks. One was an outline of human history to the present, another was a survey of other races, and the third, a four-disk set, was called *The Anatomy of Cultures: Causes and Effects.*

"What are you going to do with all these?" Cord asked, studying the assemblage on the sleeping platform.

Edwina was bouncing gently on the oversized, springy bed. She patted the viridian-and-cinnabar-striped coverlet appreciatively. "I'll wear some of them," she said. "The statuette, there, is attractive, so I'll admire it. And I'll read the books—or disks, or whatever they're called now. But there is one thing I forgot."

"What's that?" Cord, pulling off his tunic, dropped it, caught it with the tip of his tail, and flung it in the direction of the disposal chute. A tiny valet robot trundled out of a panel in the wall, scooped up the fallen garment in its claws, and stuffed it down the chute. The robot's mechanism made a faint chittering that sounded like admonition as it rolled back into the wall. Cord and Edwina both laughed.

"What I need right now . . ." Edwina began again.

"Is a bounce on the bed—with a partner? A drink? Both?"

"No—at least, not immediately. I want something light to read—a mystery or adventure story, maybe. The hotel gift shop has entertainment tapes. While you shower and order something to drink, I'll pick out something to read."

"You don't think I can keep you occupied all night?"

Edwina looked him up and down, smiling. "I doubt I can hold *your* attention that long. I have noticed your habit of tinkering with your weapons and gear at the least convenient times."

"Before, during, and after meals, possibly," Cord admitted fairly. "But not in bed."

"No, but you do get up in the middle of the night," Edwina pointed out. "So tonight I'll have something to read while you polish your rifle. I'll be right back."

She slipped out the door. Cord grinned and went to shower. This was a very nice hotel, he decided, as the cabinet shot jets of hot, scented water at him from all sides. It was reasonably priced, too, a nice change from both expensive luxury resorts and cheap spacers' accommodations. Old-fashioned but pleasant. He took his time in the shower cabinet. Cord knew Edwina well enough by now to realize that she never hurried past book tapes. It would take her a while to make a selection.

When he emerged clean and dry from the bathroom and found she had not returned, he ordered drinks. They were brought by a human servant, who asked if the lady and gentleman wished to order dinner. Cord declined, partly because Edwina would want a drink or two before eating and partly because by the time to which they were accustomed it was not yet time for a meal.

When he had finished his second cocquelicot cocktail, Cord began to wonder what Edwina could be doing. The gift shop had not contained that many tapes. Even if she had looked at other things as well, it should not have taken her so long. The shop was small: it sold toiletries and souvenirs and a few other items likely to appeal to the transient populace of a spaceport hotel.

He had wrapped himself in a velvety robe for the evening, but now he threw it off and pulled on close-fitting trousers, a silky red shirt, and a black jerkin. He added the usual knife, hand weapon, and other equipment automatically. Wryly he thought he was probably overarmed for the expedition. No doubt she had stopped to have her nails done at the cosmetician.

He stalked the silent passages of the Garden Pavilion. The murals on the wall, gold and umber and sepia-toned with age, were mentioned in every guidebook to Shaqin, but Cord swept past them with the barest of glances.

The lobby was spacious, furnished with a small fortune in antiques and objets d'art. Around its edges were an array of shops for the convenience of the patrons: a confectionery, a tailor, a drugstore, and the gift shop.

The clerk, dressed in a black, well-cut version of the Shaqin workers' uniform, remembered her. "Yes, sir, a green-haired lady in a green dress to match. She chose two tapes."

"When did she leave here?"

The woman told him, and Cord, translating from Shaqinese to standard time, began to be worried. So long! He asked, "Did you notice in which direction she went after she left?"

A faint crease appeared between the Shaqinese's symmetrically arched brows. "Truth, sir, I did. It is not my habit to take notice of the comings and goings of my betters, but I happened to look after her, thinking what a pleasant-spoken lady she was."

"Go on," Cord urged, reflecting that life must occasionally be difficult on Shaqin. The greater part of the population was so downtrodden.

"She seemed about to turn left, toward the stairs

and the tube. Then a gentleman came up beside her and they went out the entrance."

"What did he look like? Did he speak to her? Did she seem to know him?"

The clerk's expression grew anxious. "I hope I didn't do the wrong thing, sir. It did seem to me that the lady was taken by surprise—and wasn't really glad to see him." She paused.

"If you noticed anything else, anything at all, please tell me," Cord requested. "It could be important."

"It did seem to me that she didn't want to go with him. When he came up to her, he put his arm around her waist and whispered something in her ear. She looked startled."

Cord could imagine the embrace and warning: *That's a knife you feel against your right kidney. Come with me or I'll see how much of it I can remove with one easy stroke.*

"As to what he looked like," the clerk continued, "he was tall. Almost as tall as you. He appeared to be Terran-human, or else one of the undifferentiated stocks. He had pale hair—white, really—and green eyes. Not true green, but brownish green."

"You were very observant. Did you happen to see what he was wearing?"

The clerk blushed. "Yes, sir, I did. He was handsome, so I took particular notice. He was dressed in a dark blue tunic and trousers and matching belt trimmmed with platinum. It was a tailor-made outfit, I could tell."

"I'll bet you could," Cord agreed. "Was he thin or muscular? Heavily built?"

The woman considered.

"He wasn't as ... muscular as you are, sir. Although a dark business suit will minimize such things. I would describe him as slim but strong-looking."

"Thank you," he said with a warm smile. "I wish I

could thank you more adequately." Cord tipped the clerk generously and went to a computer terminal in the lobby.

In a city of three million, his chances of tracking Edwina and her captor were slight—particularly in the available time. However, thanks to the spacer, Cord knew the kidnapper was likely to be working for Ashek. It was probable he would want to exchange his prisoner for cash quickly.

There was a ship scheduled to depart in three days which would call at Komonor. It would drop at several other worlds, first, but it was the only vessel listed to visit Ashek's planet at all in the next planetary month. Unless the mercenary had his own ship (unlikely because of cost), he would surely intend to be aboard that liner. Had, in fact, probably made his reservations already.

Cord strode out of the hotel and signaled for an auto-cab. When the lozenge-shaped red groundcar pulled over to pick him up, he was momentarily surprised to see that there was a driver. The auto-cabs he knew were robotic.

"Where to, sir?"

"The spaceport," Cord told him, and named the company that owned the liner bound for Komonor. Of course, he meditated, many jobs done by robots on other worlds were held by humans on Shaqin. It was why he intended to visit the port offices. On any advanced planet, most clerical positions were filled by androids, cyborgs, or robots, none of which could be bribed. Human beings, on the other hand . . .

During the ride, Cord stared moodily out the plastiflex window. Shaqin depressed him, no matter how carefully he kept his guard up, the anxiety, hopelessness, and actual hunger of many of the city's inhabitants mentally chafed at him. Certainly there were fine buildings and extensive gardens—but they

were built on human unhappiness. It was the way of
the world—of most worlds, for that matter—but it
made things uncommonly painful for an empath. Life
had sometimes been hard back home on Mehira, but
no one went without medical treatment or was hungry or cold. Strange that anyone would think such
deprivation acceptable. Even stranger that the con-
trast between the rich and the starving seemed to
pass unnoticed.

The driver dropped him outside the shipping office,
and thanked him profusely when Cord handed over a
five-credit note and waved aside the change.

The shipping office was exactly what Cord had
hoped for, a one-clerk operation: small, plain, and
seldom visited. Most booking was done by computer
terminal and through travel agencies. The woman at
the counter, though, was not precisely what Cord
wanted.

She was about Cord's age, with a pale, square face,
dark hair that curled around her forehead, and a short,
straight nose. Her mental emanations indicated she
was good-humored. Cord, open to psychic impressions,
felt her curiosity and amusement as he entered the
office. He rapidly revised the rather simple strategy
he had planned. He doubted that mere flattery would
work with this woman.

"May I help you, sir?" Her voice was low and
pleasant.

"Yes, if you will," Cord replied honestly. "Are we
likely to be disturbed here?"

A tide of pink rose in her face almost simultaneously with a surge of surprise. To reassure her,
Cord added, "I must talk to you without danger of
interruption." He smiled.

Cautious, she said, "You are the first customer today.
I doubt anyone else will come in, sir."

He considered asking her out to dinner, as it was near the end of office hours, then discarded the idea. With some, a little mild seduction would work; others it only made wary. Besides, the information he needed was here, in the office.

"May I ask your name?"

"It's Marana Korsic, sir."

"Ms. Korsic, I need to know if a certain man is on the passenger list of one of your ships."

"That information is not usually made public," Marana answered. Her psychic output remained cautious, but there was a growing tinge of curiosity.

"I understand that; I'm glad to have a person to deal with, rather than a robot. Marama—if you'll let me call you by your first name—you are obviously reliable, or the line wouldn't leave you in charge here." He sensed he was walking a tightrope. By her mental reaction he could tell that she was inclined to dismiss even that mild compliment as manipulative flattery. He changed his approach slightly. "Whether or not your employers appreciate your competence, I know that you must have to use your intelligence and initiative oftener than they realize. And this is a case which calls for discretion."

She was mollified and increasingly interested.

"The circumstances would have to be very unusual before I could even consider making an exception to the rules," she said. That she had mentioned the possibility was a sign she was weakening. She might have refused outright.

"I'm a private detective," Cord said, knowing the statement rang true because it so nearly *was* true. "I have reason to believe a kidnapper will attempt to leave Shaqin with his victim, who is my client's daughter."

"But the authorities could arrest him," Marana pointed out, reasonably.

"Unfortunately, since neither my client nor the kidnapper is Shaqinese, the local police are unlikely to involve themselves. As you can see, I'm from offworld, too, so they won't feel impelled to give me any aid," he added disarmingly. This was the truth, naturally. Cord had no objection to lying except when the other person was sure to recognize it as such. "My client is well known on certain other worlds, but he feels that the more quietly this is handled, the better."

"Can't the girl do anything to get away?"

"He's been keeping her under control with drugs. I'm not asking much, Marana—all I want is to see if he's on the passenger list. If he is, I'll know what to do. But if my information is wrong, and he's not going to board that liner, I'll have to start looking elsewhere for him. And time is vital: it's a big galaxy. If I lose him here, the All-h—my client may never see his daughter again. There's more to it than simple ransom. She's a political pawn. This man's employers may decide she's a liability and kill her. Or she may spend the rest of her life in a cell. Or worse," Cord finished ambiguously. It was a pretty good story, he thought. He hoped Marana thought so, too.

The woman regarded him from level brown eyes.

"Or she could be traveling willingly with the man, who may be perfectly honest and respectable, while you are the kidnapper," she observed.

Internally, Cord winced. He liked intelligent people, but there were times when a fool was preferable.

"Do you really want to gamble that I'm not telling the truth? After all, there's a woman's life at stake. And if I were a kidnapper, would I have bothered trying to deceive you? This office is isolated. It would have been easy for me to overpower you and retrieve any data I wanted from the computer. I'm sure it isn't a heavily protected program."

Marana Korsic's mind rippled with unease. "It would

be easier to lie. That way, you couldn't be charged with any crime. Whereas if it came out that I'd told you, I might be fired—so *I'd* have to lie, and pretend you were never here. I still lose."

"True—but if I were a criminal, and didn't want to risk charges of assault and computer trespass, I'd try to bribe you. Being amoral myself, I would have failed to recognize that your character would not allow you to be bought." Cord winked and Marana laughed.

"I don't know why, but you impress me as being honest. Or at least basically nice, though that isn't the same thing, is it? What's this alleged kidnapper's name?"

"I don't know what he's calling himself at this moment"—or any other time—"but the listing includes descriptions, pictures, and handprints, doesn't it, to prevent any confusion?"

"To keep people who don't have exit visas from sneaking offplanet on somebody else's tickets," Marana explained. "If you can give me any details, it will help."

"He's a tall human male with white or very pale blond hair. He's an offworlder—I don't think he can be posing as Shaqinese."

"That's something," she said. "Let's see what we have...." The terminal's screen displayed twelve pictures. Most Cord could eliminate without hesitation.

"Number four." The man was easily recognizable from the gift shop attendan't description. "M. L. Gerard," Cord read. "Terran. Prospector." Prospector! In a manner of speaking, perhaps. The fellow had a sense of irony. Cord memorized the local address given. Who knew? Gerard might be there.

"He has reservations for two," Marana commented.

"So I see. Thank you, Marana," Cord said, letting his eyes linger as they passed over her well-rounded body. He would enjoy the exploration of her topography.

He felt the yearning in her mind, and it intensified his own.

"Isn't it quitting time?" he asked hopefully. "Would you care to have dinner with me?"

"Almost. I could lock up now," she replied, and then blushed charmingly. "But food wasn't what I had in mind."

Marana seemed almost to be sleepwalking as she locked the entrance door and engaged the computer system. No one could disturb them in the office now.

Marana took Cord's hand and led him behind a partition. The second room was smaller than the outer office and seemed to be used for storage. There was a washroom too.

Blushing again, Marana said shyly, "I've been rather impulsive, and I've got to take, ah, precautions."

"No need. Our species are too different to crossbreed. That's the advantage of interspecial sex," he whispered. His hands and tail caressed her as she stripped off her worker's uniform.

She was starved for it, he sensed. Poor Shaqinese were often deprived even of the comfort of sex by their crowded living conditions and by lack of contraceptives. The ruling classes saw to it that the poor remained fertile. In the expanding, industrialized Shaqinese economy, a large pool of cheap labor benefited the wealthy.

Her breasts were large and white and sweet, like melons. Her hips . . . oh, her hips. Well rounded and strong. A man could get a grip on those and never let go. He shed his own garments with alacrity. Marana's eyes and hands and lips roamed his body admiringly.

"I'm afraid there isn't much floor space," she breathed.

There wasn't. Cord regretted the absence of a bed, since this lady deserved plenty of room for a tumble. Still, one makes do. Cord braced himself against the wall, clasped her waist, and raised her. She was light in his arms as he lowered her carefully onto his organ. Marana realized what he intended and guided herself onto the spear, wrapping her legs around his thighs.

It was not as leisurely as he preferred, and he would have liked to have shown the inexperienced Marana a few special tricks, but under the circumstances it was enjoyable. Particularly for Marana, who had never had a lover so practiced or so unusual.

He left her at the office and stopped to make two purchases. Marana would never have accepted money from him, but he thought a gift would help brighten her drab life. He arranged for flowers to be delivered to her office. Then he went into a store selling sundries to purchase a map. No computer-generated maps on Shaqin; it was not sufficiently advanced. But the regional map he selected was printed on a fine sheet which was guaranteed to lie flat and never to wear at the folds. Also, the print glowed faintly in the dark. He stopped by a fountain in a square and studied the map. To his surprise, the address Gerard had given was on the outskirts of town, almost suburban. It appeared to be a residential district, rather than one of hotels. Cord wondered whether the other bounty hunter had given a false address, and concluded it was unlikely. There must be some connection: given the uncertainty of ship arrivals and departures, passengers were requested to leave addresses where they could be contacted in the event of a schedule change. Would anyone who needed to get off world (and rather badly, at that) risk missing such a message? Cord did not think so.

He knew enough about Shaqinese life from his study of educational tapes and from observation to realize that the size of the dwelling, its location on the city's edge, and the modest fenced garden surrounding it indicated that its owner was prosperous but not of the elite. Most Shaqinese lived in dormitories or barracks owned by the factories or in miserable shacks or tenements. The wealthy owned country residences. This quiet neighborhood suggested the middle class— those who had to live near the city to commute to their management-level jobs, who could afford one or perhaps two servants, who were educated but not idle. Solid, practical people. Cord recognized the neighborhood from a dozen other worlds. It was surprising to find a bounty hunter in such sedate surroundings, however.

His observation of the house was brief and stealthy; he could not take the chance of being seen. But he got close enough, under cover of night, to open his mind to Edwina and to sense that she was within.

The confirmation was reassuring, and he left to plan Edwina's "liberation" for a second time.

Chapter 16

By the next night, he knew much more. The house was owned by a Shaqinese who headed the Guardians, a local branch of a multiplanet security service. Guardians supplied watchmen, bodyguards, and private detectives. They also installed alarm systems and even trained secret police. A large organization, their advantage over smaller competitors lay in their network of contacts and resources. Guardians had a reputation for efficiency and quite reasonable prices.

It was late when Cord began to check the fence with a current-and-beam detector. The owner of this home, at least, would understand protective systems. Cord was right; two separate alarms were engaged, set to be triggered by different things—the interruption of a beam of light or the weight of a body on the garden wall. Cord smiled coldly. He had spent much of the day in research, and by now he was an expert on Shaqinese alarms and booby traps, and consequently on evading or disabling them. The local devices were adequate against the local criminal element—but against Cord the Hunter? Hardly. Once he thought he caught sight of a movement far down the road, and froze until he was convinced he was mistaken. Reassured, he continued his work.

He took the cage he had brought and opened the screened door, taking care that the creature within did not dart out. He gripped its harness and drew it out—a being the size of a Mehiran or human baby, but bone-thin, six-limbed, and covered in fine fur. It meeped softly, annoyed at being disturbed. Cord held it against his chest, rubbing its wedge-shaped head until it calmed and began to nuzzle him. Its claws grasped his tunic and pawed at his pockets. Holding the emul with one hand, Cord pulled a ball of orange-tinted aromatic gum from his belt pouch. The emul strained to reach it, cooing coaxingly. Cord held the globe of sweet paste just out of its reach, then deliberately tossed it over the fence. The emul's three eyes all followed the gum ball's arc. It whined. Cord placed the emul on the fence and produced several more balls. The beast put out one claw to grasp one, clinging to the woven lathe. Cord threw them all over the fence in quick succession, and the emul darted over the barricade in search of its treats. Pursuit and enjoyment of its favorite delicacy should keep the creature active in the garden for some time.

Cord watched. A light or two was still on in the lower floor of the house, but now lights came on upstairs as well, a sure sign the alarms had sounded. Cord swung himself over the fence and dropped onto the brick-paved yard, then melted in the shadow of a blossoming shrub as light flooded the garden. His eyes were dazzled by the sudden change from darkness to bright light, but he heard a door open. He could sense and then see, when his eyes had grown accustomed to the light, a man standing in the open door of the house. The room behind him was dark, making it difficult to see him. His right hand held a blocky, glinting shape.

The intoxicated emul skittered across the courtyard, enlivened by the mulein gum. The man started; Cord was sure he would fire before realizing that the beast was harmless. But although his weapon's muzzle followed the fast-moving emul, he did not pull the trigger.

Cord's twitching ears caught the other's harsh crack of laughter.

Someone called out from the house. Cord could not catch the words but he heard the gunman's reply.

"Only an animal—"

A second figure appeared behind him. This time Cord heard Shaqinese-accented Multi-Lang—the first man's host, he assumed.

"It is an emul," the Shaqinese said. "There is a quarry for you, Gerard. They do not run wild in these parts, so it must be an escaped pet. There may be a reward."

The suggestion was faintly insulting, though the tone was friendly, but Gerard took no offense. Instead he laughed again and answered, "That's what comes of working for an assembly-line business like the Guardians—you get fat and credit-conscious. What's that it's chasing?" he asked.

The shorter man behind Gerard seemed to peer out into the lighted yard. "Probably a toy—oh, a ball of mulein." After a moment, he added, "That's strange. I wonder how it got here—the emul didn't bring it. You see the effect it has on the creature. Cord the Hunter couldn't have traced you here, could he?"

Only Gerard's pale hair stood out clearly in the dark. "How could he?" the mercenary responded impatiently. "He doesn't know anyone else was after the woman—most likely he thinks she ran away. He was foolish to let her go out by herself—I could scarcely believe my luck when I saw her. I'd been trying to think of a way to separate her from Cord, and there she was, almost a gift. It took only seconds—considering that most people don't observe at all, it's probable that no one saw us leave the hotel."

Gerard's psychic emanations were calm, even complacent, while the Shaqinese's remained nervous. Now was the time, Cord decided.

With one fluid movement he leaped from his hiding place. One leg swung up, and Cord's foot connected with the gun in Gerard's hand. A second kick, this time to Gerard's crotch, disabled Cord's most formidable opponent. As he shoved the human aside, Cord wondered if human males' arrogant aggressiveness stemmed from the vulnerability of their private parts. At the same time he fired his dart gun past Gerard's shoulder.

The Shaqinese seemed to fall back, but Cord didn't have time to make sure he was down: Gerard, gray-faced, hunched over in pain, had managed to draw another weapon. The first shot missed Cord's shoulder by the length of a fingernail, detonating noisily against the garden fence and blowing a fair-sized hole in it. Cord fired automatically, knowing the anesthetic could not take effect quickly enough. He slipped sideways, pivoting on one foot. When the second tiny bomb hissed past him he was already throwing himself at Gerard. He slammed into the hired cutterman at waist level, sending him reeling against the wall. Cord's fist drove into the other's stomach, doubling him over. Cord snapped one muscular knee up, catching Gerard's chin. When the human staggered back, he gave out no psychic emanation beyond the low-level background noise of an unconscious mind.

Gerard had fallen in the doorway. Cord dragged him inside and closed the door, stepping over the Shaqinese. Deliberately he shot Gerard with an anesthetic dart too, guaranteeing that the bounty hunter would stay unconscious for some time.

Only then did Cord venture farther into the house, going cautiously, all his senses alert.

The house was pleasant, not too large and not too old, with low-ceilinged rooms and high grilled windows. It was, Cord decided, a very desirable residence for someone in his line of work—or its owner's. Now where was Edwina—upstairs or down? Recalling the more generous windows of the upper levels, and their balconies, Cord opted for the cellar. The elevator was in the center of the house—literally, since the floor plan was circular. The cylindrical elevator dropped him with breathtaking speed. When he stepped out into the basement, he was as impressed by it as he had been by the main floor. Here the space was divided into several sections. The first was a workroom with a variety of equipment, though none of it was very complex: what a hobbyist might use, no more. Cord wondered what hobbies a local Guardians' chief pursued. The next section was more of an armory than a storeroom. It would have been possible to equip a small guerrilla force with the cutter rifles, antipersonnel missiles, and tactical gear on the walls or in boxes. Somehow the workroom seemed more understandable. Here the Shaqinese had the ability to repair or modify the tools of his trade.

In the next section there were half a dozen heavy doors with small windows. Cells—and Edwina was in one of them. Cord could feel the restlessness of her mind, like white-capped waves on the sea. She was very close.

He looked through the pane in the first door. Eureka! Edwina sat huddled on a cot, staring at the floor. But as Cord's face darkened the glass panel, she looked up. As she recognized the unhuman silhouette of his head, she leaped up, grinning, and ran to the door. She said something, but the words did not carry though the thick glass. Cord nodded reassuringly to her and stood back from the door to study it.

This was not complicated. It did not even have a control board to open and close it and to control temperature, humidity, pressure, and atmosphere. Primitive. The Shaqinese had probably installed his private prison himself, unable to hire an electech, perhaps, because he preferred not to have the presence of cells known. There was a massive lever. Cord moved it experimentally. It had pointed left. As he tugged it to the right, he could almost feel the bolt it controlled sliding back. When the level pointed to the right, Cord pulled. The door came open, grudgingly, and Edwina emerged from behind it.

"You found me, oh, Cord, you found me. Let's get out of here," she whispered frantically. "I'm sorry I went out to get a book tape—it was a mistake. He came up to me as I started back to the room and made me go with him. Hurry. please—before he finds out you're here."

"Hush," Cord told her. "It's all right, I know all about it. Gerard and his friend are taking a nap. We'll be long gone when they wake up."

But Edwina was still shivering when he led her out of the house, through the garden, and down the side street to his groundcar. Still, once they were in the skimmer, she was composed enough to ask, "Where are we going?"

"First, to a cheap rented cubicle in a part of town where nobody notices anything," he replied, guiding the orange groundcar into a maze of back streets where one vehicle in five was orange.

"Are we staying here long?" Edwina inquired, gazing around her with distaste.

Cord grinned at her reaction: the room was pretty bad. It contained a bed that folded up into the wall, a lavatory, and a telereceiver without a computer hookup. The walls were grimy in spite of their impermeable finish; the color was years out of fashion and had not been attractive even when new. The uncushioned floors were scuffed. The local communications network he had switched on earlier was broadcasting a program of music and dance.

"Not long," Cord replied, setting a small case on the wide shelf meant to serve as table and storage place and unfolding it.

Edwina watched with interest as he began to remove clothing and less identifiable objects from it. Cord tore open a foil pouch and removed a cylinder of flesh-tan material. He pulled up one end and it unrolled into a large oval of thin, rubbery substance. "Gather your hair back," he ordered.

Edwina complied without asking questions. Altogether, Cord thought, she was very easy to work with. He slapped the plasti-flesh over her face, smoothing it to blend with her skin at the hairline, under the chin and jaw, and in front of the ears. A muffled protest came from behind the featureless sheet of plastic.

"It's all right, Edwina, you'll be able to breathe in a moment." He used the shaper provided with the theatrical makeup kit to open nostrils, eyeholes, and a slit for her mouth. Then he pinched, kneaded, and coaxed the pliable dough into ridges and furrows that changed the topography of Edwina's face and added years to her age.

The telereceiver routine came to an end—half a dozen virtually identical dancers in beaded pantlets and bandeaus—and a new broadcast took its place. Cord did not bother to switch to a different channel, being fully occupied with molding Edwina's face. He was not paying it much attention, since local news was of little interest to him, until his ears pricked up at the words "legal authorities."

". . . have revealed new facts in the recent sex and torture slaying of a worker woman. Medical evidence indicates that the woman had had sexual relations with at least two men shortly before her death. This only highlights the dangers facing workers who misuse their time and cheat their employers. The woman apparently entertained her lovers on her employer's time and on his premises. She was rewarded with hours of agony and ultimately death, a lesson to all who are tempted to shirk their duty."

"Self-righteous hypocrite," Edwinda muttered furiously. "Back home some half-wit might have said she was asking for it, but he wouldn't have dared spout that kind of nonsense on the news. I'm glad we aren't staying here, Cord."

"No, it's not my kind of place, either," he concurred. He supposed that on a world as socially repressed as Shaqin, sexual psychopaths would be common. He turned the receiver off and made a few adjustments to Edwina's mask. He surveyed his work critically and decided she would pass muster.

"Don't touch the plastic, and try not to move your face for a few minutes." He added, "That will give it time to set."

Turning to the mirror, he took out another roll of plasti-flesh and began work on his own face. He cut the eyeholes first this time. Edwina watched with rapt attention as he made his nose wider, his jaw fleshier, and his cheekbones more prominent. Under their newly wrinkled lids, Edwina's eyes grew large.

"You can talk now if you wish," Cord said, with a last tweak at his chin. "It's my turn to be quiet." While he waited for his own mask to firm, he took more plasti-flesh and molded a pair of ears—the human kind—and pressed them onto the sides of his head. They would not withstand close inspection, but they wouldn't have to: his wig, shoulder-length and shaggy, would cover all but the occasional glimpse of an earlobe or tip. His own ears would not be very comfortable, flattened down under the weight of a wig, and he would not be able to hear very well, but those were drawbacks he would have to endure. The discomfort wouldn't be for long.

The ears in place, he rubbed a skin-tinting agent

onto his hands. All that would be visible of him, hands, face, and "ears," was now a human color—an undistinguished dull tan.

"I can hardly believe it," Edwina marveled. "You look so different! If it weren't for your body and ... tail, I wouldn't know you. Or myself, either," she added with less enthusiasm, catching sight of her own elderly face. "But I always thought that no one would appear to age in the future. Where ... when I came from, it was already possible to continue looking pretty good until quite an advanced age. Hair coloring, wigs, face lifts, makeup, false teeth, and exercise. You have more resources than those, so why would anyone want to look like this?"

"There were things I didn't understand when I left my own world, too," Cord admitted. "What you're forgetting is cultural diversity. On some worlds the old are venerated for wisdom—or the toughness to survive long enough to be old. On the planet we are going to claim we come from, it's considered dishonest to tamper with one's appearance."

"Won't we be conspicuous?"

"Yes." Cord laughed. "Extremely. This time, that's all to the good. I'm counting on Gerard and his friends to assume we'll try to be as inconspicuous as we can."

No luxury ship this time. The *Janci* provided the cheapest possible star transport for those who traveled from necessity rather than for business or pleasure. Once a freighter, the *Janci* transported passengers in dormitories where tiers of bunks, each one provided with sliding panels for privacy, accommodated hundreds.

The panels cut off sight of the others, but did not block out sound. As they lay close, listening to the rhythmic buckings and moans from the bunk above,

Edwina whispered, "This is certainly an *experience*. Any resemblance to our last trip is purely coincidental."

"It doesn't have to be *pure*," Cord replied, raising himself on his elbow and beginning to explore Edwina's body with hand and tail. "I've never made love to a middle-aged lady before, but there's always a first time."

The trip was a featureless round of meal packs eaten in their bunk alternating with games of chance and talk. Cord's second favorite leisure activity, tinkering with his weapons, was impossible. Middle-aged civil servants emigrating to settled colonies did not carry weapons—at least, not weapons like Cord's. There were, in fact, not supposed to be any weapons in the dormitory at all, considering the cramped and difficult conditions. Cord's knives, anesthetic ring, and the other devices he'd brought in his luggage were not easily identifiable. His more obvious tools—cutter rifle and dart pistol among others—were packed in the cargo hold. It made him uneasy to be without them, but there really was no choice if he wished to conceal his identity.

Which made it the more annoying when he made his mistake.

Cord was standing in the narrow passage between two tiers of bunks, talking with another would-be colonist. The man was a veteran of a planetary civil war who wanted to start fresh, away from all reminders of several years of hard, bloody fighting. He was headed for Mte-4 also.

"See, I know it was a military base, but I figure I can handle that—it wasn't my war. At home, it was seeing the buildings and parks and people I'd grown up with blown to atoms that got me. Out there—"

Someone pushed past Cord, throwing him onto the veteran.

"Old fool, you are in the way," a harsh voice said.

Before Cord could reply, the veteran reached out; he caught the other's shoulder and spun him around.

"There was enough room to get by without pushing my friend around," he said. The Kamean responded with a curse and struck the soldier's hand away. "An old man and a cripple—a good pair," he sneered.

Cord had restrained himself with difficulty, bearing in mind what he was supposed to be. But his new acquaintance surprised him by lunging at the Kamean. His movements were awkward, however, and his target sidestepped easily and brought his fist smashing down on the soldier's temple. The veteran fell against the closed panels of a tier of bunks and dropped to the deck. The Kamean, with an ugly smile, turned to walk away.

With a hiss of anger, Cord leaped after him and whipped the bully around. He rammed his fist into the Kamean's jaw, sending him reeling back. Cord admired Terran-style boxing; unlike many forms of personal combat, it required little space. He advanced upon the dazed Kamean and doubled him over with a swift, brutal blow to the belly. The man's flattened psychic output indicated he was knocked out. "Pardon me," Cord said as he turned his back on him and knelt by the veteran.

Cord knew enough first aid to be sure there were no serious injuries. Carefully he lifted his acquaintance into his bunk, noting the unlifelike weight and feel of the veteran's artificial legs. Then Cord went to an emergency call panel to summon the ship's doctor.

As soon as the physician arrived and Cord had described the cause of the veteran's injury, Cord withdrew.

"Was it wise to get involved?" Edwina asked when he returned to their bunk.

"No. But he got involved orginally on my behalf.

There's no point in worrying about it now. I doubt our Kamean friend will care to push it further."

It was true, and it reassured Edwina, but Cord knew that the real danger was that the incident would provide their enemies with a clue to their whereabouts. An elderly civil servant beating a Kamean ruffian? It was sure to be talked about. There was no point in worrying about what could not be changed, Cord realized.

Chapter 17

Yevren had followed Cord and Edwina to their Slum Town room and saw them emerge later with their newly old faces; that Cord would resort to such a guise did not surprise him. What he did find baffling was their choice of destination.

What had brought the bounty hunter and the woman here? Yevren stared around at the military-surplus buildings of Mte-4's main city. There were no ships due out for days; this was not a busy terminus. He had checked on that while still aboard the colony ship. Nor should it be easy to find a tramp pilot— there was nothing here to attract them.

No, he thought. Mte-4 was a colony world, pure and simple, with the roughness of all frontier planets and an extra grimness he had previously associated with military bases. Until the Indil-Waro Conflict the place had been virtually untouched. The Indilisi had used it as a staging area and command post. The uniform tan-and-brown buildings of the city were their legacy.

Still, the colonists themselves remained individualists even in the face of their regimented surroundings: people of several races who minded their own business, were loyal to their friends, and were not too ready to bow to authority. Not an ideal planet by Yevren's criteria.

He followed Cord and Edwina to their hotel—barracks converted to rooms, but with little in the way of amenities. He knew, because he took a room, too. It provided the best lodgings in the city, almost the only accommodations Mte-4 had to offer. The other half-dozen people who had disembarked were also staying there, with the exception of a couple who had relatives nearby. Once checked in, Yevren sent a subspace message to Duke Ashek, advising him of his arrival. The code he used was simple and well known to the Komonori police, but would prevent the message from being understood by the inquisitive or talkative. The communications center staff, for example. It had been his intention to ask that the duke send back Tanet or some other police agent, since surveillance was easier with two than with one, but after seeing Mte-4, Yevren changed his mind. Here another stranger would only be conspicuous, especially as there were no other Komonori on the world. Besides, Cord and Edwina could not easily lose themselves here, not the way they could in a big city.

The next day he followed them to the land office, waited until they had come out, and then went in.

"I want to ask about renting or buying some land," Yevren said, thinking how odd it was to be able to buy land. On Komonori, the nobility owned land. They might occasionally acquire more by marriage or inheritance but they never sold any. It was illegal.

"We've got it," the Warese said with a grin. "How much do you want and where?"

Yevren produced a sheepish chuckle. "Well, now that I can't say, offhand. But this seems like a planet that's wide open, and a nice place to live. What kind of folks are taking up land here? Farmers? Small manufacturers? I saw an old couple leave here a while back. What are they going to do?"

The Warese shook his head. "They're going into

manufacturing cosmetics and toiletries. They took a lease on a surplus installation. They aren't much of an advertisement for their products, though."

Yevren and the Warese laughed together.

"Suppose *I* wanted to lease an installation, instead of buying land?"

"You could have your choice of dozens."

"All located near that old couple's?" Yevren asked, shifting in his seat.

"Absolutely not," the Warese protested. "All the installations are scattered. Theirs is about two days' travel; their nearest neighbor is a day away. But you don't have to choose such an isolated area." He pulled a map out of his desk drawer and pointed. "They are here, at Battleground; you can choose from any of these others." He indicated a scattering of pyramidal symbols.

"May I have this?" Without waiting for a reply, Yevren folded the map and placed it in his pocket. "And Battleground—what's that, a town?"

"No," said the Warese uneasily. "It's an old-time battle site, dating back to the first colonists. There was an, ah, misunderstanding between them and the natives, but that's all over and forgotten now."

It took more time to learn further details, but it was time well spent, Yevren thought. He discovered where Cord's leased property was, what facilities there were, how to get there, and which outfitter the Warese had recommended to Cord. Finally having exhausted the land agent as a source of information, Yevren said he'd have to get in touch with his brother about setting up in business together before picking a site.

The same technique worked well at Pou's Surplus and Equipment. Careful questioning revealed that Cord and Edwina had already been there, and would be picking up their purchases in the morning.

"They need something big to carry it, I guess," Yevren remarked.

"They've got a crawl they bought here, but it's being overhauled. They're picking it up early tomorrow."

Yevren invested in some gear himself: a small all-terrain vehicle, a light camping kit, and a ray rifle.

"I've never yet seen a world that didn't have some kind of predators," he remarked, checking the battery pack.

"There are some small animals—more a nuisance than a danger. But if you see something humanoid around your land, don't shoot. Not to kill, anyhow."

"Oh? Why not?" Yevren looked up from the rifle's sights.

The clerk shrugged and said, "It's not a good idea to kill the natives here, that's all. It brings bad luck."

Yevren laughed shortly, "I'll bet they spread that superstition."

His informant laughed uneasily. "I guess so, but it's an unwritten law around here. And some people hold it's almost as bad to kill anyone. I used to think it was silly, too, but after you've been here a few years, you'll understand."

"Every world has its own customs, I guess." Yevren paid for his purchases with the colorful Warese scrip that was Mte-4's currency.

It was now late in the afternoon. Yevren turned into a foodery. It was full enough to suggest that the meals were good and busy enough to ensure that he would be inconspicuous. He took a table for two in a corner, pushed the order button inset in the table rim, and asked for the Chef's Special.

The other diners paid no attention to him. Several of them looked as if they might have secrets of their own; if they'd been on Komonor Yevren would have had them arrested just on suspicion. He gazed dispassionately at his surroundings until his meal came. The short, capable-looking woman who brought it was not sufficiently attractive or vibrant to interest him.

The food was a mixture of slices of coated deep-fried meat tossed with noodles and slivers of vegetable. It was all right but it wasn't Komonori.

He finished, paid, and left, knowing that no one in the eating place would remember him. It was best not to be conspicuous, on his current assignment, but on the whole he preferred his existence on Komonor, where at least he was well known to the criminal class.

He walked aimlessly for a time, partly for exercise, partly in the hope that he would find a house of prostitution of the right kind.

There were several houses of pleasure down on Port Row, but to judge by their advertisements none catered to his particular needs. His mind went to the furry piece of tail he'd seen Cord with on the *Sen Ru*. He'd like to get one of her kind in police headquarters on Komonor. It would take days to subdue a half-savage, half-animal like her.

At last he started back to the hotel. There was nothing for him here.

It was late by frontier standards. At the hotel's front desk, the robo-receptionist had been switched on; apparently the owner had retired for the night. Yevren met no one on the way to his room. Cord and Edwina's room was at the end of the hall. On an impulse Yevren went softly to their door and listened.

No sound; and the close-fitting door made it impossible to tell if there was a light inside. Several plans occurred to him, only to be dismissed as impractical. Tomorrow . . .

"Hey, what do you think you're doing there?" The words were not spoken loudly, but coming from a pace or two behind Yevren, they startled him.

The young human male confronting him looked pugnacious.

"I heard something in there as I passed—a bump or thud. I wondered if something was wrong," Yevren improvised. "If this is your room, you'd better be careful going in." He recognized his questioner as a young veteran who had arrived with Cord, Edwina, and himself on the colony ship.

"It's not," the ex-soldier said, "but they're friends of mine. So maybe we'd better make sure they're all right." His glance at Yevren was full of suspicion as he stumped forward.

If he alerted Cord, Yevren might as well go back to Komonor and report failure to Duke Ashek. The bounty hunter had not survived and prospered by trust. Let him realize that someone was watching him and Yevren would have no further chance. Noting the young colonist's strange, stiff gait, Yevren gambled.

As the Terran passed him, Yevren's fist chopped down on his neck. He caught the veteran as he toppled. The only sound had been that of flesh and bone striking flesh and bone. He half-carried, half-dragged the man to his own room, let himself in, and secured the door again. Then he sat down on the hard platform of the hoverbed to consider his alternatives.

The colonist would go to the local authorities as soon as he revived, naturally. Yevren would be arrested—or at least charged with assault, which was bad enough. Worse, Cord would be alerted. No explanation would lull his suspicions, Yevren guessed. He might notice Yevren's Komonori features, or hear that Yevren's identification showed him to be Komonori. That must not occur—not now, so close to fulfilling his task.

So the man had to die.

It was unfortunate, Yevren thought, but the fellow had brought it on himself by his inquisitiveness. On

Komonor, Yevren would have flashed his police brassard and the meddler would conveniently and selectively have lost his memory. Yevren began his preparations by taking two ampoules of Hypnoze from his travel bag. One wold wipe out all tension and anxiety in almost any species of humanoid, making it possible to sleep. Two would knock out that same humanoid for two sleep periods. Although the veteran wasn't going to be around that long. . . .

Each ampoule had a tiny needle at one end. Rest it against a convenient vein, give the capsule a sharp squeeze, and the drug was in the bloodstream. Yevren administered both in the veteran's left wrist. He trusted the body would not be found, but if it was, the authorities (who were not too sophisticated on Mte-4) might think the man had overdosed.

Now came the tricky part. It was so late that there was little danger of being seen. Yevren opened his window wide and looked out. The only other lighted window was in the far end. Even if someone glanced out, he would be unlikely to see Yevren going about his work.

The smell of damp ground and vegetation stole into the room. He had chosen a room at the back, facing the undergrowth that came up almost to the building, thinking that it might be useful if he needed to leave his room secretly. His foresight was vindicated.

The drug had had its chance to work on his prisoner. He would not struggle or make a sound at an inopportune moment. Yevren dialed off the room lights, waited until his eyes had readjusted to darkness, and then shouldered the still form. The window sill was low. He stepped over it, paused to close the window all but a crack, and then moved as quietly as possible into the brush and trees.

He remained in sight of the hotel, although the foliage screened him. Straight in this direction, and he would come to an open field that was used for sports events. Edge around that, keeping to the concealment of the trees, and he would encounter a large lake. A few of the colonists took primitive watercraft out on it; many others fished at the edges. But no one lived around it, and the water was deep, even by the shore. He rolled the sleeping man into the water and watched him sink. Even if the body was found tomorrow it would appear an accident.

Yevren's muscles ached as he stood up. The veteran had been a heavy load and the walk had been long. He stretched briefly and started back—there was no sense in lingering at the lake. He went as quickly as he could in the dark.

The incident had left him uneasy. He felt, somehow, that he should have handled it with more finesse—even though he'd rather messily killed a woman just a short time ago. But that was a crime of passion. She had refused to answer his questions about Cord, at first anyhow, and then, inflamed with anger and lust, he had forgotten himself.

He should have been more cautious. Under the circumstances, the duke would understand the need for the murder, but he might not be pleased.

Later, lying in bed waiting for sleep, he thought about Cord's plans. Apart from the fact that he'd leased property, his purchase of so many supplies was revealing. The clerk at Pou's had been as helpful with gossip as with merchandise, so Yevren had a fair notion of what Cord had bought. He was planning a long stay, then. Which meant either that he and Edwina were simply hiding until the search for them was called off, or else that Cord wanted to experiment with the ring. Obviously, Edwina had confided in him; she was not Cord's prisoner. They seemed to be on excellent terms. What had the bounty hunter offered her that Duke Ashek had not? It wasn't important. His chronometer alarm was set for an early hour; he needed sleep now more than riddles. He needed a woman badly, too, but he would have to wait. He would take Edwina back tomorrow, perhaps, and then there would be the exquisite pleasure of inducing her to tell how the ring worked. His resolution to be cautious was forgotten as he fell asleep dreaming of tortures and pleasures.

Chapter 18

Edwina stood with her arms crossed, hugging herself, dwarfed by the trees and the mound. The road disappeared into the forest in either direction, if you cared to dignify the dirt track with such a title, Cord amended. It was slightly wider than the military crawler in which they had arrived, and which was now safely inside the mound and out of sight. Aerial surveillance would show nothing but a winding, badly made road leading up to the shore of a river which had not yet begun to be exploited when the war turned the colony into a military base.

The installation Cord had leased contained laboratories and cells. On the whole, Cord preferred not to speculate about the reason for such facilities. The point was, he had gotten it cheaply, it was distant from the port and the only town on Mte-4, and when the portal was closed it was virtually impenetrable.

The bunker's slanting sides and slightly arched roof had been planted with moss to conceal it; now the spring growth was thick and interspersed with jewel-like wildflowers.

He opened himself to Edwina and abruptly felt a mixture of strange sensations. Edwina was uneasy. The cause of her jitteriness was understandable to Cord, although she could not detect it herself, except subliminally. The cool air, full to the scent of foliage and bog, was also full of emotion.

Cord's muscles tensed for action. The area surrounding the bunker was supposed to be deserted, his nearest neighbor a day away. Ears twitching, he tried to make some sense of the signals.

They were faint, but not from distance, from some other cause. He didn't think they were animal-created, but they didn't seem to come from live humans either. It was very puzzling, and then he relaxed. He realized the emanations were old, very old, a residue of something that must have happened here long ago. It reminded him of the way cherished objects picked up traces of their user's personality, so that years later it was possible to feel the psychic imprint. It accounted for his race's veneration of ancestral keepsakes.

This imprinting was old but strong, as though the forest now contained a soul—a very sad soul. Wisps of anger, hatred, horror, and death floated around the bunker area—and the longer his shields remained open, the more the depression grated on his nerves. His psychic shields came down, shutting out the blackness.

"Let's go in," he called to Edwina. She gave a nod, smiled, and ran forward to meet him.

"Good idea," she agreed as they passed through the great door. "It's getting cool out there, now that the sun's going down."

Cord paused to throw the lever that rolled a slablike, stone-faced door into place. Other levers turned on the lights and life-support systems. The bunker was now impervious. He turned and led her through the cavernous space meant for the motor pool. At the far end was a portal.

Cord had already memorized a map of the bunker. Beyond the door were large storage areas, Stores and Central Supplies, now just as empty and deserted as the garage they'd passed through. Only their all-terrain crawler stood in this vast cavern.

Cord bypassed the warehouse section and led Edwina to a second door, opening into the housing and living quarters. It was extremely spartan, and Edwina wrinkled her nose in disappointment. Simple cots, drab blankets, colorless furniture that looked as though it had been formed in badly made molds—and this was to be their home for months!

"Let's go to the lower level," Cord said quickly. "It may be more interesting there."

The laboratories were on the next level and could be reached by elevator or by a spiraling ramp. Although the electricity was functioning smoothly, Cord took Edwina's arm and led her to the ramp.

"If the mechanism fails," he said wryly, "it could be a full planetary year before anyone comes looking for us."

His teasing did nothing to lighten Edwina's mood as a mutinous look stole over her face. They took the ramp slowly. There was one more level below the labs, and it contained cells. He certainly wouldn't take her there; in fact, he refrained from mentioning them.

There were half a dozen independent laboratories on the lower level. Many were fitted up for biological studies; one seemed suitable for a physicist. Each contained an equipment list in plain sight. As he scanned them, he thought he recognized the purposes of most of the devices. None were identical to those he had learned about on Mehira, and all were superior in sensitivity and instrumentation. Well, Mehira had always placed more emphasis on the bio- and psychosciences than on the "hard" sciences. Any race of empaths would.

"Cord," Edwina said, in a small, taut voice. She interrupted his inspection of a cylinder-and-coil apparatus that could be anything from a plasma cannon to a still.

"Yes?" He looked up from its controls and was

surprised to see that Edwina was pale. "What's wrong?"

"I don't like it in here—any more than I liked it out there."

Alarmed, Cord straightened up. At her expression, he asked, "Did you have a vision?"

"Not exactly." She looked around furtively. "I know this sounds silly, but could anyone be hiding in here?"

Mentally alert to any danger, Cord opened his shields. He could feel nothing except Edwina's disturbance. He put an arm protectively around her shoulders and felt her shiver.

"I'm sure we're alone, but I can check out the rest of the installation if you want. But it was sealed when we arrived and the life-support systems were inoperative."

"I guess I'm just tired. I had this strange feeling that someone was watching us. Sorry, I can't explain it, but"—she shook off his arm and stood straighter—"I'm all right now."

They retraced their steps and passed through the pale gray corridors to their crawler. Unloading was easy; they used float-boxes for their luggage, Cord's specialized tools, and their provisions. They stacked all the provisions in the mess hall/kitchen area and left the tools near the spiral staircase.

Carrying the luggage, they trudged to the housing area to choose a room. There were several dozen cubicles, all identical.

Faced with such a ridiculous choice, Edwina giggled. Cord raised an eyebrow.

"I don't know whether to use one room, or"—she looked suggestively at Cord—"all of them."

"All of them, by all means." He returned her smile.

"Except"—here Edwina frowned—"these were meant to be used by only one person. Look at the size of this cot." She went over to the thin slab and poked at it. "'Bed' is not the right term for this object."

"Easily solved," said Cord. "We'll just make a pile of them and we'll be cozy in no time."

"No time like the present," she urged.

Cord put down the luggage by the door; Edwina followed suit. He turned, went out, and into the next cubicle. He came back with a mattress and went out again. Getting into the spirit of this, Edwina ran to the cubicle across the hall and grabbed up a mattress. Soon the floor of their cubicle was littered with mattresses—a wall-to-wall bed. The luggage was soon pushed out into the hall, followed by pieces of clothing and moans of delight.

He teased her with tongue and teeth until she was in ecstasy. His tail tip stroked her right thigh while the tip of his organ, extended to its full length, traced patterns on her belly and thighs.

"Oh, please—come inside," she invited. The words were husky with passion. She cried out when he slid into her. He opened himself to her emanations as fully as she had opened herself to his organ. He nearly came as the waves of her delight washed over him. He wished she could feel the psychic pleasures as well as the mere physical delights.

Again and again he brought her to the brink of orgasm, each time easing off, but leaving her more urgent every time. Her inner muscles rippled around his probing length. Her emotions focused to one burning need: the heat between her thighs. They were spread as far as they would go, which in an athletic young woman like Edwina was a considerable distance.

Her back arched and her belly and hips thrust upward. She was lost in exquisite passion—it flooded over him, bathing his every nerve fiber with fire.

It was time to give her what her body and mind cried out for—if only because he couldn't hold it much longer. He let himself concentrate on how slippery she was, how hot, the rhythmic surge of her muscles.

The blinding flood of her lust flowed over him, and then with overwhelming physical release, he flowed into her.

If she had been Mehiran, their spirits would have mingled. As it was, it remained only a joining of bodies. But it was very, very good. He lay there, pleasantly exhausted. Shields still open, he could feel Edwina's sleepy satisfaction. And suddenly—he realized that was *all* he could feel. They were completely alone. He couldn't even sense the desolation of the forest outside, nor the life of any animals and birds. It gave him the horrible feeling of being surrounded completely by death.

He stole another glance at Edwina. She wasn't affected. He had attributed her earlier uneasiness to a mild empathy of some sort; the forest had obviously disturbed her too. But now he couldn't understand the change.

Curiously he sent out mental probes—and sat up suddenly when the probe smashed into an impenetrable wall. *Ancestors!* he swore. *Of course!* He cursed himself for a fool for thinking of it as just another building. The bunker was built of many layers of material and covered with earth. It not only blocked out the exterior emanations but rendered Cord powerless to sense outside intruders.

He slumped back. There was nothing that could be done now. He had to put his faith in the bunker. It was built to withstand any assault. This was a fortress, he told himself hopefully, not a tomb. . . .

This accursed planet didn't even have a decent moon or two to light up the night sky, thought Yevren sourly. It was pitch-black in the forest, and Yevren couldn't even make out the mound where the bunker lay. He was not excessively fond of creeping around unknown places in the dark, and the strangely silent forest was unnerving. But unless he grasped the lay of the land and found some way into the bunker, nothing would be accomplished. The duke was waiting for results.

He snapped on a tiny light inside the crawler and searched for the night finder; it was a small device that would allow him to pick his way out in the dark. His hand closed around the odd-shaped box, leaving a thumbprint on the viewing screen. He wiped it off with a sleeve.

Turning the light off, he stepped out of the crawler. He'd been told no one was in the area for kilometers around, but he left nothing to chance. It was still possible a native might wander into the area and find him.

The night finder guided him toward the mound, telling him when to avoid obstacles. Spikelike trees loomed everywhere, and the ground was uneven and springy, almost as though it weren't solid earth. He could feel the ground slope upward, over the bunker. Here it was more level, more solid, and easier to walk on. He flipped another switch on the box, a sensor that would find an opening anywhere in the bunker. A vent, a crack somewhere, a secret entrance.

Yevren spent most of the night covering every piece of ground over and around the bunker. He could find no chink in the bunker's armor. Not even a vent. Apparently the life-support systems recycled completely. As the sun sent its first rays through the trees, he swore and kicked at a pile of leaves overgrown with wild flowers, destroying their beauty.

The sun was stronger; he would have to move his crawler farther out of sight, deeper into the forest and away from the main entrance. He trudged back to the crawler, cursing all the way.

He shifted the crawler into low gear, and it lurched forward, its treads gripping the forest floor. Yevren headed deeper into the forest, angling away from the entrance to the mound. He spotted a small rise and headed for it; he could hide the crawler behind it and then walk back to the bunker. Already a plan of attack, through the main entrance, was forming in his mind. There were several ways he might get in through the front door, any one of which might work. He smiled. Things were looking up.

Edwina was singing in the mess hall, cheerfully making breakfast, when Cord padded in. She'd not only put away the various foods they'd brought, but had unearthed some overlooked cans of military supplies, which were neatly stacked in a corner.

She smiled when he came in. "Good morning," she sang.

Cord had to wend his way past row upon row of gleaming metal benches; the vast mess hall was meant to feed over two hundred people. He felt dwarfed by the cavernous space.

Edwina was in a large kitchen, also completely metal. Using only a section of the huge stove, she was busy stirring, boiling, and cooking.

"You're quite chipper this morning," he commented, sticking a finger into a bowl and sampling her wares. "I guess you're feeling up to par?"

Edwina smiled again. "Thank you for using old Earther terms. It makes me feel at home." She slapped his hand away from the bowl. "Sit down and I'll feed you."

She brought spoons and two bowls of a thick, steamy substance to one of the metal benches. "This tastes a little like oatmeal; I used to eat it back on Earth."

"Tell me more about Earth. How different was it?"

A dreamy look came into Edwina's eyes. "Books.

There were books everywhere. Magazines, newspapers. Now it seems they're almost extinct. You people have computers, holopix, and speed-of-light transmissions. You don't need books very much."

"They haven't disappeared completely," he protested. "The more primitive planets still have them."

"Thanks."

"Then what about the great scientific advances that took their place?"

She shrugged. "Well, we didn't have space travel. On the other hand, we didn't have slavery either."

She took his empty bowl and went back to the kitchen, returning with the next course. "I found some military supplies left in the cupboard, but they're marked 'Desiccated Seaweed Stock' and 'Freeze-Dried Poultry Stew.' "

Cord attacked his plate with enthusiasm. "Emergency rations," he explained. "What's this I'm eating?"

"The alien version of bacon and eggs."

"You forget," said Cord, putting down his fork, "that I don't know what bacon and eggs are."

"Sorry. It's old Earth breakfast food. Bacon is strips of meat, and eggs, well, they're eggs. You know, from a bird."

"You'll have plenty of time to teach me all about Old Earth," Cord said, "while we research the ring."

"It's a deal," Edwina replied, gathering up the dishes. "I'll teach you all about Earth, and you can teach me, um, other things. . . ."

Cord laughed and helped her clean up. Then they descended to the laboratories on the lower level. The air seemed to grow colder, though Cord didn't think that was possible. The life-support systems maintained the same pleasant temperature throughout the building. He decided it must be psychological—something to do with going down into the ground. Edwina obviously felt it, though she said nothing; she had goosepimples.

It was strange that it affected both human and Mehiran, but then the two species shared many traits. It had to be sheer emptiness of the huge complex. Once it had been filled with bustling personnel; now their own footsteps echoed down silent corridors. He noticed also as they passed the biological laboratories that he was aware of tension, almost as though he could sense the unpleasant experiments that once had been carried out here. He began to sing softly in the dead quiet, a Mehiran paean of joy for all good things. It raised his spirits again and drove away the oppressiveness of the subterranean halls.

"What was that?" Edwina asked when he finished, nearly at the door of their chosen lab. "It was so beautiful."

"A song of my own people about sunlight, growing plants, fresh water and good food, lying with one's lover . . . a lot of things that are pleasant. Like you."

Edwina laughed, probably the happiest sound the walls had heard in the duration of their existence. "What are you going to do first?" she asked as they entered the room.

"I'd like to do a chemical analysis of the ring to find out what it's made of. That's what this machine is for," he replied, patting its enameled metal side.

Edwina held the lavender-silver band in the palm of her hand. "You're going to harm it? You'll have to shave off some of the metal, and that will change it. I know it will."

"No—not with this. These people didn't need to take a sample to analyze it. We just put the ring there, on the pad, and focus these five beams on it. It's important that they all be at a certain angle," Cord murmured, consulting the user's guide. "And this control ensures that they all are. Distance from the object being tested—yes, it's metal, so it should be eighteen points away. . . ." He carried on a running commentary, which probably made little sense to Edwina. She watched intently, however.

"We're ready," he said at last and pulled the lever down. Edwina moved a little closer.

Nothing very spectacular occurred. Except for a hum so low that even Cord's acute hearing could hardly detect it, the machine operated silently. Presently it made more noise, as it printed out a list detailing the ring's composition. The major metals were common enough: platinum, silver, copper, and iron.

"What a mixture," Edwina remarked.

There were more than two dozen trace elements, some of which were unfamiliar to Cord. He asked Edwina if she knew of them.

"Not by those names, certainly. Maybe if we knew what they were called in English, I'd recognize them. Or maybe not. Chemistry was not my strongest subject."

Cord held the ring in his hand and pondered. He wished his training had included more theoretical science. As it was, he was only an ingenious tinkerer. For all he knew, any piece of jewelry might contain a similar assortment of elements.

Maybe its composition was meaningful or maybe not; there were other tests to be done.

One piece of equipment would show an enlarged, three-dimensional-image of the inside of the ring. If it contained any circuit or any other sort of gadgetry, such examination would reveal it. Cord put the silvery band in the chamber and set the controls to give a printed report as well as a visual scan.

"Oh, look!" Edwina exclaimed.

In the air over the spherical chamber lines were forming. It was like watching the beams of a miniature building being settled into place without either workers or equipment to move them. The lines formed the diagram of a very short thick cylinder. Cord observed that they were not all the same color. The outlines of the ring were white but gradually patterns were forming of pink, violet, and dull green. Touches of brown, black, and orange appeared. The enlarged, "interior" view of the ring was finished. It hung there, a glowing construct in a puddle of artificial dark. With a "fffft" a silver-paper copy was ejected from a slot into a tray. But Cord didn't pick it up. He was staring at the image.

At first he had thought the colored lines reflected writing on the outer surface. Now he realized it was not so. The colors wove a complex pattern of their own, a braid of interlocking pentagrams.

"This is interesting," Edwina said, taking up the printout. "How did they do it?"

"Do what?" Cord asked absently, still tracing the interlace with his eyes. The complex twistings almost seemed to having a meaning. . . .

"It says here that the pink represents copper, the orange is iridium, and so forth. But see how fine those lines are in the image; in the ring they must be . . . well, just an atom thick. If that's the right word. How did its maker manipulate anything that fine?"

"I don't know," Cord answered. "Of course, we're dealing with someone—or something—whose science is probably more sophisticated than your world's or mine. But I'll settle for knowing exactly what it is and how it works. Tell me again what happened when you picked it up."

She repeated the story. "I'm sure I've told you everything, Cord. I've gone over it in my mind again and again. I was embarrassed, I wanted to be somewhere else, and then I was."

"But obviously wanting to be elsewhere isn't enough by itself, because you've probably wanted to be home any number of times since then and it hasn't worked,"

Cord commented wryly. His eyes went back to the projection. "It's strange, but I can't help but feel that that pattern means something."

Edwina glanced at him. "Yes, that's what I think. I don't know why it should, because it can't be seen in the ring. But it seems familiar, somehow."

Cord turned off the machine. He had already made a copy of the band of script running around the ring; now he fed that into a computer with a massive language program. He had obtained a software package which was advertised as containing virtually every known tongue. It was going to take a while to run the program, given the number of possibilities, including planetary dialects, archaic forms, and extinct languages.

"Let's go," he said to Edwina. "Let it work while we take it easy."

"I'll take it any way I can get it," Edwina replied, grinning.

Chapter 19

Somewhere, a twig snapped.

Yevren, in the middle of trying to set the dials on a small thermal bomb, froze. His head swiveled at the sound, but he gingerly aborted the fusing procedure before reaching for his blaster.

In the distance a pale figure, not human, stealthily stepped between two trees. The creature carried something in its paw or hand as it threaded its way between the spike trees. It was headed away from him, deeper into the forest.

Yevren holstered the gun and placed the bomb in his pack, still keeping an eye on the creature. He moved slowly after it, picking his way over the spongy, moss-covered ground.

Oblivious to Yevren, the alien began to croon as it walked. The object in its hand—Yevren could see a little more clearly now—was round, with a handle. As it sang it shook the object like a rattle, making strange hollow noises. Fascinated, Yevren watched the creature; it was obviously a native, praying on the sacred Battleground.

The creature itself was humanoid, but only two-thirds his size, with a pasty white skin. It had spindly arms and legs and a featherlike crest that began low on the forehead and continued back over the shoulders. Its scrap of clothing consisted of a bit of loosely draped fabric covered in a pale design.

It must have finished its song, for it stopped, turned, and looked squarely at the tree Yevren hid behind.

"You are man?" it piped in Multi-Lang.

Yevren stepped into view, hand on his holstered blaster.

"I am T'Whierl'T'Whee."

Yevren didn't know if that was the name of the creature or of its race. He remained silent.

"You pray?" it questioned.

"No. I'm, uh, lost."

The creature motioned him closer. "T'Whee show you the way."

The way out or the way to pay homage? Yevren wondered. He walked toward the creature and was startled, upon closer inspection, to see it was a female. Two long, flat breasts dangled beneath the toga. He wondered about the rest of her.

"Do you live here?" he asked.

"No!" The reply was emphatic; T'Whee waved an arm. "Live there." Yevren looked in the direction indicated and saw only more trees; she could be talking about kilometers or light-years. "No one live here. Not safe."

She turned and started to walk in another direction, but Yevren took her arm. It felt soft, warm, and strangely pliable. "Wait. What do you mean?"

For a moment a perplexed look shadowed the creature's face. Then it said, "Many turnings of the sun, more than can count, man came. T'Whierl die." She swept her free arm in a circle, indicating the forest around them.

"And the bunker?" Yevren prompted. He pointed in the direction of the mound. "Where the soldiers used to be."

"Bad place." T'Whee spat at a tree. "More T'Whierl die. Not go there again."

She again turned to walk away. Yevren tightened

his grip. This creature had been inside the bunker, and he wasn't letting her get away!

T'Whee struggled against his iron grip, but the creature was too small and frail to resist Yevren's strength. He dragged her through the trees, toward his crawler. The sun was setting for another day; this time Yevren was determined to have what was euphemistically termed "female companionship" for the night—as well as to find a way to kill Cord the Hunter.

Cord was aware of the rustling of paper, but he was engrossed in diagramming a circuit that wasn't a circuit. Behind him, Edwina stood at the computer terminal.

He felt that he'd learned a great deal this day, primarily about the ring's particular elements and the patterns they were arranged in. But he still didn't know how a braid of metal could transport itself and its wearer through time or space.

"Cord, did you forget about this translation?" she asked, breaking his concentration.

"No, but I don't expect much enlightenment from it. If the computer identified the language, we'll know where the ring was made. The inscription isn't likely to tell us how to use it."

"Well, you're right about that," she agreed. "According to the printout, it's in something called Athosian."

"What does it say?" Cord inquired, becoming interested in spite of his certainty that the inscription would not be helpful.

"There are several variations—Athosian must be a very complex tongue. The first is 'From the light against the dark.' Or 'By the sun out of the night.' Or 'Of good, from evil.' Or any one of several more."

"Well, they're fine sentiments," Cord agreed, "but not much help."

"It might help if we knew more about the Athosians,"

Edwina said practically. "Shall I call up that information on the computer?"

Cord stood and stretched, tail twitching. "I'll do it. While it's printing out, we can make dinner."

"Then what?"

"Tomorrow I'll test the outer surface of the ring—particularly the letters—for buttons. Maybe it's activated through them. I don't see any signs of such a thing. But how would I know? I feel like a primitive trying to figure out electricity."

"You'll get it, Cord. You've got to. It's the only way I can go home."

And perhaps the only way I can find Julia McKay, wherever . . . or whatever . . . she truly is. . . .

The creature had reverted to her native tongue, piping and whistling as she sat on the floor of the crawler. She shook the round rattle she still carried; in fact, T'Whee had never loosed her grip on it. Yevren supposed she was praying to her gods for rescue. No such luck, he thought, grinning. Especially since he'd never had an alien woman before, nor practiced the art of interrogation on such a creature.

The singsong chant stopped. T'Whee shook her rattle a few times and then stood. The top of her crest was level with Yevren's chest.

"Go now," she said hopefully.

Yevren reached for the rattle, and she jerked her hand away. He took the hand and snapped all four fingers. They curved but didn't break; the rattle fell into his open palm. The only sound the creature had made was a sharp whirrup.

He examined the rattle and decided it was made of some sort of wood, carefully carved and polished from use. The handle bore cuneiforms; the rounded rattle had outlines of all sorts of creatures. Since it wasn't of gold or silver, or gem-encrusted, he tossed it aside. It bounced off a wall, rattling hollowly.

T'Whee made another sound. No doubt Yevren had just broken a taboo. He reached out and ripped off the toga she wore.

The T-Whierl was barrel-shaped and hairless. She had a feathered area, similar to the crest, between her legs. With luck, she'd be humanoid there too. He hadn't noticed until now that her four toes were elongated, and that her knees were extremely knobby. Not particularly appealing. He walked around her, carefully scrutinizing the creature's physical makeup. It had just occurred to him that he hadn't the least idea where her vital organs were located. If he wasn't careful questioning her, he'd accidentally kill her before getting the information he wanted.

He also examined the toga. The garment was of a simple woven fiber, probably natural, with a crudely stamped design. The pattern could be of anything; Yevren was not familiar enough with this world to know if the design had any meaning. It certainly had no value. It was good for only one thing. He draped it over the crawler's front-facing window; it would keep the inside light from filtering out. He doubted the bunker had windows—he certainly couldn't find any— but why take chances?

With a grin, he turned back to the T'Whierl, who stood silent and shivering. When he approached, she stepped back and finally trilled in Multi-Lang, "No! No want!"

"Yes." Yevren grinned again. "Want you."

It took him a length of time to discover how to penetrate the T'Whierl. By then they were both slippery with sweat and the creature was bent into a rather odd position. While grappling with her, Yevren had tried not to damage anything vital, and she managed to put up a good fight. It only excited him further.

They'd bounced off the crawler walls a few times, and caromed into the plush driver's seat, but Yevren now had her firmly pinned to the floor. As he rhythmically thrust into her protesting body, he could almost feel the entire crawler swaying in unison. He had no way of knowing that the ground beneath the vehicle was slowly rippling, as if the very earth itself were feeling the force of his thrusts. . . .

After their meal, Cord and Edwina studied the printout. Cord had never heard of the Athosians, and the computer report could shed little light on this extinct race.

The Athosians were an insectoid race from a planet on the far edge of the galaxy. On the star chart, the distance was enormous. Their homeworld was even farther from Earth than from this sector. The planet, as well as several others, had been destroyed in an interstellar war with another alien race long before humans had found their way into that part of the galaxy. Whatever was known about the Athosians and their war came from secondhand sources—other races who'd taken part and survived.

The war was about religion. The Athosians were an extremely philosophical people, leaning toward a blend of science and mysticism . . . as the ring's inscription attested. The Athosians did not believe in death; oh, the corporeal body could be destroyed, but not the soul.

Edwina stared at the line drawing of a very tall, thin creature with several spindly arms and legs (or both) and faceted eyes.

"Great. The answer lies with a ghost."

She picked up the nearest object and threw it at a wall; it clanged and rolled away. Tears were in her eyes.

Cord tried to comfort her. "Perhaps not all of them

died in the war; there might still be some alive. Besides, ghosts *do* talk. I know."

Edwina looked at him suspiciously. "What are you talking about?"

"My people worship ghosts—our ancestors—and sometimes their voices can be heard. They even spoke to me."

"Then there's still some hope?" she asked in a small voice.

"Yes. If all else fails in the laboratory, we'll travel out to Athosia. Or what's left of it."

Edwina brightened visibly. "You know, I've been reading about ghosts on Mte-4. Did you know that this planet has an indigenous intelligent race?"

"I've heard there was. But the real estate man assured me none were in this area."

"I read why. There are several reasons. When the colonists first came here, there was a pitched battle on this site. It was short and bloody—but it was the only one. Since then the natives and colonists stay away from each other. There was another incident here, having to do with this bunker."

Cord raised his eyebrows, and Edwina went on.

"The Indilisi soldiers stationed here used some of the natives for sport, and some of the scientists no doubt used them for experiments. It was also a short-lived confrontation."

"And . . . ?" Cord prompted.

"Although the natives have no weapons, and their numbers are very small, they have an interesting supersition that saved them. When any of them is expected to die, his neighbors who have offended him come to apologize and give him gifts. They believe if someone dies with a grudge, he'll come back as a ghost and harm his enemies. So no one wants to be on bad terms with a person who's dying."

"It's been said that if a T'Whierl dies violently,

there's great anxiety all around. Sometimes everyone moves as far from the place as possible. There are even instances of the enemy of the deceased committing suicide on his grave—to avert the disaster of the dead man returning for vengeance."

"I assume there must be some truth to their ghosts, then, if these stories have persisted for so long. And if it stopped further bloodshed."

"Would it do us any good to talk to a ghost here?" Edwina asked.

Cord laughed. "I wouldn't know where to find one."

By morning's light, Yevren was exhausted. The creature had given him some information, but nothing of use. T'Whee had been inside the bunker before, but only briefly, because she had been used by the men there and then thrown out. For some reason, she was deemed not suitable for laboratory use. He still had no way inside the bunker short of blowing it to smithereens.

The excitement of the night's work had given way to disappointment. And now he still had to bury the corpse. He wrapped what was left of T'Whee in her toga and dragged her some distance from the crawler.

He returned carrying a short spade and eyed the mossy ground. He hoped it wasn't very hard; he was tired and needed rest.

The ground was spongy and soft, gray from the moss and from the profusion of short spiky needles from the tall trees. He was able to dig quickly until he was a few feet down. Then his spade turned over a horrifying sight.

On the shovel, protruding from the dirt, was a gobbet of flesh! He shook it off and dug up another spadeful. This one contained a hand! A few more shovelfuls confirmed his suspicion: this was a burial site, probably from a battle or from the bunker's laboratories. A nauseatingly sweet, unwholesome stench filled the air.

There was no point in digging further. He rolled T'Whee's covered corpse into the hole and filled it. In a sense he was lucky; if the corpse was never discovered, they'd think it was meant to be there. T'Whee had threatened him with bad luck, but the poor creature must have been confused. . . .

Satisfied, Yevren headed back for his crawler to get some sleep. He was too tired to realize he was not alone.

Several of the analysis machines worked independently of human control, so Cord took this time to make a knotted story cloth. The fiber strands wove an abbreviated diary of his adventures; it was an offshoot of the craft of making bags to contain ancestral relics and hangings for shrines.

Ordinarily Cord found it cleared his mind. It also kept Mehira alive in his memory. Now the cords were taking the shape of the interlaced braid in the ring.

He stopped knotting and paced around the small table, tail whipping. He found it increasingly difficult to relax, and he didn't know why.

The fortress's empty rooms and corridors did not depress him. Although he could be affected by the force of others' emotions, he was here only with Edwina, and she was content. He should not be experiencing such anxiety. Perhaps it was the artificial environment? Neither of them had gone out since their arrival; there was no reason to do so. It must be the laboratories. Since they were the scenes of some nasty business, probably he was picking up a psychic residue, the same way he did in the forest.

He walked out of the cubicle; Edwina was next door, reading a dog-eared book she'd found.

Cord lifted the book to read the title. It was a scientific tome.

"Haven't we had enough of this?"

"I thought there might be something here to help us," Edwina protested.

He took the book out of her hand. "I need a diversion from all this science. Come here."

He lifted her off the chair and pulled her to his broad chest.

"Is that what I am? Merely a diversion?" She made a face in mock anger.

Cord nibbled at her earlobe. "A very tasty diversion," he amended.

Edwina was more than willing to cast aside her book and provide Cord with some experienced entertainment. Their coupling was explosive and brief. When they were sated, they went back to the mattress-covered cubicle to rest. Despite the size of their "bed," Edwina snuggled next to him.

Now that he thought back, it seemed to Cord that Edwina often displayed a noticeable reluctance to be alone. He wondered if Edwina was a touch empathic and if the grisly history of Battleground and of the laboratory was somehow reaching her. . . .

Chapter 20

Yevren screamed. The cry ended in a gasp as he was punched in the stomach.

"If you can't say something worth hearing, don't say anything at all."

The squat, thick-necked pirate spat to one side, barely missing his own foot. Yevren stared at him without replying.

"Let's go through it again," the leader said. "What's a Komonori policeman doing here?"

"A high-ranking one," a female voice added. "One with funny ideas of . . . fun."

Yevren couldn't turn his head to see her. But he was sure it was the woman with the spiked red hair and the three pairs of earrings—all in one pierced ear. He imagined she was licking her lips, probably in anticipation of what she'd do to him next.

He licked his own lips; he was parched for water. He hadn't had anything to eat or drink since earlier in the day, when he had been captured. They'd tracked him to his crawler and attacked from behind—half a dozen cutter captains, the Ae's dogs, he'd soon realized. And one of them—the woman—had recognized him, perhaps from a stay in a Komonori jail.

They were by a grassy knoll, somewhere north of the bunker, where the pirates had made camp. Yevren was lashed to a tree, unable to move his upper body.

His legs were tied to pegs driven into the ground. His clothes were tattered and bloody.

"You want to lose another nail?" the man growled.

"He can't," the woman giggled, coming into view. "He hasn't got any left."

It was almost funny, Yevren thought. They'd bound his wrists so tightly that by the time they progressed to pulling out his fingernails, he couldn't feel a thing.

"Then he'll lose something else. An ear, maybe. or his nose."

"Or," the woman added hopefully, "something more . . . fundamental."

Yevren stared back at the gloating faces. There was blood in his mouth, and he had several broken ribs. He thought there was internal hemorrhaging. His hands were useless, too long without circulation to be saved, even if he was rescued. No one knew better than he the damage the human body could sustain. He coughed and tasted salt. These pirates were amateurs.

"Why don't you talk, curse you? Be reasonable and I'll be reasonable. Tell me what you're doing here." The knife was poised against Yevren's earlobe.

Yevren's head spun. This scum would not let him live, whatever information he gave them. And he would not betray Duke Ashek.

There was pain and hot dampness at his ear. With a muttered obscenity, the pirate threw something down. Warmth trickled down his neck to his collar.

Yevren grinned mirthlessly, suddenly looking like a death's-head. He would never betray his lord's secrets. Never. It had been midday when they began; it was now dark. The pain could not last much longer.

The man began sawing at his other ear.

Deeper in the forest, the ground rippled. . . .

"Who's going to bury him?" Suwa asked.

"Don't look at me," Marjane snapped back. "You're the one who carved him up."

The pirate leader kicked at what was left of Yevren's leg. The body was still tied to a spike tree; the ground around it was dark red.

"Hey, Tally!" Suwa yelled in the direction of the camp. Soon a tall, hefty, dark-haired man trudged into view.

The newcomer surveyed the remains of the Komonori. "Finished playing games?"

"Yes," Suwa snapped. "Now you can clean up."

The newcomer was unruffled. "Learn anything?"

"No." Suwa spat on the ground, barely missing his toe.

Marjane giggled. "I think Suwa's losing his touch."

She stepped back quickly as the pirate leader reached out for her—and missed. "You'll lose more than that," he growled.

"Temper, temper," Tally said.

Marjane pouted. "I didn't even have the chance to try him out. He might have been a fantastic lay."

"He was a lousy lay," Suwa said. "So are you."

Marjane reached for her cuttergun, but Tally stepped in front of her. He put his hand on hers, preventing her from drawing.

"This Komonori pig wasn't worth fighting over even when he was alive. Come on, help me untie him."

Together he and Marjane cut loose Yevren's corpse. "What shall we do with it?" he asked.

"Bury it away from camp," Suwa commanded. "I don't want to see it—or smell it—while I'm eating."

"It's getting pretty dark," said Tally. "Send Kessel over to help us."

Suwa turned back to the camp, where Kessel and the others had built a flickering fire. In a few moments, two more men appeared, one carrying a torchlight, the other two shovels.

Marjane left the three men to carry out the burial.

She also returned to camp as the three dragged Yevr
corpse deeper into the forest.

"I don't like it here," said Kessel. "Never did."

They quickly set to digging a shallow grave. "
we leaving soon?" the other man asked hopefully.

"No," answered Tally. "As soon as Suwa me
with him, he'll tell us the next step. That won't be
another day or two."

They dug faster, eager to be out of the gloomy for

"Won't be a minute too soon," Kessel said sou
"This forest gives me the creeps." He threw the
shovelfuls over Yevren's body. A slight mound of fr
dirt stood out in the glare of the torch.

Tally used a shovel to rake some dead leaves
twigs over the mound in an attempt to disguise
The odds were against someone stumbling over
grave in this deserted area, but Tally didn't lik
take chances. Especially not here, where the lege
ary "bad luck" of the natives and colonists still per
ated the air.

The pirates picked up their tools and left the fo
to its chilly stillness.

At the end of several days, a pattern was slo
emerging. Cord felt they were close to a breakthroug
a desperately needed one. Not to find a way home,
to hunt down and kill Julia McKay, not to con
time and space, and not even to rule the unive
They simply needed to leave the bunker.

The atmosphere of the bunker lay over them li
shroud. Cord had no idea why. Nor could he re
beyond the walls to seek a reason outside; the bar
made him emotionally blind. Edwina nervously pa
back and forth and hovered around him like an i
cure moth.

He shoved aside the printout he was studying
rolled off his stomach, tail twitching. He spent all

waking hours pouring over the computer results—so did Edwina. She lay a few mattresses away, on her side, flipping the pages of an enormous readout.

"This is worse than the Yellow Pages."

"The what? No, don't tell me"—he held up a hand—"it's an Old Earth phrase."

"Not a phrase, a thing," Edwina said. "The Yellow Pages was a telephone directory."

"Telephone?" Cord grinned as a wave of exasperation hit him.

"The telephone—we used it to talk to one another. It's sort of like a com screen without the picture."

"Boring," he announced.

"Dammit!" she exploded, throwing the printout at him. "If you can't hunt it, eat it, or screw it, you're not interested."

Muscles rippling, Cord effortlessly deflected the printout; it fluttered open, across the mattresses.

"Is this a new kind of bed cover?" he asked, sensitive to her changing aura.

"Back on Earth, there was a very interesting theory. It was thought that if someone slept on an open book, the information from the printed page would somehow be transferred to the brain." Edwina flipped up one of the printout sheets. "If we make love on a computer analysis, do you think our brains will somehow come up with the secret to the ring?"

"Worth a try."

They stripped quickly. Edwina snuggled against Cord's broad chest while he stroked her with hands and tail. She slipped her arms under his and pressed her length against him. Silken skin slid over silken skin, friction heating up the shared warmth. Because the thickness of the walls barred any shock waves of emotion, Cord kept his shields down during the entire time they were in the bunker. Her passion washed

over him; he closed his eyes; it was almost like b
back on Mehira. . .

Edwina climaxed easily, but Cord wanted more.
continued to fondle her lush body, nibbling paths
her salty skin. She tried to snuggle against him o
more, but he shifted her body away from his, so
her back was to him. Then he rolled her over on
stomach.

"There's one more position I haven't shown y
he whispered.

Slowly he eased himself between her firm butt
and entered her from the rear. Edwina tensed,
then slowly relaxed, and he continued to stroke
toward ecstasy. His tail came up, the tip winding
way through their tangled legs. It probed deeper
deeper inside her, until it could go no farther, fil
her completely. Then he alternately thrust and w
drew as Edwin writhed in his strong arms.

He reached up in front of her to cup her full brea
playing with her straining nipples. Low moans of p
sure slowly built into cries of ecstasy, and her d
cious emotions penetrated his mind, sending
reeling.

They moved together as he tried to keep his hol
Edwina; she was thrashing about like a wild won
When they peaked, her climax washed over him
rainbow ripples of color; his bombarded senses co
stand no more. Still holding on to each other, they
entwined, his legs around her, his tail wound arou
them both. Their breathing slowly relaxed, and C
regained control. He looked down at their brai
bodies, and, unbidden, the ring jumped into
thoughts. The pattern. The braided elements ins
the ring. It was more than a design. It was a circu

He let go of Edwina. "Get dressed," he urged.
think I've just solved part of the ring's puzzle."

Edwina moved away from him excitedly and turned to face him. "Tell me! What is it?"

"I think," he said cautiously, "that the braid of elements inside the ring is a psychoactive circuit. Where it takes you depends on where you want to go."

"But I didn't choose to go to Duke Ashek's palace! On another world, in another time!"

The memory brought tears to her eyes, so Cord said softly and reasonably, "But you did activate it somehow. Like switching on a machine, or an aircar. You can control it, but if you don't, it will still move in whatever direction it was pointed. You turned the ring on somehow, you wanted to go somewhere—but you didn't say where. So it took you to Komonor. Maybe that was the last place it had been. Maybe it was programmed to go back there. This is all supposition, since we haven't succeeded in making it work again. Perhaps your trip exhausted its power source."

"Power source," Edwina repeated, her forehead wrinkling. "Is that all that's keeping it from working now?"

"If my theory about the rest of it is right, yes. It would take energy to move you from one place to another. It doesn't draw power from the wearer's body. I can't imagine where it could get energy, though."

"'By the light, out of the dark,'" Edwina quoted suddenly. "Cord, I think I know. There's one way our tests and the times I tried it before Ashek took it away differ from the time it worked."

"What?"

"Here, we've been trying it in the laboratory; on Komonor I was a prisoner in Ashek's palace. On Earth I was outdoors. In the sunlight, Cord."

"Ancestors!" Cord breathed. "It makes sense." He checked his chronometer. "It's too late tonight. We'll have to try first thing in the morning."

"Oh, I hope it works, Cord," she said. "I want t[...]
home."

"So do I."

They walked out of the mound, hand in h[...]
carefree. Edwina kept raising her hand to look at[...]
alien ring shining dully on her finger. As they step[...]
out into the reddish sunlight and heard the h[...]
portal grate shut behind them, Cord glanced aro[...]
Suddenly he felt conspicuous . . . and vulnerable.

He was wearing his dart gun at his left hip, a[...]
did everywhere it was not prohibited by custom[...]
law. Casually he dropped his hand to the butt[...]
opened himself to psychic impressions.

He automatically snapped his defenses back in pl[...]
the anger and hatred roiling around the undergro[...]
installation were too strong for an unshielded m[...]
They had increased a hundredfold since he had se[...]
them on entering the bunker. With long practic[...]
screening out unwanted feelings, Cord was abl[...]
block them entirely.

He let his eyes go to Edwina. She had felt noth[...]
had not noticed his momentary hesitation. Not for[...]
first time, Cord marveled at the insensitivity[...]
humans.

But there was no external sign of horror. The[...]
shone as brightly as it ever did on Mte-4; the air[...]
still and scented. The odors of bog and tree and s[...]
nant water came to Cord; the clearing in the fo[...]
seemed peaceful. Cord, his stomach churning, v[...]
dered what had stirred the disembodied emotion[...]
tached to this place. It worried him, because he[...]
no Mehiran basis by which to judge it. This w[...]
and these terrible psychic remembrances were[...]
closest he had come to war. Maybe all military s[...]
were cloaked in despair and fear. If so, he would v[...]
wide of them henceforth.

Edwina took a deep breath of cool, fragrant air and said, "I'm ready, Cord."

"So am I," said a voice from the shadow under the trees. "Freeze, both of you."

Gerard stepped out into the clearing. His cutter rifle was sighted in on Cord's chest.

"Raise your hands," he ordered.

Seeing that thin, smiling face, Cord decided that his own chances of survival had become infinitesimally small. Gerard was not a man to forgive someone who had outwitted him. As Cord began to comply with the instruction—what else was there to do? Edwina was almost in the line of fire—he noticed that she was still clutching his hand. Her grip on it was tighter than ever. And then—

—Cord was sinking to his ankles in marshy ground. They were in deep shade, and Edwina's hand was still in his.

"Quick!" Edwina hissed. "We've teleported."

Cord's gun whipped out of its holster as he pushed her to the ground with the other hand. His eyes caught a sunlit flash of motion ahead of him. Some fifteen body lengths away, out in the clearing, Gerard was staring around him, turning first one way, then another. He recovered from his amazement with the swiftness that marked him as a professional and loped toward the shelter of the trees.

Cord squeezed off three shots, paused, sure that only one had hit Gerard, and fired twice more as Gerard threw himself down. The human's rifle cut through the trunk of a great fronded plant a few steps left of Cord. It toppled, brushing Edwina but it was too soft to do any harm. Edwina only burrowed deeper into her mossy tussock, further camouflaged by the fallen fronds.

In the silence, Cord was sure he could hear Gerard's ragged breathing. "Stay where you are," he whispered to Edwina, and he began a slow, wary crawl toward Gerard's last position. If only one dart had hit Gerard, he might still be conscious. The sound of his breathing suggested he was—if it was his breathing Cord heard, and not some imaginary or natural sound. He was working blind—without his empathic sense to tell him whether his adversary was conscious, he was handicapped. But in the maelstrom of past emotion here, Gerard's signal would be lost, even if Cord had been willing to open himself and listen. And he wasn't. The horror was too great to endure, even hardened as he was.

Steadily but without haste, he worked his way toward Gerard. There was no hurry; let the drug take effect. Cord did not wish to arrive in time to be shot by Gerard before the man slipped into unconsciousness.

Cord forced himself to remember the words of a Mehiran litany. As the rhythms flowed through him, his heart slowed, his control strengthened. He slid through the moss on his belly, unwilling to stay too long in one place. *As though it would grow over me if I lingered,* he thought wryly. It did grow rapidly. He'd noticed that it covered the edges of the road and had tried to get a foothold—roothold?—on the stonelike portal of the bunker.

He wished he dared risk opening his empathic sense to check on Gerard. To have to rely only on the senses a human possessed was frightening. Cautiously he raised his head above the hummocks that gave him cover.

His estimate of Gerard's position had been accurate; behind a lichen-encrusted log Cord could see a boot and part of a long leg. It was motionless, and the rest of the body was out of sight. Perhaps the bounty hunter was unconscious, or perhaps he was lying in wait for Cord to approach. Noiselessly, Cord lifted his weapon and fired. The dart buried itself in the green-trousered leg, and gave proof that the leg's owner was already oblivious; if he'd been awake, there would have been some response.

Cord rose to his feet and made his way over the humpy ground to stand over Gerard. He bent to pick up the cutter rifle, but his hand never touched the black plasteel stock. A burst of energy smashed through him, making his body jerk. Cord fell, unable even to stretch out his hands to break his fall.

He did not lose consciousness, but he suffered a period of disorientation. The soft, warm moss against his cheek reminded him of Mehiran women's pubic fur. When he realized he was unable to move, he knew he had been hit by a blast from a neuron disruptor.

Sound. The rustle of fabric against fabric, the faint creak and jangle of gunbelts and holsters, the scwudge of moss compressed by heavy feet.

"The Ae'll be pleased to hear we've found you, Cat Ears," a deep, mushy voice said.

Cord found it difficult even to shift or focus his eyes. All he could see was a pair of large, scuffed spacers' boots. Someone sniggered, "I bet the Ae would like those ears hanging on his wall."

"Those ears" would have gone flat against Cord's head if his nervous system had not been stunned. As it was, he simply lay as slack as a spacer's duffel.

"Get him on his feet and tie him to that tree while he's still cooperative," mush-voice said.

At least, Cord thought, he was giving the maximum amount of trouble. He was too limp even to support his own weight, so the two pirates who manhandled him had to drag him.

"And check his pouch and pockets for the key," their leader added. "Ashek's woman is in there, I guess."

They must think Edwina is still in the bunker. If

they didn't know she was within earshot, that was one triumph. Cord prayed to his ancestors as he had not since climbing the Spine of Arzet that she would use the ring. She had used it once, proving herself a quick thinker. This time all she could do was to teleport to the city and bring back the authorities. Cord hoped she would think of it. But even if she did bring the local constabulary, it would still be too late for him.

"Here it is, Suwa," one of the men said, holding up the sonic key.

"Good. Go get her when you've got him tied up."

Held upright by the ropes binding him to the tree, Cord could see there were six of the Ael.

"What about Martin Gerard?" a woman's voice inquired. She was at the edge of Cord's range of vision. Typical of the underside of spacer society: hard-faced, with restless, glittering eyes and cropped hair. She wore a greasy shirt over pants, looked and sounded like a man.

"Is he alive?" Suwa asked, surprised. "I thought Cat Ears here finished him after Gerard signaled us to move in."

"He's breathing." The woman shrugged.

The pirate leader chuckled nastily, hunkering down. "Well, Marjane, it's like this. You can nurse him back to health, in which case he'll get half the reward for Ashek's pillow girl. Or else Gerard can have an accident here, and there'll be twice as much for us."

Marjane's hips rotated, and she licked her lips. "He was good—but I could buy a dozen lays as good with the money."

"You want to take care of him—for old times' sake?"

"Sure." The woman smiled. She rolled the bounty hunter over with one toe, then knelt astride him, while she thought about the best way to kill him.

Cord lost interest in Gerard's problem as the pirate

who'd gone into the bunker returned. "I don't think she's in there," he said.

"You don't *think* she is," Suwa repeated. "Didn't you look? What's wrong with you?"

"The place gives me a funny feeling—like there's someone waiting for us. I didn't find anything on the first two floors except some printouts and equipment. But when I started downstairs, I got this feeling. . . . Besides, it's big. It would be better to ask the bounty hunter where she is. It'd save time."

Suwa snarled a single, ugly word. "Well, he'll be able to talk pretty soon. If you had any guts we wouldn't have to wait, but since you don't . . ." Suwa flicked a practiced finger toward Cord's left eyeball. Cord's head jerked as far to one side as his bonds permitted.

"Should be able to speak right now," the pirate muttered. "Where's the woman?"

Cord swallowed and found his throat worked. "In a cell on the bottom level."

"I don't think you're telling me the truth," the thick voice said. "I don't think you'd give in so easy."

"Use your knife," Marjane called ecstatically. Out of the corner of his eye, Cord saw she was bending over Gerard, her thumbs on his carotid arteries.

"Let's start easy," the leader replied, balling his fist and striking Cord in the stomach. Cord's body strained against the ropes trying to double over. A blow to his face cut his lip; he could feel the salt of blood on his tongue.

"Get him by the balls," the woman suggested, almost forgetting Gerard, whose face was turning blue.

"I'll leave that to you," Suwa answered, laughing. He pulled out a knife from his boot and straightened up. With its tip, he slashed a shallow cut across Cord's face.

"Where is she?" he grated.

Cord kept silent. The pirate used the knife to cut a bloody pattern on Cord's biceps.

"Where is she?" he repeated. When Cord didn't answer, he snarled, "I'll cut you into pieces. I'll leave quivering hunks of your flesh strewn over this accursed forest. I'll—"

The pirate broke off in surprise as something black thrust up through the moss beside his boot. Black, rotting fingers clamped around his ankle. The man gave an exclamation which turned into a scream. He dropped the knife and reached for a gun, but a second hand caught his other foot and pulled him down.

Two of the spacers ran forward to Suwa and tried to pull him free. Instead, the thing in the ground held on relentlessly; and as the pirates pulled Suwa away, they pulled the buried corpse of a man free.

The corpse opened its lids to reveal blackened holes; it smiled with what was left of its lips. Screaming, the pirates dropped Suwa.

More ghastly things—some of them not human—clawed their way out of the peat and fell upon the pirates. Tally drew his cuttergun, but a rotting hand shot out to wrench the weapon away. Another man had managed to get off several shots, but the mangled corpses advanced, heedless of more missing limbs.

Suwa tried to push away the creature gripping his legs, but he couldn't break its hold. Shreds of decaying flesh showered the writhing pirate. In spite of its awkwardness and decomposition, the thing was strong. It crawled up Suwa's prone body, using him like a living ladder.

Tied to the tree, Cord couldn't do anything more than stare in horror as the strangely earless corpse crept toward Suwa's throat.

Something dragged itself out of the damp earth to pull Marjane off Gerard. It threw itself on her awkwardly, hungrily, clawlike fingernails ripping at her clothing. The woman flailed at it, knocking off gobbets of putrescent flesh. The walking corpse did not seem to notice, but another came up behind Marjane and pinioned her arms. It nuzzled her neck with its noseless face and nipped her shoulder with its exposed teeth. The first tore open her garments—blackened nails scoring her thighs as it forced them apart—and then, dripping corruption, entered her.

The screaming pirates were outnumbered by the army of walking dead. Animated severed limbs writhed on the ground, reaching out for them. Tatterdemalion figures lurched through the trees, eyelessly searching for the nearest live human.

Cord threw up.

After that, he kept his eyes closed and his shields firmly in place, and endured the other sounds—the meaty ripping of living limbs torn from their joints, the wet snap of bones, the gurgle of laughter in throats rotted to liquescence. Eyelids squeezed tight, Cord gagged at the smell filling the air. He sensed the presence of dozens of—beings—as he hung in the ropes, waiting for them to notice him. He tried to remember a calming Mehiran litany, but the words kept slipping away from him at each new noise or gust of putrescence. Edwina. Oh, Edwina.

Chapter 21

For a moment he did not remember where he was or how he came to be there. His eyes, looking downward, focused on the moss at his feet. Cord realized he was bound to a tree and that his clothing was stained with something worse than dirt. He froze as memory returned.

There was no sound at all but his own breathing, and no scent on the air but the smell of his own sickness. Cord tested his muscles one by one and found that he could again control them, although he ached all over. Slowly, not wanting to, he looked up.

The forest floor's cushiony moss was undisturbed. Some distance away, precisely where he'd been when Cord's dart hit him, lay Gerard. His face was ashen, but he did not appear to have been strangled to death, so Marjane must have been interrupted in time. . . .

Cord cut off that line of thought. *What* had prevented the woman from killing him didn't bear thinking about. But if Gerard and he were alive, maybe Edwina was, too.

He called her name softly, and a second time, a little louder. There was no reponse at first. Then fronds trembled and rattled, and Cord saw Edwina emerge from a clump of fern as large as a small tree, not very far from where he'd left her. She stumbled forward, her gaze fixed on Cord. He didn't like the blankness in her eyes or the way her mouth was twitching.

"Edwina, can you untie me?" Cord asked carefully. He hoped she wasn't going to go over the edge before she freed him.

The question brought a flicker of emotion back to her face. "Cord, I don't know about you, but I'm going to survive," she replied. Her voice was unsteady, but she did not sound hysterical. "In the past year a ring has catapulted me across the galaxy and into the future, I've been raped half a dozen times, captured by pirates, sold in a slave market, and rescued. I'm not going to fold up at the sight of a few corpses, however lively." She began to work at the knots.

"Edwina, it was brave of you not to teleport away, but I hoped you would. Under the circimstances there was nothing you could do for me—until now."

She laughed, and the sound was wry but wholesome. "It wasn't all courage—we're in the shade here. To work the ring has to be in direct sun. We went from the sunlight into the trees, but it wasn't bright enough here to teleport away. Believe me, I tried." The bonds securing his wrist came undone.

"Where did . . . everyone . . . go?" he asked, leaning against the trunk, his arms hanging limp as he waited for circulation to return.

Edwina unfastened the loops around his legs and began coiling the rope tidily before answering, "Down there. Where they came from, under the moss. They took the pirates with them," she explained as though Cord might have misunderstood.

"But there's not a trace left!"

"No," she concurred.

No sign remained that the earth had been ripped apart from within, not a drop of blood or a scrap of flesh or bone or fabric, not a breath of corruption in the air.

"When the pirates were all overpowered or dead, the corpses sort of pulled them into the ground. And everything they'd ... left behind ... vanished, and somehow the place seemed nicer."

Cord thought she was trying to be funny until he realized that there *was* a different feeling to the wood. Reluctantly he let down his mental defenses and breathed a sigh of relief. The only psychic presences here were Edwina's, his own, and Gerard's.

"I think," Cord said practically, "that we should use these ropes to tie up Gerard before the anesthetic wears off."

"Already? It's only been an eighteenth rotation."

Checking his chronometer, Cord discovered she was right. "It seemed longer," he remarked. He tried to rise, but his legs refused to support him. He leaned back against the tree.

"I need a few more minutes to get my arms and legs working. You'll have to tie him up yourself."

Edwina obediently took the ropes and walked over to Gerard. As she wound a rope around his ankles, she called to Cord, "What exactly happened here?"

"You saw as much as I did. Probably more."

"But this is your time, one of your worlds. You understand what you saw," she retorted. "Why were those people buried in the woods? I thought there hadn't been any fighting on this world for a long time. Why did they come out? Is that natural on this planet? Because it would be considered pretty damned peculiar where I come from."

Her acidic summation made Cord grin in spite of himself. "It's damned peculiar anywhere. But it must be connected with the bunker, and with the natives' legends of revenge."

"But what did we do to set them off?"

"We did nothing. It must have been the pirates." Cord paused. It was obvious to him, but a nonempath would be puzzled by it. He chose his words carefully. "The pirates attacked us. We were the victims—like the remains of those poor souls. I'm guessing, now, but I think they were prisoners who were slaughtered. You never asked what was on the lowest level, and it seemed best not to tell you that it was full of cells." He could see that she was putting the information together and reaching his own conclusion.

"I've heard that anger and hatred are contagious," he continued cautiously. "Did you feel either of those emotions?"

"No. I was simply terrified."

"So was I; and Gerard was out cold. But the pirates were preparing to torture me and kill Gerard; they must have been full of negative emotions. Somehow that must have triggered the rage of the dead."

She nodded thoughtfully and sat back on her heels. "Now that we've got him tied up, what are we going to do?"

They carried Gerard down to the cellblock, and Cord noticed that the aura of chill menace had vanished. While Cord headed for their quarters to clean up, Edwina stood guard over Gerard.

"Why don't you start collecting our gear?" Cord suggested to Edwina as soon as he came back. "We may want to leave quickly."

"I'd love to," she said emphatically. "The sooner the better."

Cord stayed behind in the cell to untie Gerard, who was beginning to stir. The hired gunman did not seem to be injured, apart from the great purpling bruises on his throat. Cord drew his gun. He counted on Gerard's being too weak to attack him, but a show of force never did any harm.

Gerard's icy green eyes opened. He lay for a moment without moving, taking stock of his own condition and his surroundings. Then he turned his head—

slowly; moving was clearly giving him difficulty—
and saw Cord lounging in the open cell door. His
eyebrows shot up.

When he did not speak, Cord said, "Gerard, you
don't keep very good company. Your pirate friends
were going to double-cross you."

Gerard raised one hand and felt his neck gingerly.
" 'Were going to' or 'did'?" he croaked.

"You're still alive, so I'd say they failed."

Gerard snarled out a curse. "They've got the woman.
Why'd they leave you? Unless they thought Ashek's
reward would take them beyond the Ae's reach—and
mine," he added, more to himself than to Cord.

"As I understood it," Cord said, "the idea was to
sell Edwina back to the duke, splitting the money
among themselves, and turn me over to the Ae—or at
least show him proof of my death—and live happily
ever after. Since you'd be dead, they would have your
share too. What made you decide to join up with
them, anyway?"

Leaning on one elbow, Gerard started to laugh. It
turned into a cough. "They offered to join me. They
said they wanted you, and that we had a better chance
working together. Naturally they wanted part of the
reward Ashek was offering. I reluctantly agreed. You
made a fool of me on Shaqin, Cord. I didn't think you
could do it again, but I'd have been pleased to think of
the Ae's getting you." He watched Cord from narrowed eyes. Cord knew he was wondering just what
the situation was. What was Cord going to do? Where
were the Ae's pirates? Could he catch up with them
and recapture Edwina? Why wasn't he dead, since
someone had wanted him that way?

After a lengthy pause, Gerard said, "Maybe we
could work something out. Together we'd be a match
for that spacer scum. It would be to your advantage.
You may have escaped them this time, but if the Ae

wants you as badly as they say, his men will be after you again. I'd like my revenge on them. I have no argument with you—I took what's-her-name away from you and you took her back. We're even. Now let's get even with Suwa and his playmates."

Cord smiled. "There's only one thing wrong with your proposal."

"What's that?"

"You've assumed Suwa's gang has Edwina. They don't. I do. And unless your influence reaches a lot farther than I think it does, you won't be able to punish them."

Gerard's face twisted in a scowl, but before he could retort, something in Cord's expression or voice made him pause. "What do you mean?"

"They're dead." Cord was simultaneously pleased and annoyed at Gerard's astonishment. It was very satisfactory to have taken him by surprise but not very flattering that the man had so low an opinion of Cord's abilities.

"Yes, that does change things," Gerard admitted.

"So I don't really need your help."

"But you're standing here talking to me," the hired gunman pointed out.

"Yes, because there's one thing you could do for me."

"What? And what do I get out of it?" Gerard demanded.

"You get out of here." Cord gestured around the cell with the hand not holding the gun.

"Not much of a reward."

"Consider the alternative. Edwina and I will be leaving here soon. The rent's paid up for almost a year. You could get awfully bored in that time. And awfully hungry, if the food ran out."

"I see," Gerard muttered. "It's still a stinking

bargain, but it seems to be the only one available. What do you want?"

"Were those five with Suwa the Ae's only agents on Mte-4? There's no point in lying, Gerard. If another bunch of Ael broke in here they wouldn't bother to let you out. Why should they? They'd assume you had something to do with their friends' disappearance."

"All right. Those six were the only ones. They didn't—couldn't—leave a rearguard, because they all wanted to be in on the fun and none of them trusted the others enough to stay behind. You know how these pirates are when there is a valuable prize to be taken: no teamwork except on shipboard, no discipline, no subtlety."

"I noticed. Well, thank you, Gerard," Cord said, slipping out and sliding the door shut.

Gerard sprang up from the cot. "You said you'd release me," he hissed.

"And I will—as soon as Edwina and I are ready to leave." Walking away, Cord smiled to himself. He wasn't averse to letting Gerard sweat a little, though a bargain was a bargain. Besides, Gerard's psychic emanation had told him the truth. Though emotion was not an infallible indicator, he had detected no other feelings behind Gerard's statement.

"I was beginning to wonder where you were," Edwina greeted him when he entered their room.

"Oh, I stayed to talk to Gerard for a while."

Edwina was surprised. "I didn't know you were on speaking terms."

"We have a lot in common," Cord explained. "We're both realists. Gerard told me the pirates who were here were the only ones on this planet. So my plan is for us to stay here until we finish with the ring."

"Couldn't we do it somewhere else?" She put aside the carry-all she'd packed and sat on the bed.

"Now that we know the ring has to be used in

sunlight, the problem is finding a place to test it in privacy. If someone saw you disappear it would cause talk—and there would be more people after us than there are now. All wanting to get the ring. Whereas there's no one around here."

Edwina conceded the point. Cord dropped onto the bed and put his arm around her.

"Are you sure you want to try it?" Cord asked as Edwina stood in the cool red sunlight of afternoon. She ran a finger around the alien ring.

"It brought me here; it can take me home again," she replied.

Cord said, "If it does take you back, you won't return." It was not quite a question.

"No, I suppose not," she said, as though it were a new thought. As perhaps it was. "But then you wouldn't know if it had worked, would you? It might have transported me somewhere, but not necessarily to the past. And you've worked so hard to find out how the ring works, that would hardly be fair."

"I would like to know," Cord agreed. "If I knew it operated the way I think it does, in time I might be able to build one, using the computer analyses."

Impulsively she ran to him and kissed his lips. "I'll come back. It would only take a few moments, and then you'd know. After that, I could go home to stay."

"I will miss you, Edwina." He had not realized how much until then.

She grinned. "There's no point in getting sentimental. I'm not gone yet."

He smiled in reply. It was too late to say the only thing that was in his mind: that he was falling in love with her.

Edwina walked a few steps away. For a moment, Cord's mind flew to the day before, when they'd been interrupted by Gerard. His heart speeded up, and he glanced around the clearing apprehensively, opening his shields. There was nothing. He looked back at Edwina in time to see her vanish.

He blinked—and she reappeared in precisely the same place.

She staggered slightly, off-balance, and leaned gratefully on Cord's arm when he hurried to her side.

"That was quick," he said. "Did it really take you back?"

"Yes, damn it all," Edwina replied. "Almost to the minute, I think—Jim and Frieda were still fighting, I could hear them—but as soon as I realized I was *there*, I was here again. I don't understand it."

"Do you want to try again?"

"Yes. But first I want to rest for a while. I feel like a rubber band that's been pulled too far and let go."

"I'm ready," Edwina said grimly.

This time she did not waste time bidding Cord goodbye. She closed her eyes and winked out as though she had never been.

Edwina expected to open her eyes to the sun shining on the water in the gravel pit. Her previous experiences had taught her that it was best not to see the kaleidoscope of light and dark in the fraction of a second that it took to go from one place to another.

But even before she opened her eyes she knew she had not arrived. There was no sensation of sunlight on her skin, no scent of open air, no gravel under her feet. There was no sensation at all. Where was she?

Sick with terror, Edwina raised her eyelids to see . . . nothing.

Nothing. It was not dark. It was like being in the thickest fog ever, without the presence of anything as substantial as fog. With a qualm that was almost sickness, Edwina looked down. There was no discernible surface under her feet, yet she was standing. If she kept her feet still and didn't think about it, she could imagine she was standing on a well-carpeted floor. If she moved or thought about the way her feet felt, it was obvious that there was nothing beneath her, and no gravity pressing her down. But she wasn't weightless either.

Making these observations helped her, in a way. They kept her from thinking about her overall situation. She was neither where she had been nor where she wanted to be. . . .

Impulsively she thought of Cord and the clearing on Mte-4. She wished she were back there with the yearning of a prayer.

"The ring will not work here," a sexless voice stated.

The sound seemed not to come from any particular direction, but before her Edwina saw a figure. Edwina had not seen it approach, but she did not think it had simply appeared either. Perhaps it had been there all the while and she had not noticed.

It was possible. The figure was robed in the same color as the surrounding mist. A deep hood shadowed its face, and its hands were tucked into the wide sleeves and crossed on its chest.

"I—"

The voice cut her off. "I am a simulacrum placed here for your guidance and as a safeguard. You have twice attempted to use the ring in a manner for which it was not intended and which creates a dangerous imbalance."

Edwina intended to ask what her informant meant, but it continued uninterrupted.

"Like most tools, the ring has a potential for misuse. Its employment for time travel is one of them. We can duplicate some of the techniques of the Empire, but even they could not escape the flow of time. Nor will you. It is not permitted."

"But—"

"Alterations have been made in the psychoreactive structure of the ring. It will no longer respond to any attempt to return it to the past. This precaution should have been taken when another tried to use the ring earlier—for the same reason. We are sorry this adjustment—and others—must be made now. We advise against your attempting to return to your point of origin, as the effect of repeated closed-cycle travel on the body is not known. I scan that you are in the normal range physically at the moment, however. The device will continue to function for point-to-point travel. You will now be returned to your most recent place of origin."

Edwina snapped her eyes shut against the blur of cascading images. Her stomach was already queasy from tension—and, she supposed, from "closed-cycle travel," whatever that was. Cord must be worried about her, she thought. She had said she would come back immediately. He would think that either she'd had an accident or that she had broken her promise.

"Didn't it work again, Edwina?" Cord's voice asked. As she collapsed to the ground, she saw his erect ears tilt forward in alarm.

"I'm all right," Edwina repeated. "I'm all right. I was only terrified in the void. It's like free fall, there's no up or down. Except it wasn't free fall. . . ." Her voice trailed off.

Cord sat on the ground beside her, arm protectively around her shoulders. Edwina had spilled out her incredible story in a rush; Cord could hardly believe his ears. He had so many questions, it was difficult to know where to begin.

"You said the simulacrum referred to the Empire, and duplicating techniques. Could this ring be a copy of an Imperial device?"

The awesome power of the Imperials was legendary, despite the almost complete absence of artifacts. Even if this ring was a copy and not the real thing, the thought was staggering.

"Why, yes. I'm sure—at least, I was sure—that was what it meant. I wish I'd had a chance to ask it questions, but I couldn't get a word in."

Cord grinned, "It wouldn't—or couldn't—have replied anyway, I'll bet. It sounds like a very simple construct, much less complex than a robot. Its function was to give a warning if the ring was used in a dangerous way. Since you were trying to go back to the past, it delivered its prerecorded lecture on the impossibility of time travel. Apparently it was also capable of sensing whether you were injured or ill. If you had been, I think it would have transported you to a place where you would have been sure to get medical attention."

"What makes you think so, Cord?"

"It would be a reasonable safety feature. Given the makers' ability, it wouldn't be difficult to arrange—just another program for the simulacrum."

"Yes, but the original 'program' still confuses me. What did it mean by saying that another had tried to use it?"

"I don't pretend to know the meaning of 'dangerous imbalance,'" Cord responded, "but I'd say it has to do with how the ring got to your world in the first place. How else did it get there?"

Edwina frowned, "You mean, someone brought it back in time? But what happened to him?"

"What indeed? He took off or lost the ring, anyway."

"But he can't have stayed there—on Earth, in the past. The robed figure said someone had *tried*. So probably he bounced back to 'now,' too. Or wherever he came from. But I belong *there*. Why can't I go back?"

"I can guess. Traveling into the past might c
that past, our present, and the future," Cord sai

"But it was willing to make me into the futur

"Yes. Your being here may affect events from
time of your arrival, Edwina, but the history
affect hasn't happened yet. But if you went ba
your own time, your knowledge of what's ahead
affect what happens—happened—from then to
Things that had already occurred differently. S
can't go back. At least," Cord confessed, "that's
read it."

"I'm stuck here," Edwina summed up neatly.

"Afraid so," Cord agreed. "I'm sorry, Edwina.

"It's all right. It's not your fault, and anywa
resigned myself months ago."

Cord helped her up from the mossy ground.
leaning on him, she walked slowly back to the bu

After he helped Edwina to a cot, where she
rest, he went to complete their packing. There w
point in staying on.

What he found stopped him dead in his tracks
pile of computer readouts, left on the metal ki
table the previous day, was now a pile of ashe
ran down to the next level and through the laborat
All the machines used to analyze the ring—an
main computer terminal—were now a useless ju
of fused circuits and melted controls. A mon
work with a blaster. Simple spite on the part of
cutter captain Suwa had delegated to search the bu
The information would be impossible to retrieve;
was no way of duplicating the ring the way it us
be before the simulacrum altered it.

Their last hope was gone.

Cord slung the last of their gear into the cal
the crawler.

"Get in," he told Edwina. "I'm going to release our prisoner."

She climbed up into the cab without a word, although Cord could see she was nervous. Understandable. Ordinarily he would have been wary of letting Martin Gerard loose, too. The hired killer was too dangerous to be treated casually. Cord wondered, briefly, about what was under the moss and whether it was down there for good. . . . Gerard was not going to be happy, and if his psychic emanations stirred anything up . . .

Well, it would be Gerard's funeral, but Cord hoped it wouldn't come to that.

Gerard was slumped on his cot. His head rolled back at Cord's approach, and unfocused green eyes gazed blankly at Cord.

"You drugged me," he slurred.

"Yes," Cord concurred. "I don't underestimate you, Martin. I put a little something extra in your last meal pack. By the time you recover enough to walk, Edwina and I will be gone. Get up," he said, gripping his captive by one arm. The muscle relaxant had done its work well. Steadied and guided, Gerard could walk, but he was certainly in no condition to do so under his own power.

By the time Cord had gotten the hired killer out into the sunlight, Edwina's brow was furrowed with anxiety. Cord grinned up at her reassuringly as he let Gerard settle onto the moss by the side of the road. "If I were you," Cord said to the dazed human, "I'd take a nap, and when I woke up I'd start walking back to town. It should take you about a day and a half. I don't think we'll be meeting again, so goodbye, Gerard."

Cord joined Edwina in the crawler and guided it onto the narrow road.

"It would have been safer not to leave him alive," Cord ventured, seeking to explain to his companion

something which he felt must puzzle her. "But I d
like cold-blooded killing. And we'll be out of his rea
He was not entirely sure of the last point, but
though his excuse for not finishing Gerard off
true enough, the real reason was that Cord rem
bered the terrible battle in the clearing. If that
what happened to people who died on Mte-4, he di
want to kill anyone here. Gerard rising, rotting, f
his grave was not a thing to be contemplated.

"No, I don't think we need to worry about
now," Edwina agreed. "Where am I going to go, tho
Cord? On Earth, someone with no citizenship
almost a nonperson."

"If that's all that's worrying you, we can take o
of that. There are planets that will grant citizens
to anyone for a token fee or for a promise to se
there for a period. Or else, for slightly more mo
we can buy false papers for you. Personally, I'd ad
the former. With a forged identity, you could be
trouble if it were found out. But Voskian and Karar
citizenships are perfectly legal and safe, even if th
governments accept anyone. Of the two, I'd rec
mend Vosk. It's got a loose government and low ta
and you don't have to establish residence."

"Then there's a fee to be paid."

"Several thousand credits. Not much."

"I don't have any money, Cord."

"No, I know that. I'll buy your papers for you."

"I'm afraid I've been an expensive assignment
you," she said.

"Yes, you have. On the other hand, though
printouts were destroyed, I still retain knowledge ab
the ring. With work, someday I might yet dupli
it."

And the knowledge of the properties of a brai
certain elements was not all he had gained. C
recalled a conversation with Julia McKay about

Empire's warp. Julia had said she wanted it; she'd spoken the truth then, he thought, though at the time he hadn't believed her. If the ring used the same principle as the much-sought-after secret of the ancient Empire's method of transport, it might serve as a lure for Julia.

"Thank you, Cord. It's kind of you to offer to help me."

"Why shouldn't I help you? You're a friend of mine." She'd better not settle down yet, Cord decided. On Vosk in particular it would be easy for Ashek's mercenaries to grab her back. "Maybe you'd like to stay with me for a while," he suggested offhandedly. "We'd be quite a team."

She turned from the crawler's window to look at him. "I'd like to stay with you," she answered, squeezing his thigh.

They went straight from Rent-a-Hauler to the port. Cord wanted the next ship out as long as it connected with some busy world where they could find an assortment of spacelines.

"The important thing after losing Gerard is to avoid any of Ashek's other hirelings. Then there's always the Ael, but by now I hope the Ae's losing interest, along with his men."

"Oh, we don't need to worry about Ashek," Edwina assured him. "And I don't suppose Gerard will come after me once he learns the duke is in no position to pay him. Or any of the others. Is Gerard likely to want revenge on you, though?"

Cord stopped in the vast concourse of the spaceport and stared at Edwina.

"What's this about Duke Ashek?"

Edwina looked surprised. "He's dead. I've known for a long time that he would die, but I wasn't sure when until recently. Didn't I—no, I guess not. We

were so busy doing other things, it never seemed
the right time."

Cord spotted a news terminal. He went to it, drop
in a credit piece, and dialed Komonor. The n
broadcast it played to him did not originate on Komo
but rather on a world with close economic tie:
Duke Ashek's world.

"The rebellion is said to be under control,"
announcer's professionally modulated voice sta
"Although Komonori sources claim the uprising
in protest of the duke's progressive policies, th
familiar with Komonor's politics and cliques sug
that the rebellious minor nobility were bankro
and instigated by the Komonori emperor. The
peror is absolute ruler over four systems, but D
Ashek, the emperor's chief subject, did not always
eye to eye with his ruler. The emperor may well h
felt the duke was becoming too powerful in his
right. Any involvement by the emperor has been
nied by imperial spokespersons and by the leader
the rebellion, who have, however, sent delegate:
the emperor to make their peace. In the meanti
the emperor has appointed Senek, one of the du
sons, to take his father's place.

"Meanwhile, Komonor remains in a state of c
unrest, with all offworlders advised to remain in:
the port. Order is expected to be reestablished quic
now that reports of the duke's death have b
confirmed. A small group of highly trained revolut:
aries penetrated the ducal residence and hanged I
from his own balcony. His other three sons were
there at the time, or they might have shared
duke's fate. With the appointment of Senek, his br
ers may no longer fear for their lives but only for t
political futures.

"Once again, no non-Komonori ships are lifting f

Komonor, and all ships are advised to avoid the planet until the situation is stable."

Cord switched off the terminal, as the announcer was proceeding to give biographies of the duke, the emperor, and the chief rebels.

"I guess you're right, Edwina. We don't need to worry about Ashek. Connor Roi is probably having a field day." He laughed. "The Litheen have been waiting for a chance to revolt, and this may give them . . ." His voice failed at the sight of Edwina's face. She had gone sickly white, her lips compressed tightly.

"I'm sorry," she gasped.

Cord led her to an empty corner and sat her down on a divan.

"What's the matter? Is it Connor?"

"I'm sorry," she said again. "When she shook hands with me, I Saw, Cord. She . . ."

"Is she dead?"

"I hope so. One of Ashek's police was torturing her to find out about you and me. She must be dead now, she was hurt so badly. I'm sorry."

"So am I." He let her weep until she stopped and dug a handkerchief out of her pocket to dry her eyes and blow her nose.

"Are you feeling better?"

"No. I should have warned Connor, but I was afraid to—afraid she'd turn me in to Ashek; afraid she'd laugh, even afraid to believe I could know the future. I don't blame you for despising me. I despise myself."

"I don't, Edwina. Believe me." The anguish in her emotions was more than Cord could bear. "Come on."

"Where to?"

"We're going to board a ship headed in the general direction of Vosk. We're going to give you a new life. No regrets. No looking back."

*   *   *

Vosk was a melting pot of species. Everyone h
something to hide, but everyone was cheerful, full
pleasure in life and confidence in the future. Mon
drink, and laughter flowed freely. It seemed to Co
seated at an outdoor café near the port, that
Voskians lived in a continual state of carnival.

"I can't come with you, Cord," Edwina said sad

"Are you sure? You'd be an asset to me—and he
you'd be on your own."

"I know, and it does scare me. But I let you do
once, and neither of us would be able to forget i
can't forgive myself, and I barely knew Connor Ro
and she was a friend of yours. So I'll stay here. Th
you for everything, Cord.

"I don't know how to tell you how grateful I am, I
I want you to take this. Maybe it'll come in hand
She pulled the lavender-silver ring off her finger
held it out to him. Lying in her hand, the band seen
larger.

"Edwina, are you sure?"

"Take it. I don't need it."

He picked up the ring and turned it around
around. "I mean, what will you do here?"

"I have a talent," she said wryly. "I can see
future. People will pay for that, especially if I dres
up with a few exotic trappings."

He nodded once. "I think you're right. And my
is no kind of existence for you. If you came with
you'd always be on the move, always in danger. H
you'll be reasonably safe."

"So it's all for the best?" she asked impishly.

He nodded. "I'd better be going." He slipped
ring onto his finger, and it shrank to fit.

"The Imperial way?"

"In a ship—until I understand this better,"
answered. "Thank you." He hugged her briefly. "Th
you for everything."

Then, quickly, he walked away toward the port, knowing Edwina would be fine on Vosk. Now, somewhere, somehow, he was going to find the makers of the ring and unlock the secrets of Imperial technology. Because when he did, he would be one step closer to finding the woman with the alien trace, the woman he was going to kill.

H. M. MAJOR guards his privacy jealously. However, he is said to sport a bushy salt-and-pepper mustache and to speak with a faint accent evocative of British colonies and whisky-and-soda. His favorite sports are archery and fencing, which he feels has been spoiled by the use of blunted foils. He speaks several languages, but only when forced to. He lives alone except for a temple-trained Siamese guardcat. And where he lives is not really known, but it is probably not in the States.

JOIN THE *ALIEN TRACE* READERS' PANEL

Help us bring you more of the books you like by filling out this survey and mailing it in today.

1. Book Title: _____

   Book #: _____

2. Using the scale below, how would you rate this book on the following features? Please write in one rating from 0-10 for each feature in the spaces provided.

POOR	NOT SO GOOD		O.K.		GOOD		EXCEL-LENT
0	1	2	3	4	5	6	7	8	9	10

RATING

Overall opinion of book .... _____
Plot/Story .... _____
Setting/Location .... _____
Writing Style .... _____
Character Development .... _____
Conclusion/Ending .... _____
Scene on Front Cover .... _____

3. About how many Science Fiction books do you buy for yourself each month? _____

4. How would you classify yourself as a reader of Science Fiction?
   I am a ( ) light ( ) medium ( ) heavy reader.

5. What is your education?
   (   ) High School (or less) (   ) 4 yrs. college
   (   ) 2 yrs. college   (   ) Post Graduate

6. Age _____   7. Sex: ( ) Male ( ) Female

Please Print Name_____

Address_____

City _____ State _____ Zip _____

Phone # (   )_____

Thank you. Please send to New American Library, Research Dept., 1633 Broadway, New York, NY 10019.